THE WORSHIP OF EVIL

MARK KILROY—A twenty-one-year-old pre-med student, he came to Matamoros with three friends in search of excitement. What he found, instead, was terror...and death.

SARA MARIA ALDRETE—An honor student and cheerleader at Texas Southmost College in Brownsville, she lived a bizarre secret life—as the High Priestess of a sinister cult that practiced blood sacrifice.

ELIO HERNANDEZ RIVERA—The head of a powerful Mexican drug-dealing family, he believed it when his *brujo* told him that drinking human blood would make him invincible.

and

ADOLFO DE JESUS CONSTANZO—The *brujo*, the sorcerer, was a handsome Cuban–American known as "the Godfather." With awesome, charismatic power, he inspired his disciples to commit unspeakable acts of torture, mutilation...and murder.

CAULDRON OF BLOOD
THE MATAMOROS
CULT KILLINGS

CAULDRON OF BLOOD
THE MATAMOROS CULT KILLINGS

JIM SCHUTZE

AVON BOOKS ◆ NEW YORK

CAULDRON OF BLOOD is an original publication of Avon Books. This work has never before appeared in book form.

AVON BOOKS
A division of
The Hearst Corporation
105 Madison Avenue
New York, New York 10016

First Avon Books Printing: September 1989

Chapter One

You just did it. It was part of life, part of growing up in Texas. All winter you hit the books and did the very best you could. When spring break rolled around, you hit the road for Padre. It was tradition. You talked about it. You planned it. You enjoyed planning it. Planning every last little detail far in advance was part of the ritual, part of the fun. In the long months before, the telephone calls flew back and forth, once a week, three times a week, sometimes more often.

Mark Kilroy—handsome, forthright, serious for a twenty-one-year-old but never dull—believed in it and accepted it as unquestioningly as any of his friends.

Mark and his friends had grown up together in the little town of Santa Fe, a far suburb of Houston, out on the vast torpid flats of the Texas coast, squeezed between a distant sea and a tangled smokey horizon of chemical plants and refineries. The high school is small. The good athletes play on all the teams. Mark and his friends, all members of the Santa Fe High School Class of 1986, had played baseball and basketball together.

They had gone their separate ways to college but had stayed in close touch, nudging and coaxing each other along by telephone and during vacation visits. They were their own little fraternity, their own private buddy system, and planning the spring break trip to Padre was part of it. In fact, there was nothing to plan.

They would meet back home in Santa Fe. They had a room reserved at the Sheraton in the town of South Padre, right on the Texas Gulf Coast beach on Padre Island, twenty miles from the Mexican border. Beyond pointing the car south and going, there was nothing else to do. The phone calls were a process of turning over each detail and examining it again, relishing the thought, rubbing and burnishing the moments, taking a long yawning pause away from cramming for exams to think about the beach, the sun, the water, Mexico . . . to think about the girls.

For generations, young Texans struggling with the pressures of early adulthood have scuttled south like lemmings to the region along the Mexican border. In the 1950s, they stayed in rooming houses; in the 1960s they drove hand-painted Volkswagens out on the beaches of South Padre and threw blankets down around camp fires; now they book rooms in the row of tall hotels on the south tip of the island.

The lure is the same. Texas is a state of few mercies for the young. Hard in the core of the Bible Belt, it's a place where religious fundamentalism goes hand in hand with a worship of unrelenting hard work. There is little middle ground in Texas. Everyone knows where you stand. If you're hard at work and worshipping hard, then you're probably on the side of right. If you're playful, even for a moment, then you may be straying into dangerous territory.

But playing and straying into dangerous territory are impulses too ferocious in the youthful heart to be tamped down entirely by even the most determined Bible-thumping, finger-wagging parent. The good kids, the ones who do go on to college and who do work hard and who don't get involved with drugs, know instinctively that they need to give it a rest once in a while. They know just as instinctively that the further away from home and parents they get, the safer they will be.

And so when the colleges and universities suspend classes for spring break, the young people of Texas head down the interstate highways and the state highways and the farm-to-market roads—hundreds of thousands of young people, all drawn by the song of the beach and to the Mexican cities just across the line—Ciudad Acuna, Piedras Negras, Nuevo Laredo, Reynosa. Matamoros.

Matamoros, population 350,000, is one of the few border cities that does not have a "boystown." Boystown is a border tradition older even than spring break, dating from a time when Texas did not yet have very many colleges or universities—in fact did not have very many women in the outpost regions a day's ride or two from the border. The boystowns, or "zonas," are old whore districts where Mexican and Indian women and boys have been selling themselves to cowboys since the days of the Texas Republic. Most of them are municipally run. Before AIDS, they were one of the safer ways a restless white man from the American side could vent his pent-up ambitions and dabble in some mildly exciting racial and ethnic taboos.

In the other border towns, the zonas today look like warehouse districts. The neon signs over the doors in the sides of the large bleak buildings are all in English: Pussy Cat Club, The Golden Palace, Lipstick. There is always a shill standing just out front, and the floor show is always about to begin. The sun-scorched Anglo men stumping in over a dusty lintel all have big truck-driver wallets in their jeans, hooked to their belts by chains.

Matamoros closed down its boystown about the time that Padre Island real estate was beginning to take off. Padre is a 120-mile narrow sand barrier on the Texas coast in the Gulf of Mexico. It runs from the port city of Corpus Christi at the north end to the little fishing village of Port Isabel in the south. Until the 1960s, Texans had regarded it with their typically unromantic eye for real estate, mainly as a good place for pasturing cows.

The locals are a pragmatic people. Even today, at the foot of the long looping bridge and causeway out to Padre Island, the local saint whom they have chosen to enshrine with a bronze statue is Padre J. Nicolas Balli, for whom the island is named. His spiritual accomplishments were the sort of things South Texans admire: while serving as Collector of Finances for all of the churches in the diocese of the Rio Grande Valley in the late eighteenth and early nineteenth centuries, Father Balli amassed holdings of eleven and a half leagues of land on the island, all in his own name.

There was public resistance when the National Park Service moved successfully to set off the upper end of the island as a seashore preserve to save the incredible and unique variety of birds and flora on the island from farmers and other predators. But once it was done, the creation of the national seashore helped spawn a real estate boom at the south end, mainly in condominium and hotel construction.

A serious Texas-style development bubble got going on the island in the early 1980s, spawned in large part by Mexicans who had gotten rich during the early days of Pemex—the corrupt national oil company of Mexico. They came to Padre by the Mercedes-load to enjoy the beach and plant a little cash in foreign soil.

The legacy of the boom period was twofold. On the American side, there was so much overbuilding that, by the late 1980s, even the best hotels were more than happy to book in the spring break students. And, on the Mexican side, Matamoros had closed down its zona and cleaned up its act somewhat, aware that it was drawing a less working-class crowd than the other border towns, aware especially that it was drawing a crowd in which the boys either brought or attracted their own gringo girls.

Mark and his friends were all having tough semesters, all bearing down hard. They had one idea—to throw down their books the instant they finished that last exam, hit the road and head south. Moments after finishing his last exam at Texas A&M on March 10, 1989, Bradley Moore, twenty, the most serious of the four, locked up the mobile home he lived in near Bryan and got on the road for Austin. Two hours later when he got to Austin, Mark was just walking out of the second of two exams that day. But Mark's bags were back in his room, fully packed and ready to go.

It was back on the road, six hours home to Santa Fe. The trip was uneventful. Mark was still gabbing about school, about how he was faring in pre-med, the tests, the teachers, the girls. He was still wound up, just beginning to come down from the long grind. He worried about school, but he enjoyed it. He liked the challenge. He thought he had done well that semester. Maybe he had, maybe he hadn't. He wasn't sure. He was sure. He was worried. He wasn't worried. He talked and talked while Brad Moore drove and listened.

Mark Kilroy had attended a handful of colleges and junior colleges before amassing the credits and the grades he needed to get into the demanding pre-medical program at the University of Texas. Once admitted, he turned down an invitation to join the Austin branch of his fraternity. He was serious now. He was ready to work, almost itching for it, ready to really bear down, and he didn't want to spend all kinds of time and money on booze and parties and hangovers. He was sure he had done well. He just wasn't completely sure. He was still talking about it when Brad Moore dropped him off at his parents' home.

Brad drove on home to visit with his parents for a few hours, just long enough to wait for the carefully planned rendezvous with Brent Martin, twenty, driving in from Alvin Junior College. Brent Martin arrived at Brad Moore's house at 11:00 P.M.

The two of them threw Brad's stuff into Brent's Cutlass and headed for Mark Kilroy's house. They put Mark's things in the car and headed on down the road for the home of Bill Huddleston. Bill Huddleston, twenty-one, who had just finished up his own tasks at Texas A&M University at Galveston, was Mark's best friend, a close buddy, almost a brother. By the time the four boys were all finally on the highway headed south, it was 1:00 A.M., and they were humming. It was all ahead. They were driving into their own daydream. The world was new. Life was hot. That gray striped road stretching down in front of them was beautiful.

They drove all night, stopping several times to eat. Thick blankets of fog swept back and forth across the coast road in the rhythm of the sea; they talked about their semesters and the lives they had ahead. This was their third spring break on Padre. This probably would be the last summer when they all still would be based at home in Santa Fe, which meant it probably would be the last time they would make this trip together.

They made it to the Sheraton Hotel at ten in the morning. The main crush of spring-break students would not arrive for another day or two, but the Sheraton was already gritting its teeth. All of the furniture had been removed from the lobby, along with all those things like the sand jars that normally flank the elevator doors, that had been used as missles, battering rams or other devices of destruction during previous spring breaks. The hotel's attitude toward spring break was typical of the island. Spring break was hell, but hell paid.

A gathering of that many young only partially civilized human beings, soon to be solid members of everybody's target demographic group, almost all of them half drunk and with their minds only half made up about life, was too tempting for serious marketers to resist. The battle for their hearts would be stoutly fought on the beaches of Padre in the next three weeks. The major beer companies already had been on the island for a week, setting up a variety of free entertainments, movies, concerts, phone boutiques from which spring breakers could make free calls home.

Religious groups from around the country were coming

in, even as the four boys from Santa Fe were on their way. Most of the missionaries had booked rooms across the causeway in Port Isabel or even farther inland toward Harlingen, where rates were lower. But by that very afternoon, when the first Miss Tanline contest got going on the beach behind the Sheraton, the missionaries would be out there on the sand, too, Bibles in hand, imploring the young people to turn back from the way of all flesh. It was one tough sell.

Quickly arranging their priorities, the boys agreed that some shut-eye was in order—a small amount—and then their best shot would be to look for girls across the border in Matamoros. When they woke up in the early afternoon on Saturday, however, they found that the twenty-five-mile drive to Mexico was totally unnecessary.

This was Padre. They were young, good-looking, and they were there looking. At their age, in this place, at this time, all they really needed to do was sit in one place, and it would all come to them.

One of the beer companies was offering a swimming-pool party and free calls home, along with the "privilege" of being filmed for a commercial. Mark and his friends were just the sort of handsome youths the company was looking for. They accepted. Both Mark and Brad Moore called home. Then, when they returned to the Sheraton, they discovered that a group of beautiful girls from Purdue were occupying the room adjoining their own. Hey-hey. Why go away? They drank and talked and partied into the wee hours when finally even the last of them succumbed grudgingly to sleep.

But it was too easy. They were too restless. On Sunday they awakened just in time to stumble out to the beach and witness the day's Miss Tanline contest. They stretched out on the beach and dozed away their hangovers. By late afternoon they were bored.

The drive to Brownsville, just across from Matamoros, is half an hour over perfectly flat and treeless farmland, covered with low green nubs of young maize and sorghum.

On their way, they stopped at a Sonic Drive-In just across the causeway in Port Isabel. Sonic Drive-Ins are cultural artifacts of rural Texas, survivors of the 1950s, some of which still have carhops on roller skates. You eat from a tray with your window rolled down. It's the kind of setting perfectly designed to induce winking, giggling and soulful looks between cars. At the Sonic, the four young musketeers from Santa Fe met four very hot young women from Kansas. The women asked if the four men knew the way to Matamoros, Mexico. Boy, did they.

They all spent a long night of laughter, smooches and booze at a typical Matamoros drink factory called Sgt. Pepper's. Matamoros was packed and throbbing with American students, bottom to belly in the streets, carrying drinks and dancing, kissing and playing the fool. The old campesinos who slept in the streets worked the crowd for nickels and dimes. The conservative Mexican ladies who wear black dresses and shawls slipped along the inner edges of sidewalks and minded their own business, well aware that crowds like these were the city's major source of income, no matter how lasciviously the young gringos behaved in public.

Downtown Matamoros near the bridge has a nineteenth-century European feel, in the right amount of darkness and after just enough to drink. The crazy quilt of little cantinas and big clubs, hawkers on the street and foreign signs, give it a lilt and color that is decidedly lacking across the river in plain and sour Brownsville, Texas.

At 2:30 on the morning of Monday, March 14, Mark Kilroy and his friends and the four girls all returned to South Padre, negotiating the walk across the border and the long drunken drive home with the skill and sheer good luck that only very young drinkers can muster. Unfortunately, the boys' luck ran out at the island, where the girls announced they were returning to their own rooms by themselves.

But there was always tomorrow night, and the night after. Mark Kilroy and his friends set about the business of sleeping off the drinks and getting themselves rolling again as quickly as possible, so they could go back to Matamoros and try their luck again.

El Padrino wanted an Anglo boy this time. A spring-breaker. He wanted one who looked like himself. He was often taken for an American. He was a handsome man and wore expensive clothes. He had modern hair. He was handsome, like a movie star, and he wore the expensive modern American and European clothing of an international celebrity. He was powerful, important, and frightening. He needed someone who looked the way he looked. He needed a gringo.

El Padrino would take the boy's brains for power. He would offer the fingers to the others, maybe some of the brains. It made the others snicker and giggle to think of it. They all would share in the blood of the heart. They all would share in the power.

They would offer the blood, the brains, the heart, the tibias and the penis and testicles to the god, Elegua. It was from ancient and terrible Elegua that the problems were coming. El Padrino could stop the problems; he could drink the power of the Anglo's brain; he could make all of the family powerful and whole again, even more powerful than they had been before the troubles had begun, vastly more powerful.

El Padrino needed a spring-breaker who looked like him, who was handsome and strong and had modern hair. La Bruja would stand at his side and show the ways the spring-breaker could be dismembered. They would take one from the crowds surging in the streets that night. There would be tens of thousands of them. They would take only one, and they would feed his parts to the cauldron. They would eat his soul.

The magic comes from everywhere, from all people, from the Inuit and the Ashanti, from New Orleans and Transylvania. Wherever the sea has washed mankind, there the magic has taken root, and it is always the same. It always serves the same two purposes. The job of the magic is to hold the world together, make it green and whole and good, or to wrench and shred the limbs of the world and hurl them into the stinking void. The magic is always a way to bend reality itself to the will of the magician. The magician always has clients.

In the original cultures, there were always two magicians. The Kissi in Africa call one the kuino and the other the wulumo. The kuino is the dark magician, the denizen of night who kills and eats his victims. The wulumo is the good magician, a creature of the day and brightness, who hunts down and destroys the kuino. Whatever he is called, the name of the evil sorcerer means the same thing: He is always "The Great Night."

But from there the distinctions grow even more complex and bewildering—a web of light and darkness through which even the most experienced and clever tribesman must pick his way with terrible caution.

The only way the good witch doctor can hunt down and destroy the evil sorcerer is by entering his domain. The evil sorcerer is darkness incarnate. The only possible hope the good or "white" witch doctor may have of capturing the sorcerer is by lifting back the veil of the evil sorcerer's reeking empire and entering into the pitchy void with him.

It is a horrible step even to contemplate. The kingdom of the good witch doctor is the land of day, where life is whole and sweet and good. But the kingdom of the Great Night is an awful cesspool of rot and blood and horror. The good witch doctor must be the owner of incredible courage in order to take even one step along the path of the evil sorcerer, knowing, as he must, that he may never come back as himself.

In most of the original cultures, evil is the result of possession. At a weak moment, often in the traumatic process of birth itself, a soul is invaded and seized by evil. But it can also happen later, at any point in life, at any moment when a person is vulnerable.

One thing is both the cause and the effect of being possessed by demons: that is the condition of being different. If a person is odd or strange or different, his difference puts himself outside the protective circle of family and tribe and marks him. An evil spirit prowling through the village at night, looking for somebody to invade, will stop short when it finds someone who is deformed, or who behaves strangely, or who holds himself apart from the family by being proud, obstinate or lazy. That's the one the spirit will go after, the one whose soul the spirit will eat.

But once possessed, a person will only become more different, because he's possessed. The same thing that marked him as an easy target for the demon—his difference—will become more exaggerated once the demon takes up residence inside him.

So the tribe and the family have a lot to worry about, if one member is too much of an oddball, or even if one member is very special in a proud and haughty way. That person, by being too different, makes himself or herself vulnerable to spirit possession.

And then it works like infection. One member of the tribe is possessed. Then, working from that base, the demon may branch out and look for other souls to eat, other beings to occupy.

The Great Night is always hungry for souls, always looking. That is because he is missing half of his own equipment and is constantly hungry to fill the void. The half that the Great Night lacks is what modern people might call the conscience. In the original cultures, it's not quite that. The original people believed that human beings were made of two halves—that life itself, in fact, was made in two halves. One half is the obvious, the outward, what modern people would call the real or the objective.

The second half is the spirit dimension. The other. In a human being, it's the voice that answers inside one's heart or head when one thinks. It's what modern people sometimes call the soul. One half isn't better than the other. One is no more real than the other. But it takes both to make a full-fledged human being.

The Great Night has only one of two halves required to be a full-fledged human being. When he says hello to himself, nobody answers.

On the other hand, the lack of a "double," as it is called, is what makes the Great Night so powerful. There is nothing in him to check his will. He wants, he does. He sees, he takes. He is sheer force, sheer will. The rest of us want something, and that still small voice says, "Now, now, you know that bow and arrow belong to your cousin, Soft-Hands, and you know how hard Soft-Hands worked to make it, and you know how angry you would feel if somebody took your bow and arrow, so put it back."

Not the Great Night. He wants it, it's his. That is what attracts people to him. He is lust and greed and rage and total satisfaction, rolled into one, no questions asked.

But his lack of a double does curse him with one unending insatiable need. He does have a habit to feed. He does have to eat other people's souls, in order to put himself into full operating order. He has no double of his own, so he has to make due with other people's souls. That's why, once he gets inside your family, he will continue to gnaw from inside, and everyone will be at great risk.

All across the world and time, in the jungles of Africa and in the ancient cobbled villages of Eastern Europe, the great horror of the good people is ever to encounter the man who gazes into a limpid pond or a gilt-framed mirror and makes no reflection. Wherever he walks, he is the same. He is always known. He is the Great Night.

The way the Great Night eats the soul of a victim is not always figurative or entirely spiritual. He sometimes eats the soul by literally eating the victim, or at least by eating some key portions. Cannibalism, in the original cultures, is almost never a response to physical hunger. When a person is hungry in the normal way, he eats normal food.

Cannibalism, when practiced by a sorcerer and his followers, is a means of seeking power. It's a way to capture and eat the soul of the victim, by literally eating his body or the ritually important parts of his body. No one really knows for sure why, in far-flung cultures that have never had contact with each other, the same parts are always important. The phalanges or endmost extremities of the fingers, the face, the genitals, the heart, the brain, the eyes. Presumably it works this way because all human beings sense the working of each other's souls in those parts of the body.

Sorcery, as we call it, is after all the first practice of medicine, the first practice of religion and the first practice of psychiatry, all rolled into one. It's a way of linking the body and the things the body does and the things people do with the hidden ulterior causes everybody suspects are there but cannot see easily.

The most fundamental acts and functions of the human being and human body are always central to the rituals. Woman is always very important to sorcery, because woman is always considered the more mysterious sex in the original cultures. Her breasts and her genitals are mysterious givers and producers of life itself. She is closely related to the planet, because life springs from the soil of her body as it springs from the Earth. The most important rituals contain elements that parallel man's joining with woman. Ritual is often an evoking of woman, and woman is an evocation of the final mystery, the last part of reality that no one understands—no one, with the possible exception of the magician.

The center of centers in the ritual is always the taking of the power of another soul. That is the ultimate trick, the innermost mastery. And the way to really capture the whole power of another soul is always the same, in all of the original cultures.

You must drink the blood of the heart. You must capture the blood of the heart while the eyes of your victim are still flickering with consciousness, while your victim is still watching as you drink from his heart.

In all of this are the two magicians. The magician who

practices white magic is the good magician. The sorcerer, the nagual or the Great Night, is the opposite of good. The ultimate trick for the ordinary man who goes to a sorcerer is to know which sorcerer he's talking to—the one who will protect him and his family or the one who may doom them.

An ordinary man or woman's comfort is born of family, of tribe, of the circle of sameness, the round rim of the camp fire holding back the void of night. An ordinary human being dwells within the safe wall of ritual that ancestors have raised around the village—the way of doing things the same way, the right way, the way that everyone recognizes as the proper way, the way that holds back evil, wards off danger and tends to make the hunting good.

The Great Night is the enemy of all this. Here, in fact, we draw closer to the real nature and horror of the sorcerer. The truth, in almost all of the original cultures, is that the sorcerer is most likely to prey on his own kin. He devours the souls of his own family, because he is the opposite and enemy of family.

Into the safe warm flickering circle of family, the sorcerer comes prowling, having taken the form of a familiar, a goat or dog of the village, or having made himself invisible. His passing may be felt in a shiver of wind or the merest rustle of leaves overhead.

In Mexican folk belief, the most common avatar or other form taken by sorcerers is the jaguar. In this other form, the sorcerer is known as the nagual. In folk carvings, the nagual is represented as the body of a jaguar with the head of a man.

The nagual—an entity and concept right at the heart of Mexican Indian witchcraft—probably is a much more familiar object in a lot of middle- and upper middle-class American homes than the occupants of these homes realize. At chic galleries like the Davis Mather Folk Art Gallery in Santa Fe, New Mexico, the nagual figure is always a good seller.

The yuppie tourists who take them home often have no

idea how profoundly important, alive and disturbing is the figure of the nagual for most people of New World Indian lineage. All over America by now, there are thousands of maids who must wonder anxiously why their employers would give such prominent display in their homes to the hideous figure of the nagual.

On his own terrain, the nagual is always taken seriously. At home in Mexico, or in a rural village in Cuba, or in the slums of Haiti, a wise old woman may duck her head down deeper and clutch the blanket at her neck, nodding knowingly to signify to the others that the nagual is near. Signs are made, postures changed, incantations whispered to hold back his probing power.

And yet he prowls, searching among his own brothers and sisters, cousins and parents, searching for the one whose soul he will seize, the one whom he will deliver into a final agony. The sorcerer is the snake that dwells within the family but seeks to rend its flesh, tear out its heart and eat its brains. And no one knows who he is.

There is the difficulty. When misfortune begins to fall on a family, when bad luck comes again and again and the family begins to splinter apart, then reasonable men and women may assume that the Great Night is walking among them. They may guess that one of their number is a sorcerer or has become the agent of a sorcerer. But how are they to know which one? The Great Night is a trickster too, a clever beast who may hide his presence in artful and even witty ways. He might find pleasure in posing as a drunken uncle or even as a stern Catholic priest. In the bleak vision of the Great Night, after all, the most awful horrors are always laughable.

It is at precisely this moment that a troubled family may turn to the good magician, the one the Kissi call wulumo. The only being capable of ferreting out the dark magician, or kuino, is the wulumo. But the only way the wulumo can hunt for the kuino is by entering his realm. And the only way he can enter that realm is by mastering his magic. Everything the Great Night knows, then, the good witch doctor must learn, too, in order to defeat the Great Night. The good witch doctor must be very like the evil sorcerer in order to know how to overcome him.

Europeans have always harbored sharply ambivalent feelings about voodoo. Especially in North America, where Europeans ran headlong into Indian witchcraft over a long period of time, ambivalence over magic runs deep into who and what we really are. In the early nineteenth century, the same white ladies from big houses in New Orleans who were praying for the lost souls of the African slaves by day were out in bayou clearings by night, stripped and painted and giving themselves to the sway of the drums.

As much as white settlers were afraid of Indian attacks, they were much more terrified by Indian religions. At a time when most Europeans still believed firmly in the powers of witchcraft, the Indians in North America were earnestly and vigorously hard at work practicing it.

In the late 1960s and early 1970s, the writings of Carlos Castaneda enjoyed a tremendous vogue among young Americans. Castaneda presented the teachings of a Yaqui Indian sorcerer not as some kind of interesting exercise in anthropology but as truth. The further into the Castaneda books his readers got, the more transfixed they were, even addicted. His books were devoured, chapter after chapter, book after book, by a North American readership feverishly transfixed by them.

Once embarked on the path Castaneda illuminated, his readers snatched up each word of instruction religiously, because they believed the instructions were the only map capable of leading them home again. Once the first opening is allowed—and it is an opening priests of the established modern religions inveigh against with the harshest rhetoric they can muster—once a person agrees to allow even the possibility of real power in voodoo, then voodoo quickly takes over.

And therein is the power and compulsion of voodoo. It is not a game. It certainly is not a string of meaningless mumbo-jumbo rituals, easily vanquished with a semester or two of good solid social science instruction. Voodoo, magic, Santeria, Palo Mayombe, Abakua: it is always the same. It has always been the same. It will always be the same. It is the ultimate human adventure—a trek to the boundaries of reality, to the outermost membranes of sanity itself. It is a trip to the edge of everything. It is the journey the wulumo, the good sorcerer, must make if he is ever to catch and vanquish the kuino. It is a trip which may transform the wulumo into the very evil he set out to destroy in the first place.

The horrors are absolutely real. Wherever and whenever man has lingered long enough to form a culture, that culture has had in it certain taboos—death, rot, uncleanliness, incest, cannibalism and all the other fly-buzzing terrors of disintegration and madness. Beyond the taboos are man's nightmare fears of his own multilation and great physical pain.

In every human culture there also have been the themes of pleasure and satisfaction, reassurance and joy. It has always been man's deep abiding determination that he would find a way to reach out and control these forces, rather than standing passively with mouth agape while horror and joy and all the other shrieking and sighing elements of life pass across the taut strings of one's senses in a chaos of screams and roars. To blow and make music, to sanctify the union of man and woman, to ritually cleanse food, to protect a hut with sprinklings of blood and incantations: these are all ways to stop the world. These are all magic, all Santeria and Palo Mayombe. But we call it different things in different places.

The practices of voodoo simply happen to be a much more direct and immediate path to the edges of sanity than anything in the modern religions, which work instead to cushion and insulate people from those edges. Whether it's Haitian rabbit sacrifices found behind a warehouse in Dade County or Carlos Castaneda's dusty paperbacks up in a Connecticut attic, the basic exercise is always the same. It is the supreme test, in which a person deliberately propels himself into the very horrors that normally would drive him back most forcefully. By plunging into those horrors and mastering them, one achieves great power.

There is nothing unreal or imaginary about the power people may attain through these methods. It is the power to do anything. It is fearlessness and absolute single-mindedness. It is life without doubt or hesitation.

Neither is there anything imaginary about the perils. The power of voodoo is the power to live without conscience, totally beyond the bounds of normal human sanity. It is a power that can be attained only by killing one's own still small inner voice—one's double. One's soul. It is a power achieved at the cost of making one's self a monster. It is a power that some people will always consider to be well worth the price.

In today's world, there is another edge to voodoo. Frantz Fanon, the revolutionary Algerian writer, called it "a silent resistance to cultural domination." The European comes charging in, after all, sword in hand, to explain to the native that his beliefs are stupid mumbo jumbo, childish gibberish, that his culture is ragged primitivism and that (by the way) he, the native, is physically repugnant. Small wonder that the native instinctively tries to hold back and shelter a precious ember of himself from this dehumanizing onslaught.

The native must do two things. He must get along with his oppressor and simultaneously get along with himself. Before the revolution that threw the French out of Haiti, the political importance of voodoo increased in Haiti as the African people of Haiti were preparing their souls for the coming slaughter. The priests were teaching a Catholicism of resignation, a religion that would help people keep a lid on their frustrations, but the voodoo priests taught them to let their frustrations roar from their throats, taught them to have the heart of the lion.

Be men. Be warriors. Cleanse yourselves of the spiritual

chains the stinking Catholics want to hammer to your limbs.

The fact is that all of the religions of the world follow certain basic patterns, as they strive to answer logical questions that all human minds eventually pose to themselves. What is this? This is life. What is that? That is death. Where are we? The world. Who made this? The maker. Why do we do what we do? The maker sent a messenger to us, a lawgiver, his son or equerry, and the messenger told us to do things this way. Why do some people do bad things? After the making of the world, there were twins, one good, one evil.

But the native religions tend to answer the questions in ways that don't reinforce the pain enslaved and oppressed peoples already feel in their lives. The more aboriginal a religious belief, in fact, the more comfort it may offer for the enslaved or oppressed heart. The European religion, after all, is ruled by one monolithic god, a European god, who is very judgmental. If a man winds up being a slave, or if he is free but poor and diseased and looked down upon, the European priests would have him believe it is because their huge and all-powerful god doesn't like him.

Ah, but the gods of Africa and the gods of the Great Plains and the gods of the Amazon are much less judgmental. In those religions, the original maker of things did his job, made the world, and then forgot about it. He had better things to do. He is far far away, and he does not trouble himself with the anthill of mortal life. He has no idea what goes on down there. He doesn't give a damn.

There are intermediate gods who do involve themselves in the lives of men. But they are like men themselves. Their emotions and their motives are the models for human behavior. They are not dry figures living out some hollow notion of virtue. They are full of lust and hatred, greed and generosity, the stuff of human life but more of it and on a grander scale.

So one's luck on Earth, bad or good, is understandable on a far more human scale in aboriginal belief. It isn't necessarily that the greatest god in the universe had singled you out personally for a dog's life. It's far more probable that some small god—a schmuck—has decided to give you a bad day.

In the belief of the Yoruba, these intermediate gods are the souls of great men and women who have died. In the spirit world, they are without sex, or they can assume either sex, or they can take on both at the same time. They are expanded versions of the human being. For the Yoruba people, they are the equivalent of the saints that the Catholic priests tell about—dead people who live in the sky, who watch us and affect our lives, men who wear women's clothing, who may have a wild and bloody aspect about them and who suddenly appear in spirit visions in the world of man.

There is Olofin, who made the world, but he is so far away that he does not even have priests. Human beings do not seek communication with Olofin, because Olofin has nothing to say about the Earth. He was only partially done with the task of creating it, in fact, when he got so bored that he asked his son, Obatala to finish the job. Obatala can be reached by certain priests on certain occasions, but it is very expensive.

Obatala wears white. He abhors alcohol, because he is a maker of order. The Catholics call him Jesus. Sometimes he is a woman. Her name is Odudua. The Catholics call her the Blessed Virgin. Sometimes he is invisible, and then they call him the Holy Ghost. He doesn't have much interest in human beings.

Orunmila, or Destiny, is another story. He is a bit closer. He doesn't talk to humans himself, but he does have an assistant, Ifa, who can be reached. The Catholics call Ifa St. Francis of Assisi. If one needs to know why things are happening in one's life, one may go to one of the babaloa, the priests of Ifa, who alone can make the Ifa divination. They alone know the way of casting sixteen palm nuts on the ground and reading the 4,000 possible combinations the palm nuts may make when they fall. For a fee, they can tell a person which intermediate god, or "orisha," is affecting his life, from what direction and for what reason.

But even Orunmila and Ifa are quite distant gods, almost in the realm of Olofin and Obatala. They almost never return their calls, and their priests are very expensive. For the common man and certainly for the poor man, it makes more sense to go to one of the priests of Elegua. Elegua is Ifa's assistant—somewhere at the level of lower middle management. Elegua represents the pettier face of destiny, the capricious and often nasty face that has more to do with day-to-day events. Elegua is the orisha who stands at the center of all the paths and tends the gates of the afterlife. He is El Dueno de los Caminos, the master of the paths, and he, through his priests, can at least let a person know from what direction his problems are coming. And for a much more modest fee.

One typically makes an offering to Elegua by sacrificing a chicken at a crossroads or in front of the door of a place where something crucial is about to take place. In Miami when the courthouses open in the morning and the janitors begin to make their rounds, they are unfazed by the chicken heads and talcum powder spread in front of certain courtroom doors. Someone is going to appear in that room today in some important matter, a trial or a bond revocation hearing, whatever. Whoever it is has hired a santero, who got into the courthouse during the night and made this offering to Elegua. It is common.

If they are Hispanic or Haitian, the janitors are respectful when they clean up this mess. Like all of the gods, Elegua can change his nature, depending on the direction from which he approaches. When he approaches from the "Camino" or road of Eshu, he is the devil. But the white priests prefer that we call him St. Peter.

All of the gods can be many things at once. In dealing with Jesus Christ, it's important to know if he is Obatala at that moment or if he is his female aspect, Odudua. Odudua is the god of the dead, the underworld and darkness. It is to

Odudua, the Blessed Virgin, that one must sacrifice the blood of white chickens—one each month, at the time of her menses.

The day-to-day orishas are much more modest than this. There is Yemaya, for example, who lives in the water and involves himself/herself in the lives of sailors. And there is Ogun, the hairy-headed wild man of the forest, a big drunk, who is involved in the lives of people who use iron —the blacksmiths, hunters and soldiers especially. The Catholics call him St. John the Baptist. One always sees him standing out in the jungle dressed in the skin of beasts. It's plain what he is, even in the stained-glass windows.

There is Oshun, the Aphrodite of the Lucumi. She wears brass armlets and necklaces. She is a famous slut. She is very beautiful, like Marilyn Monroe.

One of the greatest of the orishas or santos is Shango, the god of war. He is the god of the lion heart. He is the orisha who reminds man to lust for the blood of the heart, who shows man where the great medicine can be found, where power really dwells on Earth. There is no babaloa, houngan or santero who does not claim to have the ear of Shango. It is from Shango that one learns the most satisfying secret of all—the way to find and nurture power that is sheer, that is absolute, that is savage, that is clean of the soapy stink of the Europeans. Shango is the one the Catholics call St. Barbara.

But the division from European belief is not absolute. It is all on a sliding scale. In all of santeria and voodoo, most of the practitioners consider themselves to be devout Roman Catholics. They are aware there are certain lines one must respect—that the white priest always gets irritated and may even say wounding things if one forgets and gives Shango his real name. One must always remember to refer to him as St. Barbara in the presence of the Europeans. A priest who is of the people or who has at least been in the country for a while may give one a very sharp look when one makes a reference to St. Barbara, but the thing to do is keep smiling and stare back with the blandness of all innocence and devotion, saying, "St. Barbara, father! Surely you know St. Barbara?" But all the time thinking, *"I know him for what he really is. And at night, when I go to the babaloa and hear the prayer to Shango spoken in Lucumi, the language of the Yorubas, then I know that Shango is listening and that he comprehends, that he is even pleased that the human calling him speaks in the tongue of black Africa and not in the nattering whine of the slug-colored whiteskins."*

The various cults are gradations and shadings of all this, having to do mainly with the African tribal origin of the members of the cult and with the European culture with which they collided in the New World. The widespread cult of the Lucumi or Regla de Lucumui is the belief of the Nigerian Yoruba people who wound up in Cuba. The language of its rituals is Lucumi and Spanish.

The cults of Arara are the belief of the Arara people who lived next to the Yorubas in neighboring Dahomey and wound up mixed in with them as slaves in Cuba. Their rituals are in Fon (their original language) and in Spanish. The Arara people who wound up in Haiti formed cults that conducted services in Fon and French, services now known as vodun or voodoo. All of these beliefs together are expressions of Santeria—an African-based religious system in which the African gods of daily life are replaced by Catholic saints.

Some of the cults are feared more intensely than others, both for their powers of magic and for the nature of their rituals. The beliefs of the Efik people of Eastern Nigeria, for example, have given rise to the New World cult and ultra-secret society of Abakua. The practitioners of other forms of Santeria often claim that the Abakua society practices child sacrifice.

Here we tread on very thin ice. The fact is that blood libel of feared strangers is a fundamental aspect of human culture everywhere and through all time. It is near the heart of the mysteries of human self-definition.

We live on this side of the river. What are we? We are

the human beings. Those creatures live on the other side of the river. What are they? They are not the human beings. But they look like us! What are they? They are the human-like but not-human monsters. They are the strangers. They are evil and devoutly to be feared.

What do they do? They steal our children and eat them. They always steal our children and eat them. If they are the Efik people wandering too close to the Yorubas, they are the ones who steal our children and eat them. If they are the Jews or the Gypsies, wandering too close to the settlements of the French, they are the ones who steal our children and eat them. It is always the same, everywhere.

Perhaps it is the thing we instinctively fear most. Perhaps for that reason we project it onto whomever we fear culturally. The problem, in dealing with aboriginal societies, is that the blood libel sometimes is not libel. The craving of the aboriginal soul for power does for some reason drive it like a spear into the gruesome heart of this ritual on occasion. The nanigos, for example, were infamous in Afro-Cuban culture for child sacrifice. They were hated and feared by other Afro-Cubans, which drove their cult deeper and deeper into secrecy, which made it all the more fearsome.

Finally, by the turn of this century, the scholars and the officials and even the simple people of Cuba pronounced that naniguismo was extinct. At least this deepest pit of savagery was gone, and what was left was a lot of mainly harmless hexing and sticking of needles into dolls. Imagine the shiver of horror, then, that ran through the Cuban intelligentsia in the mid-1950s when Cuban black scholar and writer Lydia Cabrera discovered that the nanigos were alive and well, deep in the most secret recesses of Cuban society.

It is called many things. One of the recurring names for it, in slightly different form in the different languages and cults, is "The Goat Without Horns Ceremony." In the early twentieth century, there were European writers who claimed to have been eyewitnesses to goat without horns in

Haiti. Their descriptions are in some ways consistent. We don't know whether it's because they saw the same things or because they read each other's books.

The priest chants and calls, gives prayers and dances to the bata—the hourglass Yoruba drum that the drummer holds between his knees and beats on both ends. There is a rising tide of orgiastic energy in the crowded and sweaty prayer shack.

Suddenly the priest stops. He stares at the worshippers and begins to shake violently. His eyes bug out. He puffs up like a blowfish or adder. A gasp runs through the shack. Everyone knows immediately what is happening. The houngan has opened himself up, and now he is possessed by Shango. Shango is in him. He is Shango. He lifts his knife from the altar.

A very young boy has been prepared outside. He is naked and painted white. His body has been smoothed with oils and dressed with herbs and garlands. He is brought to the shack on a litter. An even younger girl, a little child, has been prepared in the same way and is presented in the same fashion.

They are placed side by side.

Shango comes to the boy. He rises up over him, blowing and puffing ferociously, his eyes rolling madly. He stops. He lowers his face to the face of the boy and screams into his ears: "What do you want, more than anything else on Earth?"

The boy does not flinch. He has been carefully coached and prepared for this, the most wonderful moment of his life. He answers as he has been instructed: "I want a young virgin."

Shango falls back and leers. He rolls his eyes lasciviously. The worshippers urge him on, chanting and laughing with him, feeling his lust. Shango speaks to the boy:

"I shall give you your virgin."

He hovers over the children, chants, leans low, spreads his arms, pauses . . . and he slits their throats. While their blood runs out over the altar and their limbs kick, while their final breath bubbles from their throats, Shango dances and screams with joy. His worshippers are overwhelmed with excitement.

He returns to the bodies. He plunges the knife with both hands into the little chests, sawing them open raggedly. He hacks out their hearts. He lifts the hearts and drinks from them.

The worshippers are silent.

Shango stands and does not move. Finally he returns to the altar. He has one last task before he cedes this body back to the houngan who gave it to him for this meal of death and power. He plunges his hands into the bloody cavities of the bodies, lifts them dripping with blood and viscera, and he proceeds through the shack, smearing his hands over the eager lips of his worshippers, sealing their mouths forever with the secret blood of sacrifice.

Shango slumps to the floor. When it rises, this body will belong to the houngan again. The worshippers are not waiting around. They plunge into the night, with the children's still-warm blood smeared across their faces.

In the Spanish-speaking countries, the middle classes describe all of these beliefs as brujeria or witchcraft. It is a term of denigration. The poor people who believe in the cults may also call their leaders brujos and brujas—witches—but it is a term of respect.

The beliefs are much more than mere watered-down echoes of a half-forgotten iron-age past. That past speaks strongly in santeria and the other religious syncretisms. But the voice of the present is stronger.

For one thing, for all their African origin, these beliefs have in them strong elements of European thought. Voodoo has in it influences from the French middle class of the nineteenth century, particularly the spiritism of Allen Kardec, along with a good many French witchcraft beliefs that are alive and well in their land of origin—the Bocage region in rural Western France.

All santeros, from Rio de Janeiro to New Orleans, always say to strangers that they are practitioners of harmless white magic. They must say something slightly different to their believers. They must tell the devout that they are practitioners of white magic, because no one would pay money to deliver himself into the hands of an evil sorcerer, but they must tell the believer that they are capable of practicing black magic. For the only way to conquer evil is to know all its tricks. And one more besides.

Every time a stooped charwoman stops to buy herbs from the santero she knows that she is entering a bottomless and unwalled realm of white and black, of good and evil and that somewhere in the farthest reaches of that realm are all of the ultimate horrors of hell. There also are untold riches and rewards waiting somewhere in there.

The santero may know how to protect a charwoman's child from a curse performed during goat without horns. But in order to do it, he may have to perform goat without horns himself. Does she have another child?

Chapter Two

He was born on November 1, 1962, to teenage parents whose own parents had just brought them to Miami to flee the Cuban revolution. He was born with two gifts. One was a white gift. He was an incredibly beautiful baby, who became a beautiful little boy. The other was a black gift. He was a chosen one.

Little Adolfo de Jesus Constanzo turned heads wherever his Cuban girl-mother took him. When he was tiny, he turned the heads of admiring women who marveled at his somber beauty. When he was older, he turned the heads of men and women who wanted to know who he was. From the time of his earliest childhood, there was something in his bearing that caught eyes and made people stop to stare without breathing for an instant when he passed.

He never laughed. He was obsessively neat. Even as a very little boy, he was meticulous in ways that seemed strange to the adults around him, other than his mother. At the age of four, Adolfo already had developed what became a lifelong obsession with clothes and his own appearance. The somber little lad spent half an hour each night before going to bed carefully laying out and smoothing his clothes for the next day, then arranging his little robe in just the right position at the foot of his bed.

His days were already full of such rituals. His schoolbooks had to be packed in just such a way, and his lunch had to be laid out in exactly the right fashion each day.

On a few occasions when fellow students made the mistake of teasing Adolfo about his weird habits, the response was swift and unnerving. No one in Cuban Miami needed more than a few seconds to figure out the meaning of the bloody animal heads and other signs that appeared the next day at the front door of the offending schoolmates' home. These signs meant that anyone who teased or angered strange little Adolfo de Jesus Constanzo would put his entire family at terrible risk.

In everything, this boy was intent and serious far beyond his years. He was strange, and in the milieu where he grew up, strangeness was always noteworthy. It could mean one or more of many things. Most of the people in Cuban Miami who were around Adolfo and his mother for any length of time knew exactly what this little boy's demeanor meant and it frightened them.

It was always a mistake to get close to such people or to allow one's children to be near them. Of course they would smile and pretend to be the nicest people on Earth in public. They would even offer help with problems. But even a fool knew there was more to it than that.

His first father was with his mother only a year. He disappeared suddenly. The girl-mother and the black-clad grandmother told neighbors he had run away. When he was gone, the young mother moved to San Juan, Puerto Rico. She was a looker, and she had powers. She had been in San Juan only a short time when a businessman, a man of considerable means, took her as his wife. He was a Catholic, and he wanted Adolfo to be a Catholic boy.

As a young boy in San Juan, Adolfo was a model child. He was devout in his attendance of services at the Roman Catholic church. While still very young he was chosen by the priest for the high honor of being an altar boy. He played tennis and made good grades in school.

The stepfather's businesses prospered. He should have been happy with his arrangement, but instead he was frightened. He was especially afraid of his elder stepson and of what the mother was raising the boy to be and to do.

The mother knew all of this, of course, and ordered the stepfather to steer clear of the boy. He was only too happy to do so, pouring himself instead into the rewards of his business career.

To the outward eye, the boy was a model child. From the age of two years, Adolfo was meticulous beyond anything a child could be taught at that age. Yet he did not smile and he always carried himself with the regal bearing of the chosen one.

The stepfather could not resist pushing the boy in his Catholic devotions. In the early 1970s, the stepfather began to sicken, weaken and waste away before the very eyes of his associates. Adolfo's mother persuaded her sick husband to go with her to Miami, where she said she could find a special cure for his disease. But he died there in 1973. The cause of death was given as cancer.

Unlike her first husband who left her penniless and with a baby in Miami, this man left the comely Delia Gonzalez Del Valle well fixed. She was in Miami, again, and anything but penniless. Not long after the second husband died, a third husband took his place.

This third husband was no more comfortable with the boy than either of the earlier husbands had been. The boy was serious and well mannered in an eerily adult fashion, but the third husband was frightened and angered by the boy's air of haughty superiority. Delia warned her new husband not to insult the boy in any way, but the man drank and could not always control his fears.

Suddenly the young boy was the object of violent whippings and drunken tirades. There was something in the boy that infuriated this father, something the man wanted to root out at the core. The confrontations grew more and more violent and angry. Suddenly the third father was gone. Delia told neighbors they had divorced suddenly and that he had left the country.

The neighbors were not exactly eager to get involved in the intimate details of this particular family. People in San Juan may only have suspected, but people in Cuban Miami knew exactly what was going on. It was Mayomberia. Her mother before her had been a priestess in Cuba. It went straight back. No one wanted anything to do with Adolfo or his younger brother, Fausto.

Adolfo accepted the family's isolation as a necessary burden, an honor. He tried to show his brother that they were special people, and that they needed to support and nurture each other. Within the dense center of their secret lives, they lived as a family.

"I remember one time when I was thirteen or fourteen, it was New Year's Eve and everyone else had gone to a party," Fausto said, when it was all ended. "I was home alone, sitting outside by myself feeling really bad. I saw someone coming up the street, and it was Adolfo.

"He had been at a party, but he said, 'You're my brother. You can't be home alone on New Year's Eve. We'll spend it together.'"

By the time Adolfo was a teenager, it began to be clear that, for all his lugubrious manners and meticulous appearance, young Adolfo was not destined for the university or the professions. His mother made it plain he was too special for that, and by then Adolfo certainly knew what she meant.

His face was beginning to take on the movie-star good looks that would cause things to come easily to him. At fourteen he became the father of a child, by a 13-year-old girl whose mother took the baby for her own. The mother insisted hysterically that the girl break off all contact with Adolfo and his family. She obeyed.

At the same time, Adolfo was beginning to be valuable to his own mother. Her son was about to become something very important indeed, something for which she had prepared him all his life, something for which she had known he was chosen even at birth.

The signs were all exactly proper and encouraging. There was the business of the blessed Marilyn. Delia always had loved Marilyn Monroe and never had been able to understand why such a beautiful woman, a rich woman, a woman of great power, a goddess really, an incarnation of Oshun herself, would take her own life. It made no sense. With power and beauty of that kind, a woman should rule the Earth. Why would she kill herself? It just didn't add up. It was a problem over which Delia fretted and worried.

Little Adolfo, only fourteen years old, was already darling in a precocious boy-man way. He had raced through puberty almost overnight, it seemed, and was already sexually and physically mature. Only in his soft unmoving face—brown eyes so dark they seemed almost coal-black in a certain light, silky black hair drifting down on a smooth and ashen-white forehead—did he look remotely boyish. And even there his baby-soft features were always strangely gloomy, even icy, in a way that looked oddly inappropriate on so young and so pretty a face.

Delia spent hours pouring out her heart to her beautiful son, fretting over the business about Marilyn. He took it all in very soberly, like a judge hearing evidence in a case of national importance. Then one day he came to his mother tenderly and told her. It was not true. Marilyn had not taken her own life. It had been an accident. She had never intended to take so many pills. They made it out to be a suicide, because they were envious of her power. They wanted to bring her down, make her look dirty and stupid. But Marilyn had been everything Delia always had believed her to be. The death was an accident. Only an accident. Adolfo knew. He had seen.

A trickle of people began to come to the home of Delia Gonzalez Del Valle. A trickle, then a stream, then a river. This handsome, newly sexual boy-man who never laughed could see things. He could leave his body and travel the

universe. He could give his body to spirits. He could foretell the future. He was worth a lot of money.

Now when people stopped to stare at him on the streets,
now when they asked the question they had always asked
—"Who is he?"—his mother could answer them. She
knew what he was. He was important. He was a santero.
He was a medium, a person who could share in the life of
the gods of Santeria, a man who could see the future, a
man who was handsome, who had power, who could travel
in the sky and who soon would have great wealth. She told
them now, when they asked. She told right out what he
was, using the word that meant something like "god" to
Delia.

"He is a movie star," she said. In her book, the term
movie star described a certain station in life, a godlike pos-
sition in the universe. One way to get there was to be a star
in the movies. But another was to be a santero who possessed powers so great that they were equal to the powers
of a movie star.

In Delia's world, where Marilyn Monroe and the Yoruba god Oshun more or less moved in the same circles,
Adolfo was a movie star. Adolfo was a god.

It seemed to come true for him, almost because he and
his mother said it would come true. He had no friends his
own age, of course. And the baby was a thing of the past.
But those things were irrelevant in the life he had been
chosen to lead.

In 1980, Adolfo predicted that President Ronald Reagan
would be attacked by a gunman but would survive the assault. By then he had quit high school and was working
odd jobs. In 1981, he was back in school, taking a few
courses at Miami-Dade Community College. He was old
enough to begin amassing a permanent adult arrest record
by then and did. Twice in 1981 he was arrested for the one
type of crime for which he was to be investigated repeatedly in his life—shoplifting. In fact, even at the end he
was still under investigation for shoplifting in Mexico City.
It was a weakness he had inherited from his mother.

In 1983, his bisexual circle of friends in Miami was expanding to include older men who could offer things. In 1983, he was offered a modeling job in Mexico City. His mother took him there, and they stayed.

There he found the real money. His looks and his powers gave him instant entree into the fast track of Mexico City cafe society, where dope money and movie people swirled together in a mélange of late twentieth-century sophistication and lurid eighteenth-century voodoo. It was the perfect place, and he was the perfect person for it.

One thing must be said for the incredible rise of Adolfo de Jesus Constanzo, once he arrived in Mexico City. Some of it may have been based on relatively superficial things —his looks, his strange and compelling manner, his ability to mix the talk of ritual and mystic power glibly with the chitchat gossip and wisecracking of modern life. But there were others who could do all that.

The ability of Adolfo to attract to himself very powerful people in Mexican society was based more fundamentally on the widespread belief that he really could foretell and affect the future and that he really could cleanse his clients' souls of evil.

His successes were staggering. Now, in the aftermath, Mexican officials tend to talk about this chapter in his life with as much understatement as they can reasonably muster. "It seems that Constanzo was widely known," a high police official said after his death.

Yes. You could say that. His mother brags now that his clients eventually included the real elite of Mexico, who came to him in order to know whether or not to produce a certain record album, sell a parcel of land, do a deal, have someone killed.

Some of the clients named by the cult members afterward were famous Mexican entertainers. Adolfo's assistance in cases like these went far beyond general prognostications. He was able, his clients said, to cause record contracts to be offered.

One was a famous actress, beloved by all Mexico. Another was a famous hairstylist. There were lots of those kinds of people, the people from the shiny side of life, the people whom one might expect to find going to mystics and paying a lot of money to have their fortunes told.

But there was another much heavier element of society involved. For one thing, there were the dope dealers—some of them the biggest in Latin America. They came to the bars and cafes in Mexico City's gay whore district, La Zona Rosa, looking for help. It was in this kind of place, where the outlaws and outcasts live, that one could expect to find people of real powers. Wherever a person went in Zona Rosa, sooner or later he would hear the name of this beautiful new young santero, the Cuban who had come from Miami. Without too much trouble, a dope dealer and his bodyguards could even find Constanzo for themselves, probably sitting in front of a cafe somewhere, staring solemnly at the passing scene. With a little encouragement, Constanzo would put on one of his very convincing performances with the Tarot cards. He was an excellent salesman.

For a dope dealer who had a major deal coming down, the cost of knowing the future from this man—$8,000 to $10,000—was a pittance. And given the dangers implicit in the dope trade, the cost and the peril of dealing with a santero were a reasonable expense of doing business as well. The other side of the law could also frequently be found kneeling at Constanzo's altar. Several top Mexican police officials were regular clients. Apparently Adolfo could see to it that things could go well for them too. Apparently he could see to it that things ceased going well for them.

One was Florentine Ventura, the head of Interpol in Mexico. Ventura's fortunes had seemed on the rise in Mexico and in international police circles. And then suddenly there was an inexplicable chute. In 1988 Ventura shot himself, his wife and his own children to death.

But a person could never know exactly what role Adolfo's powers might have played in events such as these.

That was the danger in going to any powerful santero. The santero took a person by the hand and led him through the gates of Hell. No ordinary mortal could know what really had happened on the other side.

Often the people who came to Adolfo already had problems. That was where he made his real money. A rich person who came to him for one of his "limpias" or cleansings would gladly pay $30,000 to $40,000.

It is in the cleansing ritual that the beliefs of Santeria and Regla de Palo come back to the universal themes and fetishes of witchcraft throughout the world, over time and among all humans. Like the blood libel, the cleansing ritual is something that seems to leap independently and spontaneously to the human soul, as if impelled there by an external constant. Even down to the universal use of the egg, it is the same whether it is carried out by Indians kneeling near the banks of the Amazon or by crafty Gypsy ladies in the backroom of a bar in Detroit.

The underlying thesis is that some evil has been put on a person, a hex or curse, often the universal "evil eye." The santero must find this evil and draw it out of the body of the cursed person who has come to him. For some reason which defies rational analysis, these ceremonies always make use of eggs, and they always involve the capturing of the evil entity in the egg itself.

If the Gypsy lady has snared a rich man from Grosse Pointe into her lair a certain amount of chanting and mumbo jumbo will take place at a table, after which the egg will be broken and a disgusting blob of blood will spill forth from it. The Gypsy lady will shriek and draw back quickly from the table. This glob of blood and yoke, still quaking like the viscera of a living body, is the evidence she presents to her client to show that she has drawn the evil from him.

But in Constanzo's chapel, the show was much more dramatic and convincing. In the first place, it was no humdrum matter of sitting at a table. The client stripped naked and lay down on top of the altar itself, which was already bloody with the various offerings necessary to summon the proper orishas. Simply lying down there involved a substantial and disorienting jolt to the nervous system.

Then there followed a lot of sexually ambiguous rubbing down with magical oils and herbal concoctions—another serious journey into uncertainty and anxiety for the macho Latin dope-dealer, who probably often had trouble deciding whether to worry more about his privates or about the congealing goat head parked by his cheek.

All the while, Adolfo was passing living animals and parts of dead creatures over the client's body, each time making a special exhortation or entreaty in the strange African language of his beliefs. And finally there was the passing of the egg.

Again and again, the egg was passed, over and under the limbs, into the recesses and across the expanse, hunting, searching while the santero moaned and shouted his ancient imprecations. Finally Adolfo stopped. He stepped back. His eyes bugged. He seemed to bloat and puff up like a lizard. His followers muttered knowingly. They knew which of the orishas was in him. They knew that this was the moment of power.

He smashed the egg on the altar and a bloody tentacled shimmering human eye plopped out. It was the evil eye! He had drawn the evil eye itself out of his client and into the egg! This kind of power was a steal at $40,000 a visit!

It was after he had disappeared for a while, after Delia had sent him away to be trained by the "Great One," that he had returned and led his growing group of loyal followers across the final boundary. The followers in Mexico City said later that they were blindfolded when it first happened. That truth may never be known.

But they may have been blindfolded. He may have wanted to prepare them gradually, or perhaps simply to implicate them suddenly and unwittingly. Then again, there may have been no blindfolds at all.

The first time it happened, the followers may have believed that the ceremony Adolfo was conducting was one of his regular cleansings. But suddenly the room was sprayed with hot human blood, a sickening stink shot up their nostrils, the limbs were kicking, the mouth bubbling, the body cavity quaking. And the heart was at his lips.

They were there. They were there with him. He had led them there. They were in the pit of Hell itself, and the electric sexual power of Satan was pumping through their veins. He knew all of the words, all of the incantations. Now he spoke with ultimate authority. He knew the Bantu spells to cast as he sealed their lips with the blood and viscera. He was their sorcerer, their santero, he had always said it was white magic, they always say it is white magic, and he had led them to this precipice. Now, though, they had leapt over with him into the black bottomless pit of Hell.

No one knows how many they killed. Zona Rosa is full of human beings who will never be counted, never be missed. They are the chaff of life. They even know it. They would come to Adolfo, some without enough money, knowing that something was up, something amiss. Why would this great santero, this *movie-star* santero, take them to his altar without the full payment? But they came anyway. Such was the thrill and mystery of being this close to the deepest most feared and closely held secrets of Afro-Cuban belief. It was worth risking one's life. It was worth risking one's soul.

After the arrests, the cult members began to admit more and more. Independently, they piled detail on top of corroborating detail—things no one could have made up because they were things no one could imagine.

There was the sacrifice of Ramon Baez Elias. Sometimes in the street he called himself Edgar, and then on days when he was a woman he called himself Claudia. Baez was one of the ones they flayed, in the manner of the ancient Aztec priests. While he was still very much alive. They scalped him. Then they peeled the skin down off the trunk of his body. He only died when they took his heart.

After Adolfo had sacrificed his victims and after he and

his followers had shared the blood of the heart, Adolfo presided over carving lessons for the eager butchers at his side. He would show them how to take the all-important phalanges from the fingers, how to hack off the tibia and how to get the brains out of the skull. The killing, after all, was only the beginning.

Because then there was the teaching of the nanigos and the way of the nganga—the cauldron. Here were even deeper secrets. The brains were to be prepared by boiling in blood.

There is a part of the ritual that the police, the anthropologists and the psychiatrists have grilled the prisoners on repeatedly. They have been breathtakingly candid about all else. They remain consistently silent on this one detail.

The brain, the limbs, the fingers—those things are always important, and they are always eaten. But they are also usually cooked first in a soup of blood.

The blood of the heart is different. To be taken at its full power, the blood of the heart must be consumed while it is still in the heart. This is not easy to do. It means the heart must be seized from the body cavity and the blood from it quaffed before it has time to drain away or be squeezed out by an arrhythmic pulse.

In these ritual killings, the inflicting of horrible pain on the victim is typically a necessary and, to the practitioner, reasonable part of the process. The soul of the victim must be taught to fear its killer totally and for all time, in order to serve the killer loyally and forever. It must be drawn up near the surface of the body, quickened and enlivened, then broken and subjugated totally. Concerning these last details of the way they killed, the followers of Constanzo have been shy.

In the two years before Mark Kilroy was taken, Mexico City police found eight hideously tortured and disfigured corpses at the bottom of a lagoon in the Zumpango River, their bodies tied with wire to cement blocks. They were all Constanzo's. Later, after his followers began to talk, more were found.

Their tibias, phalanges and brains had been removed, along with most of their spinal columns. Some had been flayed, some not, some were beyond identification. The penises and testicles of all had been cut off. The chest cavities of all had been hacked open and the hearts pulled out.

Brownsville is a city of 70,000 on the Mexican border, fifteen miles inland from where the Rio Grande spills into the Gulf of Mexico. In the 1930s and 1940s, South Texas was as close as the American food industry ventured to the Third World in its search for year-round fruit and produce. Brownsville and the lower Rio Grande Valley were on the boom then. Trucks roared up out of the torrid heat loaded with lettuce and pink grapefruit for northern cities, and the packing houses ran around the clock.

Now times are hard. The food industry has expanded its operations to the real Third World, skipping over the valley. In recent years, the problems across the border in the Mexican economy have devastated the other local industry —selling American goods to Mexicans. A lot of the packing houses and bonded international warehouses have closed.

The major commercial airlines don't go to Brownsville. Instead one must fly to Harlingen forty miles up the highway. The sense of disorientation begins subtly at Harlingen International Airport, which is home to a group of aeronautical nostalgia buffs who call themselves "The Confederate Airforce" and keep World War II vintage aircraft at the airport.

The airport has been improved in recent years, and yet it too has a 1940s feel of wartime impermanence, of Quonset huts and browning palm trees painted white on the bottom. On the rental car radio, the disc jockeys call their terrain "Deep South Texas."

The aura of shabbiness and confusion grows as one proceeds south to the border. The city buses in Brownsville are battered faded old 1950s models of a type most Americans either have forgotten or are too young ever to have seen before. On the Brownsville city vehicles, they call it, "Brownsville, Crossroads of the Hemisphere." That might almost be true, if one were speaking strictly in terms of dope and poverty. Brownsville is a blur of a town where the political, social and economic currents of Latin America collide with the currents of the North.

Along its newer commercial strips and out in the new Anglo neighborhoods, Brownsville tries hard to be Norte Americano. Everything is there that ought to be—the Wickes Lumber store, the Wendy's, the new brick bunker with plastic mansard roof that houses the adult video store.

The Anglo subdivisions tend to display a lot of ferociously attentive lawn maintenance, a tendency born of two factors. Certainly one factor is the large and very available supply of cheap labor that swims and sneaks through storm sewer pipes every morning, eager to put in a long sweltering day of lawn work for ten dollars.

But another reason why the Anglos work so hard to keep their lawns square and tidy is the great Anglo dread of giving in to the tropics. The Mexican and Mexican-American people all around them have made their own peace long ago with the torpid blankets of humid wind that float up off the gulf. It's a hot sticky place. The thing to do is take it a little easy, live a little shabby, let the small things go. And of course for the Anglos, most of whom are red-scorched fundamentalist Protestants of typical Texan Scottish-Irish frontier descent, the very suggestion of taking things a little bit easy is an invitation to tropical degradation, intermarriage and Hell.

The Mexican-American people live in their own subdivisions. Some are in old areas near downtown. Those areas are charming in a handmade hokey way, with winding lanes, lurid paint colors, goats on stakes and walls of luxuriant roses. The new Mexican subdivisions are on the edge of town. The houses are identical wooden boxes up on cinderblock piers. There are no trees or flowers.

All the people of Brownsville strive hard to protect their

tribal integrities. The Baptists can't eat a simple breakfast together in a restaurant without touching on the topic of all the things that are wrong with Mexicans. The Mexican-Americans have gone through a lot of Raza-Unida-style political consciousness raising. They regard the Anglos with much the same baleful caution that poor black people feel for whites farther north.

But in the course of daily living, the arrangement winds up somewhere in the middle. A gang of kids spilling out of a grade school at the end of the day includes one little white-faced Leave-It-to-Beaver Anglo boy with his baseball cap on backwards, chattering to his buddies in high-speed highly idiomatic Spanish that his parents don't even realize he can speak.

Given its proximity to the gulf, one might expect Brownsville to exhibit some of the easygoing charm normally associated with small warm-weather coastal cities. But there is almost none of that—not a hint of Florida's easygoing ambience, for example. Whether it's the dope trade in the area, the political problems associated with Central America and Mexico, or just the general aura of ethnic ill temper in the town itself, Brownsville is not an especially friendly place. Except for a few hambones down at the Chamber of Commerce, no one even tries.

Outside of town on Highway 4, a large black on white highway department sign says: ATTENTION: BRAZOS ISLAND STATE PARK HAS NO PUBLIC FACILITIES FOR CAMPING OR TRAILERS.

And why should it? If they made it easy for people to camp out there, the place would fill up overnight with refugees and smugglers.

Somehow, from the hippies of the 1960s who came in finger-painted Minivans, to the bastards from Colombia with their mirrored sunglasses and open shirts, everybody who comes here to do anything other than work at a normal job winds up being a huge pain in the ass.

In the long awful weeks after Mark Kilroy's disappearance, another more inward aspect of Brownsville emerged.

Beneath all the politics and the ethnic tension, deeper within the community, the human heart of the city was deeply moved by the sight of Mark's father and mother, walking in the crowds like the beggars on the bridge, pleading for help.

Jim and Helen Kilroy were fine people—solid products of the American suburban middle class. In them, the people of Brownsville saw themselves. What happened to them could happen to anyone.

Jim Kilroy plodded from shop to filling station and up and down the streets through milling crowds, handing out fliers with Mark's picture on them to anyone who would take one. As the weeks wore on, the people of Brownsville knew better than anyone else that the end could not be good. The people of Brownsville live with the border every day. They know what it means when someone disappears on the other side.

The people who live in Brownsville, by and large, don't go over to Matamoros alone. They know the risks too well. They might even be justified in feeling that the naive Americans who go over there to raise Hell deserve what they get.

But there he was, Jim Kilroy, and there she was, Helen, with him: it's a small city, and no one could avoid seeing them out there every day. As the people of Brownsville drove downtown to work, as they walked to lunch, as they drove home again in the evening, there were the Kilroys, trudging up and down the dusty streets, pleading for word of their son like beggars.

By the end, the entire city had been moved, and large crowds of Brownsville residents gathered in outdoor church services to pray and weep for the Kilroys. Even knowing what they know about the harsh realities of the region, the residents of Brownsville could not avoid grieving for these good and strong people whose son had been taken in so hideous a fashion.

Highway 4 constricts to a narrow mottled strip of pavement just beyond the sign. Every few miles, a dirt road wanders off to the south. A mile or so down the dirt roads, they all turn into double-rutted tire tracks through endless perfectly flat fields of sorghum, maize and milo. Grain elevators and crude-oil storage tanks loom on the far horizon. Fat white thirty-foot-high standpipes for the area's huge irrigation system march off into the superheated haze like Easter Island monoliths. At the ends of the dirt ruts are ravines and sand dunes and then the river.

In those low brown dunes is a source of wealth so great that it lured even Constanzo away from his grand and pampered life in Mexico City. It is in that land that a certain Hernandez family has always hidden its dope. It is along these rutted farm roads and on down Highway 4 that they move it, when they're not moving it by plane. It is on these low ugly dust-blown acres that Constanzo saw his golden castle of dreams.

This area is combed night and day by Customs, the border patrol, the DEA, the federales and all of the local police agencies. It's just not a lighthearted part of the world.

Matamoros, just across the bridge from Brownsville on the other side of the brown trickling Rio Grande River, has a tangible spark and verve. Its nineteenth-century European-looking center is alive and chipper with opportunity-seeking optimism. This, after all, is a hopeful place for Mexicans and even for the Central American refugees who wind up here. It is a place from which one can see into the wonderland of wealth. It is a place where people tend to live by their wits, and so it attracts people who have wit.

Mexican doctors and dentists flock here. A billboard across the river in Brownsville shows an unintentionally caricatured Mexican version of an old Anglo couple— more like two gray half-dead Pillsbury dough-boys with canes—above an almost correctly spelled message: OUR HIP OPERATION IN MEXICO WAS A COMPLETE SUCCES!

The bars in Matamoros, like Hard Rock Cafe and Blanca White's, where Mark Kilroy spent his last hours of happiness, are huge drink factories, geared for the kind of serious boozing that only the very young or bingeing alcoholics can manage.

The normal hazards always associated with Mexico, meanwhile, remain in place. People drive like madmen in Matamoros; stop signs mean nothing; accidents are always disasters for Americans; the matter of the mordida, or bribery, is always delicate with the local police—trouble if you don't pay it when you are supposed to, trouble if you do offer it when you are not supposed to.

The countryside outside Matamoros is flat and haunting —the mixture of agriculture and continuous junkyard that is Mexico. Rusting hulks of farm machinery stand everywhere along the road. Neat rows of sorghum and maize— small plants that look like corn—stretch off over the perfectly flat terrain and fade into a dust-brown sky. Every once in a while along the highway, standing and staring or sitting slumped forward with his feet in an irrigation ditch, a lone campesino appears, barely looking up with Indian eyes, wrapped in the same blanket and wearing the same hat his forebears have worn through the ages.

Every evening the old square at the heart of the city fills with men singing the new corridas—the ballads men make up and sing often about contemporary events, singing to the swaying thrum of guitars. In this aspect and at the end of the day, Mexico is a soft and sweet place, infinitely more civilized than just across the river. The sweetness of the guitars, in fact, often masks the haunting edge of the words. Within two weeks of the discovery of Mark Kilroy's body, the men in the square were singing versions of the new corrida they had heard on the radio—the one about Mark Kilroy, the narcosatanistos and La Bruja Andrete. This tale, so utterly bizarre and totally beyond the bounds of comprehensible culture on the other side of the river, a source there only of terror, anger and suspicion, was already being woven into the fabric of the square in Matamoros.

In this part of the world, where culture and ethnicity shift like sandbars in the river, one population remains the same—the campesinos who stand by the road and barely look up, with shining Indian black eyes over arching copper cheekbones. They remain the same, because they are beneath and outside everyone else's culture. They are not doctors, trying to sell hip operations to the Anglos; they are not Anglos; they are barely Mexicans. They are mostly ancient people, the remains of ancient cultures, who have been here and have survived here because they were beneath everyone else's attention. They believe what they believe. They know enough not to express what they believe in ways that will draw the attention of the rich people— Mexican or Anglo.

They go their own ways, even in Brownsville. They do everything they can to avoid disturbing the smooth and dusty equanimity of their world. And they believe what they believe. They can find what they need, when they need it.

Most of the stores in downtown Brownsville sell cheap clothing, aimed at the army of crossers who come every day from Mexico. Rows of little storefronts hawk cheap watches, sunglasses, electronic equipment—shiny things designed to reach out and capture the heart of a campesino returning at the end of two or three days of hard labor with twenty dollars in his pocket.

But a quick eye and a yearning heart, scanning through the cheap radios, tacky souvenirs and phony China dinnerware, finds the object the heart really needs. There, nestled among the rich man's trash is the thing that can help an aching heart bring order to a painful and confusing world, restore order and sanity in this madhouse of monsters, rich whores and malevolent policemen.

There! There on a table just inside the door of a store on Washington Street is what the heart needs. The seven powers!

In a display marked "incense," the merchant is offering large green candles, in glass containers like oversized votive candles. At the top it says, "Siete Potencias Africanas." At the bottom it says, "The Seven African Powers."

These are not the cold distant gods of the rich people. These are our gods, the old gods, the gods of the simple people. The transference of these gods from Christian figures is a little different in each instance, depending on where the religious figures were manufactured and for which specific cultic market.

In this case, these are our figures, the gods of the campesinos, passed down from ancient Indian belief through the filter of Afro-Cuban belief, disseminated by the Miracle Candle Factory of Laredo, Texas.

In the center of our candle is a picture of the one the rich priests call Jesus Christ. He is on his cross. The flames of hell are at his feet. Before him on the ground is the serpent, the apple, the skull and the lantern. To one side is a pedestal with a rooster resting atop it. On the candle is the real name of Jesus. He is Olofin.

In cameos around Olofin are pictures of the other orishas. There is Obatala, the one the rich priests call "The Virgin of San Juan." We know she is really Obatalia, who can also be Odudua, the god of the dead, the underworld, disease and corruption. It is to her that we must sacrifice the blood of a chicken.

The others are present—Elegua, Yemallia, Ochum, Orula, Ogum. At the top is the most powerful of all—the one the priests call St. Barbara. We know that she is really what the candle calls her. She is Shango, the war god, the god who lusts for the blood of the heart. A sword is in one of her hands and in the other a chalice bearing a bloody sun.

These objects are for sale in downtown Brownsville. But, more to the point, they are sold in supermarkets in Dallas, Los Angeles, New York—in any city where there is a substantial Hispanic population. In the old black neighborhoods of cities, in tiny paint-peeling shops where white people never go, the same objects are sold, along with herbs and powders that are specific to black culture—

things Mexican and Central American people would regard as foreign.

For some campesinos, the candle for sale in downtown Brownsville would be too expensive, at $2.19. And it might even be too foreign, too Cuban, or too European. For such people there is an unpainted wooden storefront around the corner and up the street three blocks. A simple sign over the door says YERBERIA. Just inside the door, a baby is crying in a portable playpen. Her young parents are lounging against a wall that is covered from top to bottom with tiny packets, each containing a different Indian remedy or charm. The old lady in back is the one who knows the cures. This is magic that comes straight up out of the soil of Mexico.

It's all on a sliding scale. There are no clear lines of demarcation. At the center of old Brownsville is Immaculate Conception Cathedral. It's a small church, for a cathedral. Its architecture is curiously expressive of Brownsville: its attempt at Gothicism is betrayed by the humble brick and tin of its construction. At the entrance, a unique and intriguing event occurs. The extreme Gothic arch of the entryway is softened and rounded by pink vulvar contours that seem to do battle with the dry pragmatic lines of the rest of the building.

Inside, it's a darkly beautiful little cruciform cathedral. The stained-glass windows present plain, stiffly posed portraits of the Christian pantheon. The Anglos and the well-dressed Mexicans who come in always stop at the font of holy water, genuflect, and then proceed to the front of the church to worship before the high altar.

But the high altar is for high-ranking people. The poor people, the lawn men and the charwomen who are dragging footsore bodies back to where they will cross the river to Mexico, come in through the same soft pink arching door and turn immediately to the right.

There, in a grotto that is back behind the entryway, are the gods of the simple people. Odudua is there, along with the others. The bleeding figure of Obatalia is there—a figure so shiny and glowing, when one stares unblinking at it in the dusty light, that it seems almost to shimmer and vibrate.

Tucked here and there among the gods of the simple people are photographs, locks of hair, scraps of paper— tiny rags of clothing ripped small by careful fingers so that they can be stuffed in here and there in ways that will not be too visible and thereby risk offending the rich priests. Hanging by a string from the hand of Odudua is a prayer card that must be twenty years old. Certainly it has not been here all that time. Even the most kindhearted priest would allow it to hang here for only a day or two. It looks like a laundry ticket that has been carried in cardboard suitcases and overcoat pockets all this time. For some reason now, at this moment, it has been brought to Odudua.

It says: "Dear Reverend Ike: Hang this miracle faith-claiming tag in your prayer room over your church for ten days and ten nights."

Instructions on the card say, "Check Your Needs."

The person who brought it here has scrawled in pencil over a box next to the choice that says, "I need more peace in my home."

Hidden behind Odudua is a very old and faded photograph, probably from the 1950s, judging by the clothes of the subjects and the primitive quality of the color reproduction. It is a photograph of a smiling mother and her young daughter. They are both smiling deeply happy and unaffected smiles, unposed smiles. It is a portrait of a moment of great happiness and family feeling, washed far away by the seas of time.

In other nooks and crannies are written messages, asking for cures. These almost certainly were not written by the people who brought them here. And they certainly were not written for them by the priests. They were written by the curanderos: *Here. Your mother has been cursed by Ogum. You must take this card to Ogum in the Cathedral in Brownsville. Give it to him. Hide it so that the rich priests won't take it away.*

Everyone in Brownsville knows that this worship goes on. In a local survey of health conditions, one of the questions asked was how often the respondant went to Mexico to seek the cures of the curanderos. Only 6 percent admitted they did. When a rich man with a notepad asks you about the curanderos, you answer him cautiously.

But everyone knows that curanderism is a very common system of belief in the Valley and on down into northern Mexico. It's as much a part of the culture as soft guitars and lilting corridas in the square at dusk. The doctors minister to the rich. The curanderos take care of the poor.

When they trust the rich man to whom they are speaking, the campesinos will tell the full story of the curanderos and how they have affected their lives. Some have either traveled by themselves or have accompanied loved ones to the village of witches. It is a place where many of the people who would be considered psychotic street dwellers in Anglo society have gathered.

There are narrow streets lined with witches, all dressed in black, sitting and rocking on the ground, leaning against adobe walls, rocking, mumbling and screeching incomprehensible imprecations at invisible spirits. One comes here because the most powerful curanderos and curanderas live here. They are not crazy. But they live amidst the crazy people in order to absorb their power.

Far from crazy, the curanderos have perfected long spiels handed down through tens of generations, like the carefully crafted and practiced spiels of the Gypsies, designed to convince the simple folk that their powers are worth any price they charge. The curandero may move in with a family during the long years of a cure and live off the family's labor. His cure often involves animal sacrifice and the drinking of the blood of the heart in order to gain power. Beyond all the other of his skills, the curandero is a master of social cleverness. He knows to warn his clients that they must keep their visits to him secret from the rich Catholic priests.

For the most part, the two views of the cosmos have

dwelled together fairly comfortably. The people of European belief go to the front of the church in downtown Brownsville. The people of the ancient beliefs go to the back. Their beliefs always have been able to dwell together peacefully, in part because neither tribe was ever entirely sure what the other one believed.

The arrangement is one of those useful turnings away that make life possible on the border. In the end, people do what they can in the same way, and when they must be different from one another, they afford each other the useful courtesy of averting their eyes. It is a way the tribes can dwell together.

The history of Matamoros and Brownsville is a fantastic tangle of international intrigue. Even the trained eye of a historian or political philosopher would finally have to admit defeat in any attempt at making normal sense of the region. For ordinary folk, only two themes have ever made consistent sense: Family. And smuggling.

Now the obvious cultural divisions on the border have settled down to the rivalry of Anglo-Americans and Hispanic-Mexican and Central Americans, but in the region's formative years, at the middle of the nineteenth century, the area was a bewildering swirl of Texan, Mexican, Indian, French, German, English and other interests.

At one point during the Civil War, Brownsville had been seized from Union Forces by Colonel Rip Ford, a former captain of the Texas Rangers, who had raised his own extremely ragtag army of boys and old men from the scattered villages of the sparsely settled south Texas frontier. Almost all of these were males who had been passed over by every other hungrily conscripting army that had swept over the region in the last several years, but they joined Rip Ford voluntarily when he convinced them the Yankees were going to bring black troops down into Texas.

Ford and his army were supposed to be adjuncts of the the Confederate Army, headquartered on the Mexican side in Matamoros. But the Confederates mistrusted Ford and would have almost nothing to do with him. Their mistrust, as it turned out, was well founded. As the Civil War neared its inevitable gloomy end for the Confederacy, Ford was already dickering for a deal that never came to pass, by which Texas would have rejoined the Union at the last minute and Ford's troops would have joined Union troops in a war on Mexico.

The Mexicans were even more divided during this period. Matamoros was more or less under the control of the Imperialists—Mexicans loyal to the cause of the Emperor of France, Louis Napoleon Bonaparte or Napoleon III, who was trying to install Archduke Ferdinand Maximilian Joseph of Austria on a Mexican throne as his puppet. The American Confederates had made their own alliances with the Imperialists.

The Union forces, whom Ford had sent swimming for their lives into the Mexican brush on the other side of the Rio Grande, were allied with the Juaristas in Mexico, who wanted to toss the Imperialists out and set up a liberal constitutional government in Mexico City.

But much of the most ferocious fighting that took place along the Rio Grande between Brownsville and Matamoros during this period was strictly local—between the Yellow Flags and the Red Flags—and had to do with local Mexican padrones, jealous of each other's power and wealth. At the same time, ferocious skirmishes broke out up and down the river between Kickapoo or Apache Indians and whatever band of soldiers was unlucky enough to cross their path that day.

Ford and many Texans played an inscrutably complex game, ekeing out their own self-interest from the storm of dust and blood around them. Richard King and Mifflin Kenedy, founders of the commercial kingdom now best known as the King Ranch in South Texas, were Yankee merchants who had come to the area to make their money in the steamboat trade. Acting on Rip Ford's advice, they betrayed the Union, rechartered their boats under the Mexican flag and used them to transport Confederate cotton out to the thousands of European ships lying at anchor off Matamoros. This trade delivered untold millions of dollars into their hands.

The one place where all of this or any of this came to make any sense at all was in the little sandbar settlement out closer to the sea on the Mexican side, called Bagdad by the Europeans, Boca del Rio or "Mouth of the River" by the Mexicans. It was out toward the end of what is now Highway 4.

At the height of the Civil War cotton trade, when tons of Confederate cotton were being floated out to the dense forest of masts and rigging bobbing in the sea off Mexico, Bagdad was a settlement of 15,000 souls. Its sand and mud alleyways rang with dozens of languages as peddlers, deserters, conmen, gamblers, merchants, spies and whores rushed in from all over the world, drawn by the sick-sweet smell of quick amoral money.

It is the face of war that always draws a certain kind of adventurer. The Confederacy was being pushed from within by its own growing panic, and the European buyers, aware that the deals at Bagdad were too good to last, were hungry to get all they could while they could. It was a time and place when the only rule was ruthlessness. Anyone could get rich. All you had to do was stay alive.

While the top rate for labor in St. Louis was $1.60 a day, common laborers in Bagdad pulled down $10 a day, paid daily in silver. A person who owned his own dinghy could earn $40 a day. Rise to the rank of trader, arrange a few deals of your own, and the rich commissions on those deals alone could set you up with your own ships.

The downside was obvious, even from a distance. Bagdad was a place of absolutely no law, where life was dirt cheap and the only right a man had was the right to shoot first and shoot better.

In that sense, it was a place that helped set the tone for much of the subsequent history of the Mexican border. In that kind of setting, all of the parameters of life seem to loom out crazily beyond the wildest imaginings of simple men. The money to be made and made quickly at Bagdad was literally too much for the typical desert peasant to compass in any meaningful way. It was more money than he could imagine means of spending.

But the degradation and danger of life in a place like that were beyond the imagining of most decent and simple people, too. In a place where the stakes were so unbelievably high, the rate of treachery was just as fantastic. There was too much in it for the traitor. Men shot and killed their own trusted compadres with whom they had deserted from the French or the Confederates or the Union or whomever. Loyalties seemed to fray and rot in the steamy mosquitoshrieking salt wind that came up off the sand flats every afternoon.

There was great money to be made. But how could a man live in a place where there was no one to trust? Bagdad, for all its incredible promise, was a moral Hell in which the simplest task—collecting money on an undisputed plain debt—was always a hair-raising trip through a maze of doublecrossers, informers and cutthroats. Even if a man lived, he might be driven mad by the life.

But men and women always continue to look for loyalty. They must, because they cannot carry out even the simplest tasks in total isolation. To survive and especially to thrive on the border, one must have trusted comrades. One must find them somehow, somewhere.

For the people of the region around Matamoros, the answer to this dilemma was a more intense version of the same solution people tend to find in embattled and unstable regions the world over. If nothing else can inspire loyalty, then people must retreat to the institution of family itself.

Blood. In blood there may be loyalty. If a family is whole and good, then its members will be loyal to one other. They will be called by the blood, and, especially where no other call can be safely heeded, blood will out. It is the one thing a person may reasonably expect to trust, as long as a family is whole and healthy.

And making a good family—that's something people know how to do. Even ordinary people know how. If they have failed, for some reason, they know at least how to set about repairing the damage and making the family good again. A family is something people can understand. It's something people can control, in a world that is madness.

Armed with a good and whole family, a person can plunge into the madness, take what he wants and retreat again. His family will help him, and he will know that the men and women at his side can be trusted. His family is the key that unlocks the gates of complexity in a place like Bagdad. The rest—the whores and soldiers and merchants and thieves who have gathered from around the world— they are flotsam and jetsam, trash blown in from the sea. But a man with a family has a mighty army at his side. He has power, because he has people he can trust.

The rest of it—well, that's straightforward. None of the politics they all talk means a damned thing. It's just talk— foolish drunks shooting off their mouths to make them- selves seem educated, all for the benefit of whores who could be won over much more efficiently by a tight-lipped dollar. The only approach to take with all the rest of them, this swirling mishmash of ugly heathen jabbering for- eigners, is to wade in among them, find out what they are willing to trade their money for, and get it to them.

To the outsiders, the trade of the people in the region is called smuggling. They pronounce it with a curled lip. But to the people of the area, the good families, it is the only sensible and honorable commerce. It is the one commerce that makes mockery of all their jibber-jabber hypocritical politics while building the strength of the one thing a right- minded man should care about—his family. In this region, a man who smuggles for a living and who possesses a strong family walks in honor and dignity on the streets of his town, to say nothing of walking in relative safety.

Shortly after the Civil War, one of the cruel wild hurri- canes in which the Gulf of Mexico seems to specialize swept in off the sea and erased Bagdad, as if the forces of nature, having waited for the first instant when the settle- ment was no longer needed, had raged in to scour it away

forever. Today there are shacks on the sand, built of scrap
lumber and salvaged plastic tarpaulins. The Rio Grande is
one hundred feet broad and flows at a slow muddy pace by
this spot. When there has been no rain for some time, it is
possible to take your shoes off, tie your laces together,
swing your shoes around your neck and walk across the
river here without getting your ankles wet.

The major drug trade on the river moves up and down
the river in response to political pressure. At times in recent years a good deal of the smuggling has taken place
here. At other times, the trade has moved up the river into
the interior, in Starr County and beyond. But even when
the bulk of it has moved away from Matamoros, there con-
tinues to be a significant trickle.

On the Mexican side an unlighted pickup truck whines
and thumps along dirt roads at night, passing over what
were once the teaming streets of Bagdad. The truck stops
and two dark-clad figures jump out. They wrestle with
something in the bed of the truck. They could be rousing
sleeping mojados, wetbacks who intend to cross the river
here in order to get back to jobs in the United States. They
could be dumping a body. But not this time. This time they
are reaching forward with hay-stacking hooks and pulling
bales of marijuana from the truck. They hide it quickly in
an empty goat-shed. They leave.

As soon as they have left, there is a tinkling splashing
sound out in the shallow flow of the river. Two figures are
coming through the gloom from the American side, tug-
ging on ropes. They are pulling a simple sledge. Within
minutes, they have loaded the bales of marijuana on the
sledge and are pulling their cargo back to the American
side. Through the night, the sound of a pickup starting on
the far shore signals that they are on their way to Houston.

If they are stopped by the police—and they count on
losing a certain portion of each shipment to arrests on the
American side—these smugglers will look, to the arresting
officers, like more in a river of nameless, faceless, ran-
domly wandering Mexican peasants. Only at the very top

of the law enforcement community or in some few local communities, probably in Texas and near the border, will there be cops wise enough in the ways of this trade to recognize them for what they probably really are—members of an old and well established smuggling family that has been doing business on the Mexican border at Matamoros since the days of the Civil War and before.

It is this way all along the border. In the mid-nineteenth century, a U.S. official trying to make heads or tails of the smuggling trade upriver at Rio Grande City complained that smuggling was "identified with the best part of the population."

In the late 1970s, when the Federal Drug Enforcement Agency launched its ambitious "Operation Wishbone" anti-smuggling campaign in Starr County, DEA agents found that they had to penetrate not just a criminal element but the very heart of the mainstream social and family structure of the region. Starr County at that time was a place where people were either bitterly poor—half the population was on welfare—or mysteriously rich. The difference tended to be that some of its residents were willing to alleviate their poverty by swimming a few bundles of contraband across the river every few weeks.

It wasn't always dope. Then, as now, the midnight commerce on the river included everything from VCRs to antihistamines, herbal potions to automatic weapons. The smuggler does not always concern himself with what is in the bundle. He finds it in one place, swims it across and secretes it in another place. He does his job.

In fact, smuggling is the cushion that allows borders to exist at all. Borders are lines drawn by diplomats and soldiers, sitting far away and contemplating maps. They reflect troop movements, formal ceremonies of surrender and victory, discoveries and other abstractions that have little or nothing to do with everyday life.

On this border, as on all borders, the people who dwell on either side are realists. They know what all of the flags and slogans mean as well as any of their compatriots in the interior. They may be even more fiercely patriotic, forced, as they are, to deal with national rivalry as an everyday fact of life and doing business.

But the people on the border also know that boundaries mean nothing when people on the other side want something badly enough—booze or workers or dope, whores or secrets or microchip technology. The people on the border deal every day with the border's strangely ambivalent role in their own lives. It is a much more important presence in their lives than in the lives of the people who live a few hundred miles back up inside the nation. They make their livings from the border. They know what kind of flimsy fabric it is . . . and how important.

A few years ago a United States Immigration official in a major American border town welcomed a visiting reporter from a distant American city. He showed him maps of the border, thick with pins to show where the most recent crossing activity had been taking place. He talked long and colorfully about the great border agents, how they could tell real cattle prints from footprints made by illegal aliens who had tied hooves to their feet. He made a great ceremony of asking the reporter to sign long detailed legal releases from liability before he would allow the reporter to go out with an actual working agent and track illegal crossers on the border. The official, whose district this was, wanted to be sure the reporter understood the difficulty and danger involved in the work his people were doing. Once the releases were in order, the official turned the reporter over to an overworked and weary young agent, who had many other fish to fry but whose ill luck it had been to happen down the corridor at that moment.

Outside in the agent's car, the agent turned to the reporter and said, "The old Dan'l Boone routine for you, I suppose. You want to see us Amurr'can guys out there tracking down these dangerous characters with our years of know-how and uncanny instinct, right?"

The reporter said that he did want to see where and how

most people cross the border but that he only wanted to see what really went on.

"Well, in that case," the agent said, "I won't have to waste gas turning on the engine. You can just look across the street there to where those large crowds of people are walking in and out of those holes in the fence."

And there it was, indeed—the whole sievelike society of the border, passing in and out of huge rents in the chain-link fence along the border, most of them carrying shopping bags, a few with raincoats over their shoulders. Hundreds and hundreds of people, walking casually in and out of the holes in the fence.

The agent explained. The border patrol understands that a certain number of holes in the fence are the polite reality. They do not insult the crossers by knitting up those holes. The crossers would only have to open new holes in the fence, and, if they felt they were being unfairly harassed, they might do expensive damage to the fence in the process.

But the protocol is much more extensive and subtle than just that. The crossers who use the fence holes every day, for example, do not carry suitcases. That would be very bad form and would tend to embarrass the customs agents, whose headquarters, after all, are only a few hundred yards away. The crossers at this point do not travel in large family groups. Neither do they drag large bale-shaped packages through the fence with them. This sort of thing would be ill mannered.

These are mainly day-shoppers, coming into Texas to buy everything from groceries to automobile tires. They are such an important part of the local economy that South Texas reels into economic recession and worse whenever, for some reason, the border actually turns into a border and the flow of shoppers is cut off for more than an hour or so at a time.

Americans flood the other way and often for similar reasons. In Matamoros as in the other border towns, the streets are lined with the offices of physicians, dentists and lawyers, willing to take care of a gringo's problems for much less than it would cost to have them solved at home. A root canal, for example, might be accomplished at less than a fourth the rate just across the line in Brownsville, where American laws and regulations make health care an expensive proposition.

If one has more dangerous business at the border—the smuggling of dope, guns or people, for example—then one must live by the rules of the border and move to the zone where such things are done. The border is like a chess game, in which the principal action may suddenly shift from one part of the board to another, depending on strategic developments. But even at that there are rules that abide, of which the holes in the fence are a good example. The holes in the fence are proof that everyone on the border knows the realities and that no one wants to needlessly damage what accommodations have been possible.

The border—the place where one culture stops and another one starts—is an abstraction that only works neatly and efficiently in the minds of distant officials. In real life and on the border itself, everyone knows that the two nations must soak part of the way into each other's shores, like the brown waters of the Rio Grande, lapping from bank to bank. The border is not a line. It's a process.

The main facilitators of that process, the officials who are really in charge, are the smugglers. It has always been that way, on this and every border.

Chapter Three

Sara was born on September 6, 1964, in Matamoros. Her father, Israel Aldrete, an electrician, was able to give his family the Matamoros version of a comfortable middle-class life. Sara and her sister, Teresa, two years younger, were well fed and well clothed, sent to school, sent to the doctor and the dentist. Their lives were legions away from the lives of the poor campesinos who roamed the streets and alleyways of Matamoros, begging for pesos and eating offal.

But so were their lives legions removed from the lives of the rich gringos across the river. The Aldrete sisters were children of the border. Born in Mexico and blessed in many ways, they nevertheless grew up in the shadow of the bridge and all the power and wealth that lay just beyond it.

The house they grew up in was a modest but tidy little white adobe structure on a narrow street with a haunting name—Santo Degollado, Street of the Beheaded Saint. The neighborhood is small but not close-knit in the manner of the colonias of the countryside. On Street of the Beheaded Saint, people behave in the manner of people of the border towns. They are civil but allow each other a certain distance. The border, after all, is a region where it is especially unwise to go poking your nose needlessly into the affairs of others.

By early teenage, however, Sara already was a girl who attracted more than normal attention. She was very tall and strikingly beautiful, with large lively eyes and a precocious sense of her own presence. She had many boyfriends but was watched over in her courtships by the cautious eyes of her conservative Catholic mother, Teresa.

Sara attended a secretarial school, where she was a star pupil. Her instructors urged her to study at a real college, as had her teachers in high school. But, like many young Mexican girls who are warned by their mothers that their beauty will not last forever, she chose instead to marry.

Two years later, at the age of twenty, she was divorced and had returned to the home of her parents, presenting them with a dilemma. She was now a woman of the world.

In the first place, divorce is not the common thing in Mexican society that it is in the U.S., at least not in conservative northern Mexico. In the second place, the prospect of having a mature, beautiful and strong-willed daughter under the same roof with her mother and father was not a comfortable one for the parents.

Israel went to work with determination and alacrity and built a small semi-detached apartment for Sara behind the little house at 86 Santo Degollado. That way she could live at home, with the company and protection of her parents, and still have the privacy that both she and her parents would find merciful.

By the time she had returned to Israel and Teresa, their daughter had changed. She was less tractable, more restless, hungry for something. Her parents could only guess what their daughter thought she wanted from life.

It was true that, at this juncture, her options were not entirely cheering. She had always been more popular with the boys than her parents might have liked. But now she was no longer a girl. She was a woman, a divorced woman, and some of the traditional avenues of Mexican working and middle class life were less open to her than they had been when she was a teenager and a virgin.

There was always the possibility—her parents did not discuss it with her, because they did not have to discuss it—that she would go on to have the life of many young women in her position. She would work as a secretary or in some other similar position. She would continue to live in the little apartment her father had built for her behind his own house, in order that he and she both could be shielded from situations in which he no longer had any great paternal jurisdiction anyway.

And she would grow old. She would lose her looks. She was already twenty. She might have ten years left in that department. Depending on how she lived, she might have five.

If she stayed in the church and lived a decent life, she might die as a good but lonely old maid. If she gave into the powerful temptations of border life, she might die a less pleasant person.

Her parents did not discuss these things with her, because they did not have to bring them up. These things were obvious and plain, hanging over the little house on the Street of the Beheaded Saint like the moon itself, from the moment she returned home, her marriage a failure.

Sara, meanwhile, seemed determined to push her life beyond these claustrophobic boundaries. She had always been a forceful, willful personality. There had even been some suggestion that her willfulness, a not entirely desirable trait in women in conservative Mexican society, might have played a role in the demise of the marriage. Now that same will was showing its face in her refusal to accept the normal consequences of her divorce.

In late 1985, Sara applied for and received resident alien status in the United States. At the end of the year, she crossed the bridge into Brownsville and applied for acceptance into Texas Southmost College.

Texas Southmost is a two-year institution, housed in

quarters just at the foot of the international bridge in Brownsville. Its campus and buildings would seem shabby anywhere else but fit in smoothly with the surrounding ambience of Brownsville. Some of the classes are taught in small structures that look like temporary classrooms behind the two main buildings.

At Texas Southmost, Sara was accepted into a "work-study" program, which meant she was able to work for the college in lieu of a portion of her tuition. In January of 1986, she began taking classes as a physical education major. At the same time, she began to work as an assistant to Patty Galvan, the P.E. department secretary, whom Sara helped by answering phones, running errands and typing. She also worked at the school as a part-time aerobics instructor.

Aerobic dance: there was the venue in which Sara Aldrete's personality really shone. She was a fantastic aerobic dance instructor, always up, always on, always pressing for the next degree of exertion and perfection. Her students recalled later that the music and the exercise really seemed to transport her and that she was urgent and charismatic in her insistence that they be transported with her.

Sara blossomed at Texas Southmost. It was as if all the black dresses and bone combs and yellowing toile of Mexican culture were thrown off, and she was dancing out into the very cloud of freedom and fulfillment she had only been able to spy from afar during the dusty years of her childhood.

She made an unmistakable figure, striding across the dog-eared little campus in her leotards and short skirt, floating on long springy legs, her huge brown eyes laughing and her glassy fluting voice singing out hellos to everyone in Spanish and in English. There was a strength and worldly grit in her good looks and voice that people instinctively liked.

The next two years were a time of great political ferment and discontent in Brownsville and the Rio Grande Valley, especially for young Hispanics. The Mexican economy had gone to Hell; Central American refugees were flooding up to the border towns and on across the river, seeking refuge and opportunity, all of which only served to exacerbate the racism and xenophobia of the Anglo population.

Brownsville itself seemed to be suffering the curses of Job. Just when the economic and political problems already were earning the Valley unwanted bad publicity on an international scale, the roof of a large store in Brownsville collapsed, killing nine people and injuring many more.

The dope trade along the border was growing ever more vicious and daring. The mood of the police grew consequently darker.

It was a time when Hispanic kids in the Valley, the serious ones anyway, were apt to wonder where they fit in and what had happened to all the great activism of the 1960s, La Raza Unida and so on, about which they heard in such boring detail from their instructors and professors. What had all of it accomplished? Why did they seem still to be at the bottom of someone else's barrel all the time?

A new interest in things Mexican was welling in the heart of the Valley's youth culture. The 1960s types, judging by what they had to say in school today, were all for political activism and so on, all for taking on the gringo by taking over parts of his machine.

The new interest among young people was not unrelated to those earlier impulses, but it was not the same. It did not operate at the same level. In particular, there was great interest in the side of Mexican culture that had always been treated as taboo by the 1960s types, as an embarrassing evidence of primitivism that would only be held up by the gringos to prove their racist assumptions.

The young Mexican-American people of the Valley wanted to know more about the curanderos. Many of them still had grandparents back in Mexico who believed devoutly in the powers of the curanderos. Most of them had parents who pretended not to believe but who were not above making a little sidetrip, during a vacation visit to the Mexican interior, in order to consult with a certain funny-looking old campesino who might be able to help with a painful problem of arthritis. In all of this welter of belief and language, the young people suspected that something was being held away from them—some very interesting aspect of who and what they were and where they came from.

In this setting, Sara was an interesting presence indeed. She spoke perfect English; she seemed perfectly at home on the American side, where she had rented a small apartment; but she was a Mexican, a beautiful Mexican with wonderful eyes who returned each weekend to visit her friends and tend to things in the little apartment behind the house at 86 Santo Degollado.

Her fellow students elected her head of the booster club for the school's popular soccer team. She was selected for inclusion in the school's "Who's Who," a sort of addendum to the school directory showing who were the most popular and active students that year.

She was a special favorite of the faculty, earning straight A's in all of her courses. Some teachers, like anthropology professor and local political activist Anthony Zavaleta, picked her out as one of the school's most promising students, sure to go far in life, with her intelligence, wit, good looks and vivacious personality.

To Zavaleta, to others on the faculty like Jim Lemons, she seemed to be the almost perfect student, full of verve and determination, well organized, obviously interested in her own health and in living a healthy and productive life.

Never did she display to them any particular interest in the occult, which was itself an interesting fact. For one thing, interest in the curanderos and in occult matters generally was so high that some of the faculty had agreed to put together a special series of tutorials on the topic.

Several faculty members were familiar generally with Hispanic occultism, but Zavaleta was the school's presiding expert, having approached the matter from several perspectives. As a local politician and sometime sociologist, he had participated in studies to measure the role of the curanderos in local health conditions. Like many educated Mexican-Americans, his own feelings toward the curanderos were ambivalent. He was a modern sophisticated man, but he freely admitted he always made sure he was wearing a cross before going over to the other side to talk to a curandero.

He had made his own study of the beliefs of Santeria. And, in his other incarnation as a local anthropologist, he had taken part in a dig in a road construction site between Brownsville and Harlingen which produced what were probably the earliest clues to human habitation of the region.

In "The Unland Site," a paper describing the findings of the dig published in 1979, Zavaleta and his co-author came to very ambivalent conclusions about what had been the fate of the three human beings whose bones they had unearthed. The paper was also curiously vague about the date of their demise. Presumably they were stone-age hunters.

The men whose remains Zavaleta and his associates unearthed and studied had died violent deaths. That much was clear from the scrape-marks on the bones. The authors conjectured that they might have been left to die after being wounded. Later their tribesmen may have found their animal-ravaged bodies and buried them in a hasty common grave, without the niceties of burial normally so important to people of their time and culture.

But the paper also pointed strongly to another possibility. The facial bones, spinal columns and the phalanges of the fingers and toes were strangely missing.

"It must be assumed," they said in the paper, "that some activity or phenomenon prior to burial resulted in the loss of most proximal and distal ends of the long bones."

Perhaps, having stumbled on the most ancient known window into the region's human past, the authors were unenthusiastic about their own conclusions. In convoluted and extremely cautious language, they conceded finally that other findings from other digs of the same period would suggest that the absence of certain bones, of the phalanges in particular, could indicate the three unceremoniously buried Indian males might have been victims of ritual cannibalism.

Sara showed almost no interest in these matters in conversations with her teachers. But her fellow students saw another side of her entirely, especially after the man she called "my Cuban boyfriend" entered her life. For every bit the teachers seemed not to see, the other students saw more in Sara, more than they sometimes cared to see.

She met him toward the end of her first year at Texas Southmost, on a weekend, when she was back in Matamoros. She was in her town, in Matamoros, on a hot loud night with the streets full of tourists and refugees. Matamoros was Bagdad, the wonderful and mysterious border city it could be at its very best, teeming with energy and need and ferocious determination, dark with beggared tragedy.

She met him in the street. She was driving her father's car on a Sunday afternoon. Four guys in a Mercedes cut her off in traffic and ogled her—a not uncommon occurrence for her in Matamoros. But one of the men, the dark and dignified one in the back, struck her instantly as different from the others, the thuggy ones.

He was the one who rolled down the window and invited her solemnly to join him at a cafe. There, he read the Tarot for her.

He never smiled. He never cursed. He was "a gentleman," she told her friends later. She was certain at first that he was gay. Then, after sitting with him for a while, she was uncertain.

Sara had been drawn to the company of gay men a great deal since her divorce. She wasn't sure why. With this man, she wasn't sure of anything. She knew that he was terribly different, but she was not sure how or why.

He was very handsome. He was obviously rich. Early in the conversation he told her things that would amount to macho bragging under normal circumstances. He had "business" in Brownsville and "business" in Miami, "business" in Mexico City, and he commuted between homes in all three places.

It was not the most unusual story Sara had heard from obviously rich strangers in bars and cafes in Matamoros. It could mean the least mysterious of things—that he was a dope dealer. The city was full of young dope dealers. They came and went. Like anyone who had grown up in Matamoros, Sara knew who the established local dope dealers were. He obviously was not one of them. He spoke with a Cuban accent. He could have been any of the multitude of fools and crazies who float through Matamoros with a lot of dope-deal talk on their lips and who end up getting a bullet in their faces somewhere out there on the sandbars at night.

But he was not like any of them. Adolfo de Jesus Constanzo was very different, very unlike the other young men she typically met on these hot mysterious evenings in the streets of Matamoros.

There was an incredible and riveting presence about him. He spoke very very seriously about everything. He never once smiled. Not once, not at all. But he spoke very softly, almost kindly. He offered to read the cards for her.

He read the cards with great seriousness, pondering over each one, flicking at them with his little finger, turning them slightly and pondering them again, as if listening. While he read the cards, he engaged her in little bits of chatter, quiet barely mumbled exchanges about small things, personal things. She told him that she lived on both sides of the border, in Brownsville and on the Matamoros side too. He told her that he often stayed in the Holiday Inn—one of Brownsville's finer hotels. She asked him what brought him to Brownsville.

Constanzo told her that he had a very important "client" there. He said he came to service the client once every month or two. Sara's better instincts told her not to express interest in his personal business. But she discovered, almost with a start, almost with a quickly drawn breath, that she was already fantastically curious about him. She knew his business, whatever it was, was very unusual. Finally she asked him what he did for his "client."

He told her that he performed limpias. And suddenly the reading was over. He said good-bye, and he glided out into the mob-choked streets.

In the course of the reading, Constanzo had told her that a person very near to her would come to her soon with a terrible problem. She would not be able to help her intimate friend. The problem would be beyond her powers. She laughed later about the prediction, but she admitted to another friend that the strange and somber Cuban who had read her cards the previous weekend in Matamoros was very much on her mind, no matter what the value of his predictions.

And then, two weeks later, his prediction came true. The boy with whom she had been sleeping lifted himself on an elbow one night and explained why he had been so preoccupied in the last month or so. His family, he said, was in terrible trouble. Something was going wrong, something deep in the heart of the family. The family—always so strong and loyal he had thought of it as a physical entity, a thing of rock and mass—was falling apart in splinters and dust around him, and he could not imagine why.

She knew the family, of course. They were important Matamoros drug dealers and smugglers. Young Serafin Hernandez, Jr., only twenty, a student of law enforcement at Texas Southmost College, told her he was utterly lost and at sea. He had left his father's family to serve in the family of his uncle, Little Elio, only two years his senior. Unwilling to abandon all ties to the gringo life that had been his own during boyhood, he had enrolled at Southmost to take some courses. He thought law enforcement courses might give him some insight into the problems of his family, might make him useful in new ways.

His family, already a fairly major cocaine and marijuana smuggling operation, was now branching out, under Elio's impatient rule, to guns, stolen cars and rip-offs from other families.

She found Constanzo again in Matamoros on a succeeding weekend, and she told him that his prediction had come true. Constanzo took the news very somberly. He asked for details in a matter-of-fact way. She was hesitant.

He spoke again to her in his special way, which might have seemed like bragging from another man's lips but seemed only businesslike from him. He explained to her that many famous and rich people in both Mexico and the United States were his clients. He named famous actors and singing stars. Dropping his voice lower, he named the names of important people in the Mexican government and in the police agencies who came to him. Logically, she should have been put off by this information. She should have been afraid that all his bragging did was make him out to be an informer. But somehow his words had the opposite effect. She was drawn to him more and more powerfully the more he spoke.

She told him the broad details of what Serafin's family did—a commonplace on the border, really—and gave him an outline of the family's problems. Suddenly the Cuban was much more interested in her and in her story. He pressed, and she gave him her phone numbers and addresses. Within a week, she was sleeping with the Cuban and calling him her boyfriend. Young Serafin seemed to take it well. He soon was becoming the Cuban's friend, too.

It was after mention of the Cuban boyfriend began to creep into her conversation that the other students at Southmost began to notice the change. No one noticed anything at all about Serafin Hernandez, Jr., because he was too quiet and withdrawn to be noticed in the first place. But in lovely happy Sara with the fluting voice and the irresistible eyes they saw change—enough change that they began to talk about it.

For one thing, she was suddenly the campus expert on the occult. Students meeting informally to talk about it were even offended by her authoritarian manner on the subject. On one occasion, watching a videotaped documentary on Santeria, a group of students were surprised when she whirled on them and asked if they really wanted to know what Santeria was all about.

Angered by what she took as the condescending anthropological tone of the documentary, Sara launched into a long spirited monologue on Santeria rituals, how they were really carried out and what effects they could cause.

The students fell silent as she went on and on, telling them of rituals in which the participants drenched themselves in sacrificial blood in order to bring about their "cleansing." On more than one occasion, she slipped out of the third person and described the participants as "nosotros" or us.

One boy watching her performance was especially taken aback. He had always admired her. He called her "the all-American girl." She had spoken to him often of her "Cuban boyfriend," but he had never taken that connection too seriously. He happened to know of Constanzo. Constanzo was a known commodity in the gay community in Matamoros. He was not a serious suitor for a woman like Sara Aldrete, and this boy liked to harbor the hope somewhere in the back of his mind that he himself might be such a man.

But Sara's bizarre speech about voodoo rites had followed a little too closely on other experiences this boy had had with her in recent months. He had noticed one day she was wearing a very unusual necklace, made of string. Unthinking, he reached out to touch it, and she recoiled sharply. She spoke to him angrily, warning him never to touch the necklace again.

He had withdrawn sheepishly, thinking his mistake had been to make too physically familiar a gesture.

But she stuck her finger in his face and made a strange speech then too. She told him she was only angry because she was trying to protect him. "This necklace was given to me, and nobody can touch it," she said. "If you touch it, everything that has gone wrong against me, every evil, will go to you."

A few weeks later, he noticed the same necklace. Only this time it had changed colors. It was a dark brown-red now—a color that made him uneasy. He asked her about it.

"Yes," she said cheerfully. "It's red. It has been purified with fresh blood."

He waited for another opportunity to talk to her. When it arose, he asked her what all of this business was about —the weird speeches and bloody necklaces. She told him that she had visited Mexico City recently and that, while there, she had been examined by a Haitian voodoo priest. The priest had found several marks on her body.

The marks, she told the boy, meant that she was a priestess, a chosen one. "You are not going to believe the extra powers we have," she said.

According to the first statements Constanzo's followers made to police after their arrests, Sara's initiation in Mexico City was quick and thorough. One member of the group attempted later, in public and under Sara's gaze during a press conference, to recant. But the first statements were detailed and damning.

Sara, they said, took part in the horrible Zona Rosa killings. She was there. She wore a white robe and stood at Constanzo's side, her face frozen in the same somber ghoul-priest expression he wore.

In a chaos of blood and screaming agony, she was serene, they said. She made suggestions. She invented embellishments. According to this version of events, Sara was an avid student.

What she gained in bloodlust, Sara soon lost in another department. At some time in early 1988, only months after he first slept with her, her Cuban boyfriend no longer needed her in his bed. He needed her for something else— to exercise a power she had possessed since teenage. He needed her power to get someone else to sleep with her.

It was Elio's turn in bed with Sara. Serafin, after all,

was a powerless novice. And by this time Constanzo already had her firmly under his spell. But Elio. Now there was the man with his hand on the purse strings. She saw to it that Serafin introduced her to his uncle. She did not miss her mark. She and Elio were in bed together for the first time within a week of their first meeting.

And did she have a deal for Elio.

He knew vaguely about limpias. She laid it out for ignorant half-literate hotheaded Elio: his problems weren't with other dope dealers or the police.

His family was being poisoned. A curse had fallen on them. The nagual was prowling among them. At least one member of the family, perhaps more, had been taken by now, their souls gnawed from within.

His only hope was the limpia. The poison might be within him too, by now. He needed desperately to be cleansed, in order to save himself, in order to save his family.

Limpias are ritual cleansings of the soul. A limpia is carried out by a curandero who has the power to locate evil and curses that have been placed on a soul by another sorcerer or directly through the offices of an orisha.

The limpia is another of the many primeval rituals that echo again and again through all of the original cultures. An unreligious person might say the Roman Catholic practice of confession is a form of limpia. Certainly there are forms of group therapy that are modern secular limpias.

The form of limpia Constanzo performed for people, jotting records of each client and each ritual in Bantu in his little journal, was the ancient precursor of all these. In it he was the high priest, medium, sorcerer and soul-catcher. While he passed his hands over the bodies of his clients, he sang the songs and muttered the hexes his ancestors had sung down through the eons.

If there was a bit of Gypsy flimflam at the end, having human eyeballs blop out of eggs and so on, that was always the way of the sorcerer. Any deception he could use to trick and crack the minds of his followers was fair if it worked. If they believed he had drawn the evil eye out of the body of his client, then they would go away having been profoundly affected by the experience. And that was what they followed him for.

Once she was in the bed of Elio, Sara did not have a difficult time convincing him he needed more serious help. He was a boy, barely in his twenties, overwhelmed by crushing challenges. The smoothly operating machine his older brother Saul had put together was coming apart at the seams.

His own impetuosity—the need of a very young man to prove himself to other men—had impelled him into an incredibly dangerous position in the dope trade. Other dope gangs were gunning for him, including some of the major families of northern Mexico. He had gotten himself implicated in the war between the Mexican state and federal police to take over the dope bribes and the business itself along the border. And, for all he knew, he probably had some Colombians mad at him, too, somewhere up the line.

And yet, in order to keep it all going and in order to keep that vital flow of cash moving through the pipeline, he had to continue to go out there into the night every night and meet airplanes.

Why not trust this Cuban curandero with his problems? What could it hurt?

Within an amazingly brief period, less than two months, Elio had become totally enthralled with Constanzo. Beginning with the Tarot cards, proceeding to the limpia and then quickly on to the darker rites, Elio plunged into Constanzo's world because it offered him solace, and strength, and the power of resoluteness. Constanzo's world was in many ways hideous and frightening. But Constanzo's world was better than Elio's world.

At the end of 1987, shortly before Christmas, Elio made his own pilgrimage to Mexico City, where he received a physical exam from the traveling voodoo doctor. Lo and behold, by astounding coincidence, Elio's body bore the same rare and mysterious marks Sara's had. He too was one of the chosen. He too was a priest in the Church of Palo Mayombe, or Abakua, or whatever it was at that particular point in time—the church of the sliding scale.

Once she had won her way into the bed of Elio, the curtains of mystery lifted. She and Adolfo could see deep into events of the recent past. The first thing that came clear in this window was the double assassination a year ago. All Matamoros had whispered about it. Everyone knew it was a very serious event, because of how it was done and because of the people who were killed. But now Sara and Adolfo knew the all-important thing. They knew why it had happened.

The people who had done the shooting were soldiers in a huge family reaching out over most of the border and controlling vast amounts of drug movement and other crime. This family controls other families. It is an old operation, and some people say it is getting fat and slow. But it is huge and cruel. No one ever would take this family lightly.

One of the men machine-gunned that night had been Elio's brother, Saul—the hot one who had founded the Hernandez operation. The man standing next to Elio, the man who died with him, was even more notable.

That man had been a person devoutly to be feared. Tomas Morlet had been in Matamoros only three years, but he had arrived with bone-chilling credentials. As mighty as the local families might be, they were only locals, after all, northerners, born and bred in the conservative, cynical capitalist border region.

Tomas Morlet was a creature of higher realms. His decision to come to Matamoros had been the result of an executive transfer of sorts. He was a high official in the most feared and powerful drug cartel in Mexico. He was an agent of the Mexican federal government.

True, his position was no longer official by the time he arrived in Matamoros, but no Mexican who met him or knew of him had the slightest doubt what he was. He was a famous man, after all. He had figured in important international events. He had served the national government as a martyr of sorts. There were vast forces and powers behind him.

In February 1985, United States Drug Enforcement Agency agent Enrique ("Kiki") Camarena and Alfredo Zavalar Avelar, his DEA pilot, were tortured and murdered by Mexican drug dealers connected both to druglord Felix Gallardo and to top Mexican law enforcement officials. The killings were breathtakingly cruel.

Camarena had been beaten and tortured, his rectum violated with a stick and his skull punctured with a tire iron. Avelar also had been brutally sodomized—a trademark of Latin drug and military torture.

Authorities believe Camarena was killed slowly, then dumped in a grave. The pilot was tortured but not killed before burial. He was alive at the time he was thrown into the grave with Camarena's corpse. He died of suffocation beneath the soil they shoveled onto his staring face.

Top Reagan administration officials, deep in negotiations with Mexico over support for the Contras at the time, had tried to pass off the Camarena murder as the sad but predictable death of a soldier who had been doing his job. But an outraged Congress and some mutinous mid-level Reaganites refused to let Camarena's murder pass off so easily into the void.

Representative Charles Rangel (D–New York), chairman of the House select committee on narcotics abuse and control, and Senator Paula Hawkins (R–Florida) were adamant in calling for a meaningful reckoning in Mexico. Even within the White House, officials who had dealt with Mexican officials on the killings were angered by their obvious lack of interest.

The Mexican point of view was, so what? Mexico had lost over 400 policemen and federal agents in the drug wars in recent years. If you come to Mexico to fight drugs, they said, you run the risk of dying, even of dying horribly. Why should an American cop in Mexico expect anything different?

The problem was that the American cops who had been in Mexico fighting drugs since the 1970s had come to take a less than admiring view of the way the Mexican police operated in this realm, even of the way they died. Too many of the Mexican cops who died, it was believed, bought the farm because they were drug dealers themselves.

It was sometimes hard for an American to figure out just what the term *police* was supposed to mean in Mexico. The average police salary was $2,400 a year—a pittance, even in the Mexican economy. No one remotely expected the Mexican police to live on what they were paid.

They were expected to take bribes. They were expected to control violence and crime in much the same way gangs inside American prisons actually run the prisons. They control the violence by taking it over. They control the crime by seeing to it that it is well run, that people don't go to excess, that they stick to business and don't try to act bigger than they have a right to act. It's a mentality that accepts a level of violence, cruelty and depravity as a natural aspect of human existence.

The United States had plunged into the Mexican dope control business with both big feet in the early 1970s. More than 7,000 Mexican troops, joined by 30 full-time agents of the U.S. DEA and armed with $95 million worth of American helicopters, guns and super-sleuth technology, moved against peasant marijuana growers in Guerrero, the state that is home to the type of marijuana known as Acapulco Gold.

The peasants of Guerrero had supported a modest guerrilla effort since the 1960s. With the aid of the American anti-dope money, the Mexican federal government was able to stamp out the guerrillas, shut down all forms of peasant land occupancy or land protest of any kind and totally militarize the state. It continued to be a military enclave, in which the top Mexican police official simply took over the narcotics industry himself, becoming one of the nation's most estimable dealers.

The basic underlying thesis of the American anti-dope campaign in Mexico was one that made a certain kind of sense both to American officials and to the top Mexicans. For Mexican president Luis Echeverria and to the Nixon people who launched the policy, including G. Gordon Liddy, it was obvious where marijuana came from: poor people made it. Poor bad people. Communists. People made dope out there in the Mexican boondocks because they were bad.

The U.S. continued to push its anti-dope crusade in Mexico into the 1980s, and the effect of each new escalation in the war was to drive the dope corruption up higher into the Mexican government.

What ensued, according to the most convincing accounts, was a grim and messy mélange of ineffectual dope-fighting and very effective political repression. In 1977, the College of Attorneys of the city of Culiacan (the bar association) complained to the United Nations that Mexican anti-drug police, assisted by the DEA, had engaged in torture of suspects, including the use of electric shocks, rape, gouging of eyes, jamming heads into toilets full of excrement, forcing gasoline and soft drinks up noses until the prisoners were deaf or blind or just drowned. Other tortures caused miscarriages and necessitated the amputation of limbs.

The DEA stoutly denied that its agents had taken part in these events. Behind closed doors in Washington, DEA administrators claimed it was not possible for them to be associated in any way with the Mexican police and not be associated in the public's mind with these kinds of incidents. However unfair the accusation, they said, the Mexican public would always assume that anyone who worked with the Mexican authorities took part in torture.

The pattern that developed over time was an especially frustrating one for the many DEA people who were serious about their objectives and honest in the way they pursued them in Mexico. As their counterparts in the Mexican federal law enforcement community got deeper into the rural dope trade in Mexico, they saw more and more clearly just how much potential for profit was out there.

Meanwhile, all of the traditional Latin American anxieties and resentments over Yanqui interventionism grew stronger, the longer the DEA stuck around. The public professions of determination to root out dope corruption in Mexico seemed to mask just the opposite process.

In 1978, before his election as President, Jose Lopez Portillo had said: "Corruption is the cancer of this country." One of the first official acts of his successor, Miguel de la Madrid, was to fire Portillo's chief of police in Mexico City, Arturo Durazo-Moreno—for corruption.

In 1984, DEA agents triggered the discovery of a single cache of 10,000 tons of marijuana, enough to satisfy the entire U.S. market for one year—all of it right under the noses of Mexican police. In 1985, de la Madrid publicly admitted there were substantial "criminal links between narcotic traffickers and police agents in Mexico" and fired hundreds of federal judicial police and agents of the especially vile Directorate of Federal Security, many of whose agents had been acting as bodyguards for major dealers.

Camarena himself liked to tell a story he had heard from a Mexican informant about what happened when the Mexican cops dropped down out of the sky in their impressive American helicopters to raid the big dope operations. His informant said first there was the thwacking sound of the rotor dropping low, and then there was the thwacking sound of the money being counted out into the palm of the helicopter commander, and then there was the thwacking sound of the helicopter rotor lifting off.

As the DEA grew more frustrated and stepped up its efforts to get to the heart of dope corruption in Mexico, the Mexicans grew more itchy and uncomfortable with this pushy nosey foreign presence in their affairs. In the meantime, the very Mexican police officials with whom the

DEA was supposed to be working were working their own way deeper into the dope trade.

Camarena's mistake was to get too close. He was bulling his way in closer and closer to the operation of Felix Gallardo. And that was too high. Too big. Too near the power structure of Mexico itself.

Some people weren't satisfied, though. Senator Hawkins and Representative Rangel insisted that Mexico was supposed to be our friend, according to the fat foreign aid payments we made every year. And Mexico was our neighbor. And we could not just let this one pass.

Some people in the administration, a little farther out in the field, more in touch with daily life and less beholden to the big picture, agreed with Rangel and Hawkins. One of them was acting DEA administrator Jack Lawn. Another was Willy von Raab, the U.S. Commissioner of Customs.

Outraged over the whole thing and under constant pressure from Lawn, von Raab decided he and U.S. Customs were going to carry out their own little version of American foreign policy. What von Raab did and the events that resulted closely parallel the behavior of Customs and the outcome in the Mark Kilroy case. On both occasions, Customs was able to force the Mexican soil to open and disgorge the rot-blackened bodies of missing Americans.

But there was more than mere coincidence, much more than bureaucratic routine or political similarity linking these events. Destiny moved from the first place in time to the second in the form of a human messenger—one Tomas Morlet.

After a year had passed since the Camarena kidnaping, it was obvious the Mexican authorities had no sincere interest at all in helping the United States track down the killers of Camarena, whose body still had not been found. Acting on his own, without consulting Secretary of State Schultz, von Raab put out the order that he wanted every single vehicle crossing the border from Mexico into Texas to be stopped and thoroughly searched.

The result was chaos, furor and frenzy at the border.

From Matamoros to Tijuana, the bridges became madhouse scenes, and the economies of the Mexican border regions began quickly to grind to a halt. At the same time, U.S. Ambassador John Gavin began hinting to reporters that he was prepared to ask the State Department to haul out the one weapon Mexico could not resist:

The Travel Advisory.

Tourism is Mexico's second-biggest source of foreign currency after oil. And the oil business was already deep in decline. A travel advisory, warning middle-class people in Michigan that Mexico was too dangerous to visit, giving American tourists the impression Mexico was some kind of Third World war zone, that it was a place like Beirut or Teheran where people just weren't safe, was the one thing the government of Mexico could not allow to happen.

On a dirt road near a ranch in the state of Michoacan, a peasant found two rotting bodies dumped on the ground in bags. Someone had disinterred Camarena and his pilot and had placed them near where a group of DEA agents conveniently had been summoned by an anonymous tipster. In response to the threat of a travel advisory, the Mexican soil had yielded up grisly mysteries.

But there was more. Mexican authorities, speaking in somber and saddened tones, said it was true, as the DEA and others had quite correctly suspected, that high Mexican law enforcement officials had been involved in the Camarena case. At a press conference set up especially for TV in Tijuana, Mexican police presented the brains behind the Camarena kidnaping—one Tomas Morlet, a high official in the Federal Security Directorate (DFS). In his twenty-two years with the DFS, Morlet had been entrusted with high profile and prestigious assignments such as guarding the Shah of Iran and Henry Kissinger. He was a prominent person.

The Mexican press called Morlet and the two assistants arrested with him "sacrificial lambs." The arrest of such a high-ranking person in so terrible a crime was greeted with a shrug. It was an ancient truth that danger could only be warded off and power acquired through the giving of sacrifice. So it was Morlet's fate to go to the altar. He would serve a greater good, if the offering of his career turned out to be sufficient to get the borders out from under Willy von Raab's screaming eagle grip and banish forever this terrible talk of travel advisories.

It was enough. The difficulties passed from the border. The Americans took home the mutilated bodies of their dead and buried them. Life returned to normal.

And so did Tomas Morlet. He spent no more than a few days in "custody," and then was quietly released by the federales, along with his men. The federales told anyone with the temerity to ask—foreign reporters mainly—that they had discovered, to their great embarrassment, a lack of sufficient evidence on which to pursue the charges against Morlet.

It was at this point that Tomas Morlet left his long and distinguished career at the DFS, departed from his beloved Mexico City and decided to reestablish himself in the distant border city of Matamoros as a major dope dealer.

The feeling among the federales had always been, after all, that these anti-socialist half-Yanqui politically traitorous families in the North were making entirely too much money. It might help to have some people who were not currently officially in uniform up there softening up the beaches for an eventual takeover. After all, if the gringos are determined to spill their patrimony out all over Mexico in the form of cash for their beloved drugs, then it's best to see that this ugly but hugely profitable industry is in politically correct hands. And it's always nice to get filthy rich in the process.

But even with his awesome credentials and with the obvious source of power behind him, where would a man like Tomas Morlet—new in town and without local connections—recruit his army? With whom would he make his coalitions?

One family in particular in Matamoros was a likely target for Morlet's affections. The Hernandez clan, richer and more powerful every day in Matamoros, still had the stink of poverty up its nose. Only ten years ago Saul Hernandez, the patriarch, had launched the operation. They were starving poor then. There is a fierce heart beating in a family that can still remember what it feels like to die from lack of money.

Saul had started the way everyone starts, swimming the river with little bundles stuck to his gut with duct tape. He had graduated to pickup trucks and bales hidden in shacks out on the moonlit dunes. Saul was a comer. In all the anthill of operators out there every night, scoring their little scores and counting themselves rich, Saul Hernandez was one of the ones Elegua the god had chosen for a larger role.

Saul saw quickly that the secret to making the big money was the arrangement called "farm-to-arm" in the heroin trade. One must control one's own business along the entire vertical path, from production to marketplace. One must lust for control and for profit. One must hate sharing a single peso with outsiders. One must have the soul of John D. Rockefeller.

Within a few years, Saul had dispatched his older brother, Serafin Hernandez, Sr., to Houston, where Serafin had set up his own reliable distribution network. At the same time, Saul was using his profits to buy up marijuana fields in Oaxaca and Yucatán.

The younger generation of the family was being trained in the ways of dope warriors. The Hernandez family business ran smoothly, without violence, but one never knew when it might be necessary to have men with hearts of lions at the ready. It was important to keep the heart fierce. Disdainful of the old men and soft spoiled boys of the other local families, the Hernandez family always fought on the other side.

Several members of the younger generation hired themselves out as guns to "El Cacho," a loco and a killer. He stole dope from them and tried to sell to their customers. There were many shootouts, and finally El Cacho was wounded.

In May 1984, El Cacho was recovering from his wounds in a clinic in Matamoros. Six men with machine guns entered the clinic. They walked through and methodically sprayed bullets through every living thing they saw. El Cacho was killed. So were six entirely innocent and unrelated men, women and children.

It was, in fact, the violence between the dope families that was changing the whole nature of the business, the nature of life itself in Matamoros and in northern Mexico. There always had been violence associated with the dope business and with smuggling in general. But, with the outbreak of interfamily rivalries and now with the grim presence of a figure like Morlet in town, the violence was taking on a new and utterly bone-chilling level of intensity.

There was just too much money in it. There had always been wealth in the dope trade—exciting, numbing rivers of cash beyond the wildest dreams of simple peasants. But now there was more. There was money in a whole new magnitude. As recently as the 1960s, the dope trade in and through Mexico had involved money on the order one would expect to find in any of the major criminal activities, amplified by the fact that Mexico had a fat rich neighbor who always overspent for whores and bootleg booze, gambling and forged documents, little boys and dope. It was always big money, but it was big criminal money, snatched up in little fistfuls of cash on dirty streetcorners.

But in the 1980s, the amount of capital involved in the Mexican dope trade was more on the order of a major national industry. The straight world could see the money only in occasional peeks and glimpses through the fence of secrecy, but those glimpses were enough to tell the story. A Chicago branch of one of the Mexican farm-to-arm families was pulling down $60 million a year in profits, according to DEA estimates.

That family was a typical nightmare for drug authorities. It included over 2,000 members, bound together by the ferocious tie of Latin family blood and virtually impenetrable to almost all of the conventional police methods.

In 1988 alone, the U.S. Customs Service seized 22,654 pounds of cocaine in the Mexican border region—three times the total amount seized in 1987. Customs, the DEA, the FBI, the state authorities, all made the same plea. The amounts of dope washing into the country over the southern border, pulled in by a voracious demand on the American side and a willingness by American users to pay any amount, was simply overwhelming the American authorities. The authorities needed more money. It was happening at a time when Americans had decided they wanted to spend less money on government, not more. And so the tide of dope continued to swell.

When police were able to crack the wall and catch the smugglers counting their money, they found that the smugglers did not bother counting. They didn't have time. They weighed the money. Through these discoveries the DEA came up with the arcane knowledge that twenty pounds of hundred dollar bills is equivalent to $1 million, while 100 pounds of twenty-dollar bills equals $1 million.

The money, in other words, was coursing into the hands of the smugglers and producers literally in bales. Using fairly simple methods, the dope dealers were able to cleanse this river of cash of its criminal origin and then spend and use it as if it were the legitimate profit of a legitimate industry. The money man in a dope family would take 1,000 pounds or so of hundred-dollar bills to a friendly bank in Miami. The bank was required by federal law to report any deposit over $10,000 to the IRS. Normally there was no check or review whatever to see if such papers were being filed. Once through the bank's system, the money was gone, vanished, invisible. The fee for forgetting to file the proper papers with the IRS was 2 percent or twenty pounds, at a value to the banker of $200,000, cash, clear, tax free, in the pocket, and won't Mommy be pleased.

The friendly American bank sent the money by wire to a bank in Switzerland, Panama, Hong Kong, the Bahamas, the Grand Cayman Islands in the Caribbean, one of those places where privacy laws were strict and other nations were barred from prying. The receiving bank deposited the money in the account of a bogus corporation.

The bogus corporation loaned the money to the dope dealer. Not only was the money now clean, but it was tax free, because, of course, it was a loan. The government went after some few banks. In 1982, the Great American Bank of Dade County was charged with laundering $96 million. But the only way for the government to catch anybody was for an informer to be there and see it happen when it happened. In the vast majority of cases, it just happened.

The actual origin and path of the dope switched around over time like an angry river. Whenever some piddler/ meddler came along and tried to build a levee, the dope river leapt across and ravaged fresh countryside somewhere else. In the 1950s and 1960s, the top importers had been Italians, brokering in heroin from the Middle East. In the 1970s, Mexicans began producing their own "Mexican brown" heroin and importing it by family, swimming it across on rafts of lashed logs, moving it up into the States taped to truck bumpers and stuffed inside air filters. For a while, the Mexicans were making the mafia look like chumps.

But the Vietnam vets came back with a whole new world of narcotics connections, eventually driving Mexican brown from the streets with stuff from Southeast Asia. By the 1980s, the major region of source had switched to the golden triangle—Afghanistan, Pakistan and Iran.

By then, however, the middle classes of the United States were becoming far more important junkies than the poor thieves on ghetto streets who barely scraped together the cash for each dose of heroin. Suddenly people who dressed for success and had good jobs in solid Midwestern cities were willing to spill their patrimonies into the gutter for cocaine. Suddenly there was real money in dope—a huge chunk of the earned wealth of the great American bourgeoisie was now in play.

With that change, the focus of the international narcotics industry changed sharply to Colombia, Bolivia and Peru. By the early 1980s, officials in the United States were beginning to be aware that entire state governments and, in some cases, national governments, were being taken over by the cocaine industry in South America. The United States did what it could. In the summer of 1986, exploiting a brief political window of opportunity in Bolivia, the U.S. Army sent a wrath of army blackhawk helicopter gunships out into El Beni rain forest to blow up cocaine labs and capture bad people.

Except for one hapless teenager, all of the bad people happened to be absent on the day of the big U.S. raid. Within months, the Bolivian cocaine industry was back to normal, and American military officials were describing all of South America as a 4,000-mile-wide Ho Chi Minh trail for dope smugglers.

As American efforts to shut off the supply in Latin America increased, the Latin producers were churning out so much of the stuff that they created a glut. In the early 1980s, cocaine still cost something in the neighborhood of $50,000 a kilogram, delivered in Miami. By the late 1980s, the same amount could be bought for $5,500.

Through all of these changes, Mexico never ceased to be crucial to the smugglers. No matter where dope came from originally, the easiest place to get it into the United States continued to be the 2,000-mile border with Mexico. The best estimates now are that a third to half of all heroin entering the United States comes across from Mexico; a third of all marijuana comes through or from Mexico, which is itself the second largest marijuana producer after Colombia; the vast majority of all controlled barbiturates and amphetamines are produced in and smuggled from Mexico; and almost all of the cocaine consumed in the United States transits through Mexico.

Until recently, the traditional attitude of people in the rural states of Mexico has been that the drug smugglers—the Mexican ones anyway—are social and political heroes, in the line of Zapata and Villa. Viewed as Robin Hoods, the smugglers are revered, sometimes quite literally.

A good example is Culiacan. In Culiacan, only a few blocks from the headquarters of the federal police, there is a shrine—a public chapel—devoted to the worship of a turn-of-the-century drug smuggler. The smuggler, Jesus Malverde, was captured and hanged by the federal police in 1909. Every day, people walk reverently into the chapel, a structure of blood-red steel frame and colored glass walls, to offer prayers and light candles to Malverde.

Culiacan is the stronghold of the great druglord Felix Gallardo, recently arrested in a major show of force by the new Mexican president, Carlos Salinas de Gotari. Gallardo probably was the one who ordered the kidnaping and torture-murder of DEA agent Kiki Camarena. It was the investigation of the Camarena murder that led to the firing of Tomas Morlet, who later died at the side of Saul Hernandez in the streets of Matamoros.

The people who come to pray to Malverde are the peasants of Sinaloa—the Pacific-coast state where the United States carried out much of its Vietnam-style Operation Condor—another helicopter gunship campaign against dope growers in 1978. Like the peasants of Jalisco and the other producer states, they make their money from American markets one way or the other—by growing tomatoes or by growing poppies and marijuana. The heads of both industries are often the same people.

The police are often the same people. Since 1986, when the current governor of Sinaloa took office, 1,200 state and local police officials have been fired and 200 prosecuted for drug running. But no matter what the governor and his new policemen may profess, the peasants will continue to assume these actions are merely part of a reapportionment.

The arrest of Gallardo was an earth-shaking event here.

And the new anti-drug prosecutor, Javier Coello Trejo, has said brave things—that drug runners are never politicians, they are always only drug runners, and he will treat them as such.

But no sooner had Coello made his grito than he was forced to announce the arrest of his own most trusted assistant, Gregorio Corso Marin, a relative of his wife, whom Coello said had taken $23,000 in bribes in two months in return for selling sensitive information about Coello's efforts.

The money, in other words, is hunting, hunting and nosing its way around, and sooner or later it will find the soft place, the rotten place where it can plunge in and work its magic.

The smugglers, meanwhile, are plain and generous in their relations with the peasants. They are like fathers, who keep track of their extended families and see to it that people have money when a loved one must enter the hospital, that they have help when there is a misunderstanding with the police. The peasants, in return, love them.

When guitars ring out and the handsome male sound of Mexican folksinging fills the air in the cantinas of Culiacan, the words of the corridas they sing often are about the smugglers, from Malverde to his present-day incarnation in Gallardo. These are the heroes, the men who are close to the campesinos, the men who share their wealth with an open hand. They fly on the wings of night and face great danger in order to bring money to the hungry peasants of Sinaloa.

The favored method of smuggling now is by plane over the border. Old DC-10s are the preferred packhorse for heavy loads of marijuana. Cocaine comes over in small planes like the Cessna 210 and 206, the Cessna 172 and 182, or the fast twin-engine Aerocommander and Aztec series. In order to keep the planes up for long hauls from one obscure airstrip to another, the smugglers fit them out with illegal bladder tanks—sometimes as simple as a waterbed full of gasoline, stuffed in the luggage area and connected by tubing to the regular tank.

In Mexico there are 2,300 airstrips, almost all of them available to smugglers. On the Texas side, they may land at hidden strips or they may put down on dirt roads or out on an expanse of hard-packed Sonoran desert.

The Texas ranch families keep their eyes on the dinner table and say nothing when the telltale roar of a twin-engine craft comes low across the ranchhouse roof. They all know the tales of the families that have been found riddled with bullets. The dope smugglers, especially the Colombians, operate by a strict code. No one who sees them, no one who even glimpses them by accident, may live.

The weapons they carry with them grow more terrible with each bloody slaughter. At first it was the shotgun, then the Uzi-B, which could spit out 600 nine-millimeter slugs per minute. But then it was the AR-15, at 650 bullets per minute, and then the Sturm-Ruger Mini 14, at 750 little deaths per minute, and now it is the MAC-10, which spews out a veritable wall of bullets—1,100 per minute. If they look down, if they even point the gun, they can send down thunderstorms of death and mayhem on impulse and instantly. Their eye is truly the evil eye.

The money involved is equivalent to the entire legitimate national production of many Third World nations. The stakes involved go beyond the realm of simple wealth. In Colombia, people who have starved and weakened to die in their early adulthood for generation after generation now find great wealth on their common doorstep, thanks to the insatiable lust of the fat rich whore to the north. To oppose them in this trade is a political step, a step into the place where national destinies are settled.

What has happened instead in most of the producer countries, then, is that the established political power structure has done what it could to take over the dope trade. That process began early. Even in 1978, when the United States was carrying out Operation Condor in Mexico, spending a hundred million dollars in a vain attempt to wipe out Mexican brown, dissident Mexican officials complained bitterly that the U.S. money was only financing a government takeover of the heroin industry.

Victor Gomez Vidal, the top state police official in the state of Sinaloa, said: "Operation Condor is a way for some federal authorities to make themselves very rich. They have their own jail. Nobody knows who comes and goes but them. It's a closed system.

"And once inside, they torture people to see who has the money and who doesn't, and it's their word against ours."

If there is a fear now in Mexico, it is because the sheer cruel force of the dope trade now has grown beyond the historic proportions of smuggling in this land of smugglers. The amount of money involved and the huge and ruthless international forces competing for it have done much to disabuse people of the notion that there are still Robin Hoods in this affair.

Everywhere in the dope business in recent years, physical torture has become its lingua franca. It is not, after all, the sort of thing that lends itself to a lot of public debate. It is a huge and vastly profitable industry, locked inside a kingdom of night, where secrecy is the only universal rule and where breaking open a secret is the quickest route to riches.

The Latin police authorities had their own long tradition of torture to bequeath to the industry, of course, both by example and by direct application. The kicking, electric prodding, slow sexual mutilation and the universal trademark of the Latin American police—savage sodomizing with tools, the universal and very sexually ambivalent other face of macho—were commonplace in the business by the mid 1980s.

The amounts of money on the table made the players capable of doing anything to win. The result was horror. The face of horror. It is the ultimate weapon on the ultimate battlefield.

It is the ultimate test and has been since the beginning of time. It is the test of soft and hard. It is the question of where a man can go and not lose himself in madness, of where reality ends and dream begins and whether dream will empower or destroy. To walk in horror and hold together, to confront horror on every side but keep the world centered, one must have the heart of a lion. One needs powers that go far beyond wealth, far beyond politics, beyond warfare itself. One must have the power of the nagual—the ability to slip these bonds, to soar out across the great night and scream in the teeth of fear.

In the drug business, the Colombians are the most effective. They are the most feared. To do business with them, one must have a very strong nerve. To double-cross them in any way, one must be crazy. Their eye is the evil eye. Always.

The Colombians kill everyone who crosses them. Everyone. But they do not merely kill. That would not be enough. The fear of death has nothing to do with horror. The fear of death is a mild thing, a natural thing. It occurs to a child. It means nothing.

Horror is quite different. Horror is a hand that plunges out, that rips through the veneer of reality, the bloody hand that smashes through the day and clutches its victim by the neck, yanking him deep into the blackest night of all holy Hell.

The latest form is the necktie killing. The Colombians take entire families. They go to the home of the man who has crossed them, and they take him, his wife, his children, the maid, the neighbor, the visiting aunt.

Chairs are lined up. All of the people to be killed are seated in the chairs, in a row against the wall, facing the door from which they will be discovered. Like little soldiers.

Then, one by one, the killer proceeds down the line, slitting the throat vertically, reaching in, grabbing the tongue and yanking it out flat through the front of the throat, so that it hangs down on the chest like a necktie. The victim bleeds and suffocates slowly, dying in a bubbling foam of his own mucus, breath and blood. Those who have not been killed must sit and watch while the killer works his way slowly to them, killing each of the others one by one, methodically, leaving them jerking and sputtering in their chairs.

That is not the horror.

The horror waits. It may wait for days, time for the flies to come and the stink to rise. The horror is for the men, women and children who gather at the door and gaze in when the police finally break it down. The horror is the sight of them all, lined up neatly against the wall in their chairs with their black and bloated tongues on their chests.

The lesson is clear, visceral, immediate, brutal, profound. It is a lesson that makes people run and scream, piss on themselves, throw up and void their bowels at the same time, collapse gasping and beat their heads against the wall, trying to make it stop, trying to make the stink and the buzzing go away. It is a lesson that reaches deep into the throat of time and yanks out the most primitive pulsing heart of humankind.

Everyone—every single person who even glimpses it for an instant—knows exactly and immediately what it means. It reaches around all language and learning and through every defense of will or posture. It is the language of the Great Night.

Chapter Four

Saul knew, and Serafin Senior knew. There is no trick. They didn't rely on tricks. The trick is not to rely on tricks. The trick is to do everything perfectly—fly deep into Mexico, fly back up high into Texas, far from the border, land where there is not one vestige of an airstrip, load the dope in trucks almost instantly, be gone, and own the hell out of the local cops. The trick, if there is a trick, is to do it all. Buy the cops. Hide out. Be fast. Carry a lot of guns and use them if one small little thing goes bad.

They knew that small aircraft are more adaptable than the average citizen may imagine, especially with an experienced smuggler at the stick, especially if the owner assumes a certain amount of damage as a cost of doing business.

All it takes to land is two pickup trucks, preferably white, a couple bedsheets, a dozen short wooden stakes with white paper plates nailed to them, some flashlights and a good set of radios.

The receiving crew on the ground drives out at night to the agreed-upon landing site, usually nothing more than a flat pasture, where the rocks and mesquite trees have been cleared, the grass grazed or mowed short and the livestock moved and fenced off by an obliging landowner. Good-eyes are posted on high places to look out for any cops who don't have written invitations. Everybody stays in his pickup truck with the lights off and a gun ready on the seat, listening to the code-word chatter on the radio.

When the twin propeller engines of the dented and lumbering old marijuana plane thrum up out of the night, the ground crew makes a last check with the radio, listens for the all-clear from the good-eyes, and then it's on.

The truck engines screech alive, the trucks lurch to the two ends of the strip and put their bright beams down it from either end, the pickup doors fly open. Racing toward each other, one man spreads a bedsheet at one end of the instant airstrip, the other spreads his sheet at the other end. They crab-claw toward the middle, stooping to hammer the little stakes with the paper plates on them along both borders of the strip. Then they take their positions and begin to circle the beams of their flashlights in the air.

And there it is—O'Hare Airport in the middle of nothing. The pilot throws a beam down and sees the white trucks, their beams, the bedsheets clearly marking the beginning and ending of the strip. His own landing beams hit the paper plates, and they light up like blazes. He's down. The bales are off and in the trucks. He's up again. The landing strip disappears. The trucks are gone. The sky is black and silent. It's over.

Ten minutes.

It happens scores of times every night, up and down the 2,000-mile border. There are not enough airplanes in the possession of the air wing of Customs to monitor more than a fraction of the low-flying smuggler flights. And up and down the border, on the American side and on the Mexican side, there are families who live in comfortable new brick homes, who drive expensive new trucks, dress their kids well and even put together the cash for some college tuition, whose total source of income is this single simple operation with the bedsheets, the paper plates, the radios and two white four-wheel-drive pickup trucks. The American side is nicer duty in some ways, because America is a richer country. But on the American side, they have to go through the bother of maintaining day jobs as a front. Different members of each smuggling family often take turns keeping their families on one side or the other. It's a living.

That was just the kind of operation the feds and agents of the Texas Department of Public Safety thought they had working in Grimes County, early in the winter of 1987.

Grimes County is in the corrupted rural sphere of Houston. On the surface, it still looks like the East Texas farm and ranching county it once was. Down deeper in the economy of Grimes County, the fact is that most people there are dependent one way or the other on Houston for their money. They live in the country, they say they hate the city, but their lives are at the short ends of sticks that are stuck right in the eye of Houston.

In 1986, trusties in the Grimes County Jail got word to federal authorities that things were not right in the jail. That much, of course, would hardly have amounted to news. Things are seldom right in any county jail in Texas, especially in the rural counties, even more especially in the rural counties that abut urban areas. It is a stubborn and intractable aspect of Texas culture that most rural sheriffs will eventually make some sordid attempt to beat some kind of petty extortion out of the miserable almost entirely penniless wretches who people their jails.

In this case, the trusties said Sheriff Bill Foster was using trusty labor to make improvements and do other work on his private ranch. That alone would not have interested the feds one whit. It was the rest of the story—that, while on the ranch, the trusties had witnessed extensive dope smuggling—that caught the federal ear. As a matter of courtesy and practice, the feds had involved the Texas Department of Public Safety (the state police) in the sub-

stantial investigation that grew out of the tips from the
Grimes County trusties.

The climax of that investigation was to have taken place
on the night of January 4, 1987, in a remote field owned by
Sheriff Bill Foster's good friend of thirty years and neighbor, Gerald Pat Arrington.

Earlier that day, while investigators watched from a hiding place, Arthur William Brito flew his Cessna 207 into
Easterwood Airport in Brazos County, Texas. Brazos
County borders Grimes County and is forty-five miles
northwest of Houston.

With surveillance close behind, Brito drove to the Quality Inn in College Station, where he met with Serafin Hernandez, Sr., and Javier Hernandez. Brito drove back out to
the airport, took a set of golf clubs and the backseat out of
his Cessna, took off, flew down across several hundred
miles of Texas and disappeared into Mexico.

That night, two late-model Ford pickup trucks wound
their ways out to a desolate pasture at the intersection of
Farm Road 3090 and Grimes County Road. The land
where they stopped their trucks was owned by Sheriff Foster's old friend, Gerald Pat Arrington. Mr. Arrington, in a
stunning display of Grimes County hospitality, drove out in
his own Chevy pickup to meet the two Ford pickups that
had appeared on his land at such a seemingly untoward
place and moment.

Two years after these events, an armed federal strike
force appeared at the Grimes County Jail with a court order
forcing Sheriff Foster to surrender custody of a trusty
named Ronnie Morton. Once in federal protective custody,
Morton, whose word may or may not have been any good,
told a part of the tale of the Grimes County stakeout that
cops on the scene that night—the honest ones anyway—
could not have known.

Morton claimed a certain "sheriff's department official"
learned of the Hernandez stakeout only an hour before the
Cessna was due back from Mexico. The official rushed out

of the jail as soon as he learned what was about to take place.

The agents on the scene knew only what they saw with their own eyes. It was all happening exactly according to plan, better than they had dared to hope. The landing strip was laid out. The ever-cautious Hernandez family was not physically present, but other pertinent people were, including Mr. Arrington. The adrenaline was pumping. The plane was coming down low. It made three slow checkout passes, coming so low the agents could see the big bales stuffed inside where the seat had been removed. This was it. They were ready to jump.

All of a sudden, the plane jerked straight up into the air, banked, put the pedal to the metal and squawked off like a buzzard scared off its roost.

Then there was a scramble. The agents, furious that the dope was gone, closed in anyway. The men down on the strip broke for a nearby stand of trees and brush on foot. When the agents had rounded them all up, they searched them and their trucks. Mario Carlos Brito, a relative of the pilot, was carrying $13,520 American, a 9-mm Beretta pistol with forty-five rounds in the clip and a .25-caliber Beretta with seven rounds. In his truck the agents found eleven portable transceivers for sending and receiving signals and voice conversation with aircraft, six battery chargers, four antenna cables, one large white bedsheet, a "Home and Office" memo book, and a small amount of marijuana. In the memo book, he had written, "List. Give everybody $, make sure you check winds, put down sheets. Ask Pat what time is best."

Pat Arrington, the sheriff's friend, must either have been contemplating or just returning from a hunting trip when he motored out onto his property to chat with the people with the bedsheets. In his truck the agents found a Smith and Wesson 44 magnum revolver, a Marlin 357 magnum rifle, and several other weapons.

Everybody else was similarly equipped. Earl Leslie Harris, a local, was carrying one Johnson model PPL 6000 portable transceiver, 15 radio antennas, one Yuasa 12-volt battery, one Rossi .38-caliber revolver, one Marlin 30–30 rifle, Mr. Brito's golf clubs and six wooden stakes with white paper plates nailed to them.

The agents nabbed Serafin Senior and Javier Hernandez out on a lonely stretch of Highway 105. They had no guns in their truck. They did have two maps of the area around Pat Arrington's property in Grimes County, with directions noted in both English and Spanish.

At some point during the next few months, Reserve Deputy Wesley Alford, a jailer at the Grimes County Jail, went to federal authorities with the story of the last-minute tip-off that he said had aborted the landing on Pat Arrington's ranch. On July 19, 1987, James Mann, a twenty-nine-year-old prisoner of Grimes County, made a break.

During his escape attempt, Mann was armed with a gun owned by Sheriff Foster's wife. He used that gun to shoot and kill deputy Alford. After killing him, James Mann drove to Sheriff Foster's ranch, where he abandoned the car he had stolen and went for a walk. He was apprehended on foot. In his subsequent trial, he pleaded self-defense and escaped the death penalty.

Serafin Hernandez, Sr., meanwhile, had been brought to the Grimes County Jail with the other prisoners from the aborted plane-landing incident. He was not in jail long before bonding out on racketeering charges. He was in jail long enough, however, to attract the attention of Ronnie Morton, the federal snitch who was subsequently removed from the jail by an armed federal strike force.

Morton told federal authorities that Serafin Hernandez, Sr., had told him his family owned the Grimes County cops. Owned them flat. Morton said Hernandez had said more than that. Morton told the feds that the jailbreak in which Reserve Deputy Alford was killed had been a fake. Morton said Alford had been a witness to some of the goings on around the sheriff's department, particularly to the incident in which a member of the department had rushed off to send a radio message an hour before the aborted landing on Pat Arrington's property.

Sheriff Foster, for his part, offered the quite reasonable thesis that Ronnie Morton was a jailhouse nutball. He said Morton had concocted the entire story to make himself look big.

But quite aside from all of the jailhouse intrigue in Grimes County, there was another question humming with a low, barely painful but relentless voltage through the minds of the Hernandez clan. Why, indeed, had all of those policemen been out there ringing that field that night? If things had been taken care of properly, if the trick had been not to use tricks, to do everything properly and see that everyone was paid and taken care of, what had happened? What was going wrong?

Smuggling, in the end, has nothing to do with airplanes and paper plates. Those are mere paraphernalia, to be cast aside like soiled napkins the minute they cease to work. The system itself—the arrangement, the scam—is only paraphernalia. Saul Hernandez, the patriarch, had started by swimming the river with little pouches of cocaine stuck to his chest with duct tape. The basics had not changed that much. The family still hid its dope in the sand dunes and the cactus pasture down along the river, out near where the town of Bagdad once stood, and it still found one means or another of getting the dope across. The means were almost unimportant.

It was the essence of the task that counted. It was the meaning of smuggling—the spiritual meaning. The saying was that whores were involved in the most ancient commerce. But that was not true. Smugglers were.

Wherever there have been two tribes and a river, the smugglers have plied their hazardous craft. The tribes have always had strict rules—dietary rules, sexual proscriptions, rules to govern everything from elimination to the most profoundly sacred rituals—all designed in the end to answer the fundamental questions. Who are we? We are the human beings. Who are they? They are the manlike not-human monsters. How do we know the difference between us and them? By our rules.

The rules of the tribes have defined the limits of humanity itself, and by those limits the individual members of the tribes always have ordered their private and individual sanity. A person who deliberately violates those rules must be viewed with great fear by his own tribe and by the other. He is a different person, a person who lives outside the circle of his own people but does not belong to the circle of the other people. He goes between. He is an outsider. He is a threat to all people. He is a changeling who goes by night.

But he has great stuff. He has those terrific bone bracelets that the manlike not-human monsters wear over there. Where do they get them? They must spend the summer up on the coast. And he sells our things to them. He brings back a good return to us. He is daring. He is a brave man, who soars above his own people. He is the smuggler.

For him, the game has nothing to do with the specific conveyance by which he moves his bone bracelet shipments across the river. The game—the spiritual game—is the building of a network of changing and artificial trust, trust that is bought, not born, by which he may move between the two cultures safely. It is the merest silken spiderweb of a construction, put together here and there with bribes and threats and sheer force of personality. One man over there, who guards the rim of the camp fire, agrees to look away. Another man, who fishes over here, agrees to hide things in his basket.

It has always been the same. It is a filament of agreements, spun out through the great night by the smuggler himself, allowing him to scuttle from one branch to another, invisible and alone. Unless he has a large family.

There, in family, may be a substance of trust that will partially compensate for what the smuggler loses by deliberately leaving the ring of his tribe. The call of blood, at least, can be trusted in the deep of the night, when the twin engines of a big old dented DC-10 are welling up over

Grimes County and the pickup trucks are screeching alive, racing out onto the pasture to put those beams down, spread those bedsheets and hammer those paper plates into the ground. All of that—the mechanism and the technique —that's all good and important as long as it works. But it's what lies beneath that is the smuggler's real stock in trade. It's the network, and, even beneath that, it's the family.

From the moment Saul Hernandez was cut down with Tomas Morlet in front of a nightclub in Matamoros, something had started to go wrong. The network was not working. The fundamental ligaments of life—the ties of blood and family—were weakening from some poison.

The same low aching discomfort, meanwhile, was working in the minds of the people on the American law enforcement side. Sheriff Foster may have dismissed Ronnie Morton as a nutcase. But the state and federal agents were not at all comforted. Wesley Alford, the reserve deputy killed during the break, was very dead. The man who killed him had driven straight to Sheriff Foster's ranch. It was not the sort of scenario likely to inspire confidence in cops who were all going to wind up together out there some night with guns in their hands, facing down a gang of smugglers who were armed to the teeth and primed to kill.

That was the dilemma in this business about the border. Corruption was the starting place for the smuggler. You always paid the man who guarded the rim of the camp fire to look the other way, long before you ever considered risking any major shipments. When law enforcement people started prying and pulling and trying to take these arrangements apart, they inevitably found themselves out on the same moonlit sand dunes with the smugglers, guns glinting in the white light and nobody just exactly sure who was working for which tribe.

At this point, the federal authorities made a move which people in their position often wind up making in Texas. They went to Texas Attorney General Jim Mattox. Given the uncertainty of the terrain, they just wanted to have Mattox in on it.

Jim Mattox is a strange kind of human lightning rod. He attracts controversy, but he also attracts incredible and ferocious devotion from an almost unimaginable spectrum of Texas society. Born tough and little on the hardscrabble streets of East Dallas, Mattox always had three things going for him: big thick glasses, an electric brain and a willingness to fight anybody anywhere at the drop of a hat. As an assistant D.A. under the legendary Henry Wade in Dallas, Mattox quickly became known as the single young prosecutor a really bad crook in Dallas needed to worry about most.

But his own youth as a poor kid had made him a much more complicated figure than your average Texas hardcase. Mattox had an emotional and fervent concern for the plight of the little people, the poor people, the people he grew up among in East Dallas. In Congress, he made a name for himself as an uncompromising populist—a reputation that gradually lifted him to the very top of the hate list for every J.R. Ewing–type in Dallas. They had deliberately built the John Stemmons Expressway up on stilts through East Dallas so that the J.R.s whizzing over in their chauffeur-driven Benzes wouldn't even have to see the kind of people Jim Mattox came from. But here he was, rising up in local politics, rising up in the Congress, always lifting that tough little bit-mouth jaw up where he had no business and making trouble for his betters.

The little people of Texas kept lifting Jim Mattox up higher and higher, electing him to offices where the J.R.s wouldn't be able to avoid his glare. As attorney general of the state, he went straight out after the sacred sanctums of the old Texas power structure, ripping into big oil, lashing at the fat smug bond lawyers who ran local governments from their red leather chairs in Houston and New York. His role as lightning rod grew more and more dramatic, so that at any given point in time his office seemed to have its own private political tornado roaring permanently just above the roof.

One strange sidelight of Mattox's fiery profile was that even the crooks—the very people he had blistered so badly as a local prosecutor—seemed to trust him. In rural Texas, dope money and a wildly fluctuating oil and real estate economy were making it harder every day to know whom to trust. More and more it seemed that every thief or smuggler in the business had decided that his or her best shot at an honest man in Texas probably was Jim Mattox.

The feds brought Mattox into the Hernandez mess because they needed somebody in Texas they could trust. And there was always the chance Serafin Senior, would trust him, too.

Saul had been the leader, because he was intended to be the leader. Of all the muddy mojados swimming their little packets of dope across the river at night, Saul was one of the very few who was able, through the power of his own ruthless will, to lift himself up out of the sandbars and the mosquitos and make himself a king. Nothing stopped Saul. In 1984, the gringos busted him in Michigan with 20,000 pounds of marijuana. He slipped back down into Mexico and resumed operations as if nothing had happened. In 1986, two reporters for a Matamoros newspaper, trying to write about corruption in the city, made the mistake of sticking their noses into the affairs of Saul Hernandez. He murdered them.

Saul was thirty-eight years old when the machine guns filled him with black bloody holes at the side of Tomas Morlet. It was the way everyone always had expected him to go. It was the way he would have wanted to go.

But now he was gone, and his family faced the dilemma every wealthy and powerful family faces when its founder passes on. Someone would have to take over. It was not immediately clear which one had the heart for it.

Serafin Hernandez, Sr., Saul's older brother, was a

likely candidate. At forty-five, he had lived much of his adult life on the American side. He believed that the role of jefe belonged to him by right and by succession. As soon as Saul was buried, Serafin announced to the rest of the family that he was taking over.

But it could not be that simple. No jefe can simply seize the reins without first being tested. Serafin Senior faced a stiff test immediately in the person of his own little brother, Elio. Elio was only twenty-two, but he was a special member of the family. Named for the patriarch of the family, Little Elio always had been the baby and the darling of the clan. Under Saul's reign, Little Elio had headed up the entire Mexican side of the operation. Little Elio believed that he should succeed Saul as the jefe.

It was a galling suggestion. Little Elio was only two years older than Serafin Senior's own son, Serafin Junior. It had been difficult enough, all those years, for Serafin to work for his first younger brother. Of course, with Saul, there was no debating these things. But everyone had worked hard. Now Saul was gone, having begged for and finally earned his own death with his crazy behavior. It was fitting and proper for Serafin Senior to take over, and it was insulting for the spoiled brat in Mexico to assert a superior right.

Bad words came out, as they tend to do when families allow themselves to argue too bitterly. Serafin always had doubted the ability of the old man to father a son as late in the game as Elio's arrival. The open suggestion that Elio's father was an unknown person did not help advance discussions in a productive direction.

But there was even more pain, much greater pain than this for Serafin Senior in particular. Incredibly enough, many members of the family were drifting toward a sympathy with the pretensions of Little Elio. Many in the family said Elio was crazy and ruthless in the way Saul had been. The family needed a man with a savage heart at the helm.

Serafin Senior was finding himself in a bitter dilemma indeed. Having made the sacrifice of leaving family behind, leaving Mexico and living among the gringos to advance the family business, he was now being considered as suspect for that very reason.

But it was inevitable. He should have seen it coming long ago. Perhaps he had seen it and had simply denied it. If so, it only made the suggestion all the more enraging when it finally was openly made. It was always the belief of the people on the Mexican side that life on the gringo side made people weak and flabby, like the gringos. Mexican men move over there, and they put their children in the gringo schools, and their wives start painting themselves like clowns and whores the way the gringo women do, and soon the tale is told. They have become Americans. How could they resist? It's a rich life. A soft life. Even a happy life for some. But it's hardly the life one would devise as training for a warrior.

But even this was not the ultimate wound that Serafin would suffer in these black days and months. There was something far worse than this that his heart would have to bear. In the middle of this debate, he had moved his family back to the house he kept in Brownsville, so that his son, Serafin Junior, and his daughter, Myrna, could attend college at Texas Southmost.

A few months after the move, little Serafin Junior, only twenty years old, left him and joined the side of Little Elio in Matamoros.

It was as if Serafin Junior believed what Little Elio and the others were saying of his father. It was as if Serafin Junior suddenly believed it of himself. Forced now suddenly to stop and examine himself, he looked in the mirror and feared greatly that the reflection looking back at him was exactly the soft gringo girl the ones in Mexico said it was, instead of the Mexican man who should have been staring back.

He had never attempted to become everybody's favorite Mexican kid in the Aldine Independent School District, just west of Houston Intercontinental Airport. At Nimitz High, he had majored in auto mechanics—the kind of thing Hispanic kids do in order to stay with each other and away from the gringos.

But try as he might and in spite of the peer pressure to contain himself within Mexican culture, he couldn't resist being drawn out into the larger school population, and, once there, he couldn't help it if the other kids and the teachers liked him.

He was shy with most people at first, the way a lot of Mexican kids from strict families can be. He had perfect manners and never misbehaved. But once they got to know him, people saw something more, something they always liked, something that tickled them. The baseball coach was the one who drew him out first.

In two years of coaching him, Del Ninze couldn't turn young Serafin into any kind of a ball player, but he liked having him around anyway. He liked him for his smile and because he was "somebody to joke around with." He made him the team manager.

Of course, none of the Anglo students or teachers understood that Serafin had his own quite serious reasons for wanting to maintain his privacy. At night, when other kids were doing their homework or watching videotapes of ET, high school student and baseball team manager Serafin Hernandez, Jr., was out in the black empty night of central Texas with guns jammed in his belt, helping to flag in that night's shipment and wondering whether some cop or, more likely, some rip-off dope gang was about to explode out of the brush and blow his brains out. It was the kind of private life that tends to produce fairly private people.

It was also the family business. It was the reason why they were there. They had not come to Houston in order to become managers of high school baseball teams. His father always assumed that young Serafin knew how the world was arranged and what the family was about in life.

But the life in Houston was also very sweet. How tempting, how foreign, how soft and easy it must have looked to the kid who sat with his legs around the ice bucket in the dugout, exhausted from last night's brush with death, watching while all of those mothers and fathers out there in the stands cheered and cursed and paced the ground, as if this game were the most important thing in life. The most exquisite pain of the heart, after all, is the pain of yearning for what does not belong to you.

A year after he had graduated from Nimitz, when the split came, Serafin Junior examined himself, his life, what had become of him, what was becoming of him, and he made his choice. He went over to Matamoros to serve Little Elio. It was a decision that came only after extended counsels with other members of the family, many of whom were beginning to side with Elio, too. Soon after he joined Elio, the two of them were joined in their new organization by Serafin Senior's other brother, twenty-eight-year-old Ovidio.

Only weeks later, on a dark night in early February 1987, the federal and state agents came racing down on the landing strip in Grimes County; Serafin Senior was arrested; the cops were all at each other's throats; the dope dealers were at each other's throats; and all the long years of Saul's ruthlessness and Serafin Senior's painstaking care fell into the black void. The network—the spiderweb of bribes and deals that they had woven through the great night—collapsed. And worse.

The dispute in the family now had progressed to the level of betrayal—the sort of thing that always brings death in the drug trade. With the federal agents and people in Jim Mattox's office doing everything they could to egg him on, Serafin Senior was stewing in his own paranoid suspicions about the Grimes County bust. How could it have happened? Things like that don't happen by accident. Something bad has to go wrong, something foul in the very heart of the operation, in order for something like that to occur.

Elio's branch, meanwhile, had its own very serious concerns. This whole enterprise, after all, functioned on a basis of absolute trust and blood ties. It was too easy to do away with a rival or a pain in the ass simply by slipping a little jinx in the system. A tip-off here, a tiny bit of snitching there.

And it wasn't simply a matter of the gringo police. They were, if anything, the least of what Elio's rough-hewn little fledgling organization had to worry about. Eager to show his heart to his followers, Little Elio had been branching out. It was no longer to be a matter of the old mojados slumping their fat loads of marijuana across the border every night. Little Elio had a taste for the really hot stuff.

Under his direction, the Matamoros branch of the Hernandez family was branching out into gun running, a trade that required getting to know and doing business with rival operations. And they were going farther than that. Taking up where Saul had left off in his war with the local crime families, Little Elio was taking his band of quick young gunmen out more and more often to rip off other gangs. They stole huge amounts of marijuana, which was one thing. They also stole cocaine, which was quite another.

Stealing cocaine meant that, somewhere back up the line, somewhere in the chain, the Hernandez family was now doing something tantamount to shoving its guns up the noses of Colombians.

It was more than war. It was terror. The sheer bloody terror of ripping off cocaine and risking the wrath of the Colombians was so terrifying that it was enough to make a man grow faint suddenly, gasping for breath without any warning, just because the enormity of it had suddenly flashed before his eyes. It was the kind of life a man can stand only if he runs hard and drinks hard and forces fear from his own heart savagely. Somewhere in the back of every Mexican dope-dealer's mind is the image. They have all either seen it or heard it described in indelibly convincing detail. The entire family, sitting in chairs like little soldiers, with their black tongues stuck to their shirtfronts and ants crawling on their eyes.

All it took, in this kind of life, was the tiniest rent in the fabric of the family trust, and anyone and everyone could plunge through straight into Hell. And now here was Serafin Senior, feeling bitter and betrayed, with an American federal indictment on his head, with the gringo cops offering him a new deal nearly every day, and with too many years of the gringo good life behind him. Suddenly Serafin Senior was a lot to worry about.

Eventually, the only important member of the family who stayed with Serafin was his son-in-law, Jesse. Serafin's own son had left him, but Jesse stayed.

Through all of this, the two sides of the family continued to do business with each other, because they continued to be the best connections either side had. It was a large family, and the family's tastes and needs had expanded to require the income of an ongoing smuggling operation. It wasn't cheap. Houses had to be maintained in several cities, airplanes, trucks, guns, radios. Cops had to be paid. Salaries had to be met. The business couldn't afford simply to stop, suspend operations and take a few years off while everybody agreed on a reorganization.

But dealing with each other was getting harder and harder to do. In July of 1987, Ovidio Hernandez came over from Matamoros to do some shopping at Brownsville's Amigoland Shopping Center. He brought his two-year-old son with him. When Ovidio and the boy failed to return home, the clan back in Matamoros was desperate. They had no idea what had happened or what to do. Perhaps it was the terrible other shoe falling from the dope rip-offs— the hand of the Colombians. They had no idea. They took the unusual step of reporting the disappearance to the police in Brownsville. Police are supposed to be good for something, anyway.

But within a short time after the disappearance, Little Elio's branch of the family learned that the gringo police were not going to be able to do anything for them. They received a telephone call that shocked them even more than they could have been shocked by news that Ovidio and his son had been taken by the Colombians.

Ovidio and his son had been kidnaped by Jesse—Serafin Senior's only remaining trusted lieutenant. It was about the money. The $800,000. It was about family money. Jesse Hernandez had kidnaped Ovidio and was holding him and his baby at gunpoint somewhere over family money.

The $800,000 was just one of those things. Serafin claimed it was owed. Elio said it was not. In the last few months, the shifting of cash back and forth between the branches had become the stickiest point of their dealings. It was natural. When business partners fall out, the first thing they tend to argue about is money, no matter what the real cause of the dispute may be.

So they were arguing over some money. So what? It was $800,000. They were moving 2,000 pounds of marijuana alone over the border a week, to say nothing of the guns, to say nothing of the stolen cars, to say nothing at all of the cocaine. That amount of money, less than a million dollars, was petty cash. It would have been worked out. In better days, if nothing else, Serafin would have written it off and made it up somewhere else rather than risk wounded feelings within the family.

But now look at this bastard! Look what these bastards thought they were doing. Over $800,000. They were insulting and demeaning a member of the family, making him look helpless in front of his wife, frightening the hell out of his little baby. Did he think this stuff made him like Saul? Saul was the opposite of this kind of man. Saul would blow the face off any man who got in his way or the way of his family. He would never have turned on his own blood this way, certainly not for money.

The situation presented Little Elio with the most difficult test of his reign to date. It was a situation that called for more than mere savagery and courage. It was a bad business within the family—very bad. Solving it would require real power.

This was the kind of problem that required more than brute strength and more even than the cleverness or sophistication of a man. A thing as terrible as this—a poison in the well of the family—required the ancient powers themselves. A day after he learned it was Jesse who had taken

Ovidio, Elio went to a curandero and sought his help. Word that Elio had taken this step was forwarded quickly, of course, to Jesse.

Within a short time after word of the curandero's involvement reached Jesse, the matter of the money was settled and Ovidio and his son were returned to Matamoros. The family contacted the police in Brownsville, informed them the matter had been cleared up, thanked them and asked that it be dropped. The Brownsville police were only too happy to oblige.

Now all eyes were on Elio. By calling on the curandero, he had brought a swift end to a problem that might otherwise have meant his own swift and brutal ruin. Under the circumstances, all it might have taken for a major bolt of loyalties was a persuasive demonstration by Serafin Senior that Elio had no guts. Elio had shown he had guts.

But by bringing in the curandero, Elio also had made an implicit admission of staggering proportions. If he needed the power of the curandero to set the affairs of the family right, it meant that the power of the family was in decay.

It had been one thing, to deal with the problem of Serafin. He had behaved badly. No one likes that, but it happens.

This was quite another thing. This was proof that the fundamental underlying bonds on which all of their lives were built were coming apart. Given their lives and what they did for a living, it meant that they were all suddenly and horribly exposed. The family was falling apart deep in its innermost heart, and they were all staring into the jaws of Hell as a result.

Little Elio carried a new burden, one he had not forseen when he had leapt into his role as Saul's successor. With the ferocious heart of a young man, he had assumed that taking the role of leader would be a question of courage, ruthlessness, and a savage compulsion to dominate and win. He had all of those.

But now there was a problem that seemed beyond even his own considerable strengths. Why was this happening now? Why had it not happened during Saul's rule? Why on Elio's watch? What was causing it? What force could be so great and so black that it could worm its way into the heart of the family and turn the family's hand against itself? These thoughts turned over and over in Elio's mind.

Chapter Five

Constanzo led the others in gently at first, gradually, as he had been led by Delia and then by the Great Master. It is always done this way. The progression is always from secrecy to deeper secrecy, and there are good reasons for it.

The secrets themselves, in the first place, are not kept for the simple pleasure of secrecy itself. The more dearly a cult holds its secrets, the more likely it is the cult is engaged in activities that would call down the wrath of the law, in a civilized setting, or, worse, the wrath of the neighbors in an uncivilized setting. In other words, the more violent and macabre a cult's practices, the more serious are its practitioners about keeping what they do a secret.

One always claims at first to be involved in some other cult or practice than the one in which one is actually involved. There is a loosely arranged reverse progression. If one's neighbor finds some suspicious candles in one's house and has the temerity to mention it, one tends to claim membership in the next most proximate cult or religion in line, closer to legitimacy. If you get caught with a candle with a bunch of orishas on it, you don't claim to be a Baptist. You say, "Oh no, you misunderstand. That's not a picture of Chango on the candle. That's St. Barbara. I'm a devout Catholic, you see."

Chicken heads are a little harder. But at least you can say, "Well, I'm a practitioner of 'Christian Santeria' or 'white Santeria.'" There is always some way to put a better face on it.

Deeper into the Afro-Cuban and Haitian voodoo cults, the going gets stickier. Palo Mayombe is a bad one, in part because it is almost always practiced by people who are in some way involved with violent criminal life. It is a part of what the Mexicans call "La Vida Loca" or the Crazy Life. The Crazy Life is a sort of cult of its own—a culture that vaunts violence, daring, living outside the bounds of law and civilization. In the American prison systems in the Southwest, the Crazy Life is associated especially with Indian criminals, some of whom have an entire belief system based on savage violence.

Criminologists and sociologists call such behavior "psychopathic." They often tend to explain the Crazy Life as a psychopathic culture syncretized by criminals from elements of macho and daring and rebellion against authority. And that may be. But it does not explain why the culture of the Crazy Life gets more pronounced and more frightening the closer one moves through a prison population toward the Indian gangs and the closer one moves toward voodoo.

No matter what the ethnic background of the practitioner, anyone in the criminal and prison worlds who is associated with voodoo is more to be feared than someone who is merely crazy. And even at that, there are still degrees. Even if a person is sort of a vato loco, and even if he practices Palo, at least he is not Abakua. Anybody who has ever been around the Cubans, either on the street or in the joint with the Marielistos, knows about the Abakua. The Palos use a lot of bones, dig up bodies, boil brains and drink some blood. But at least they're not Abakua.

The Abakua are the ones everybody else is convinced

practice torture, human sacrifice and mystical cannibalism. People have been convinced of that since the early nineteenth century. Therefore, if you're Abakua, you say you're Palo.

Palo is bad enough. If you say you're Palo, property values will not rise in your neighborhood. It's sometimes called Palo Mayombe, sometimes Palo Monte. A mayombera is an especially evil kind of witch or bruja—a black witch. Palo is from a Spanish word meaning branch. Palo Mayombe is a branch of Latin witchcraft, or brujeria. The secret language of the cult, as it is usually practiced, is Bantu. The people of Bantu descent in Latin America are sometimes called Congos. Palo Mayombe, therefore, is also known as Regla de Congo or simply Congo.

The mayombero, or Tata Nkisi, is the Great Night. He is himself an incarnation of the limits of reality and sanity. Where sanity ends, the Tata Nkisi begins. He or she is the border by which we know how the understandable universe is shaped. He is very savage and very un-European. Compared to him, the average santero is a Mormon. He is especially active in the destruction or repair of family bonds and may take possession of family members in order to carry out his terrible bilongos or spells.

When Adolfo studied with the Great Master, his initiation involved rites of which Delia may or may not have been knowledgeable. Adolfo was being passed back up the chain of secrecy when his mother sent him away. Because he was so special, because he possessed power on the order of the power of movie stars, he may have been ushered into realms that were closed to his mother.

The ceremonies of initiation into the status of Tata Nkisi involve two of the key fetishistic elements of Palo Mayombe—the ceiba tree and the human tibia or shinbone.

Adolfo, wearing clothes that were taken from a grave, sat beneath a ceiba tree while a ring of mayomberos looked on. He wore a crown of ceiba leaves, designed to lure the spirits of the dead into his brain. When the observers decided that his own soul was dead and that he was now owned by the spirits, they presented this new mayombero with a burning candle and a human tibia—the scepter by which he would rule the dead.

The next step in his training was the preparation of his first nganga—the cauldron that would form the center of his new universe. Ngangas are objects of enormous fear, dread and power in all voodoo and Santeria-related beliefs. The mere mention of them is enough to produce sharp gasps and fast exits. The actual sight of a nganga is something most Latin and Caribbean people hope never to encounter in their entire lives. To look into a nganga is literally to stand on the rim of Hell.

The principle of a nganga, however, is a common one in all Santeria, in all primitive belief, in fact. It is based on the practice of catching spirits in fluid-filled vessels. It is not unrelated to Gypsy beliefs about the chicken egg. It is a primal feral belief that occurs independently and simultaneously in all human cultures.

In this case, so terrible a vessel is created, filled with so horrific a fluid, that it is capable of capturing an entire universe of dead souls, all of whom become the slaves and agents of the mayombero in the working of his curses. When Adolfo's first nganga had been properly prepared, and when it was taken to the proper feeding ground (almost always a cemetery, sometimes a battlefield), it became a powerful magnet, sucking into itself the souls of the dead.

Like all of the elements of original belief, however, the nganga is never static. It is never complete. It is never satisfied. It must be fed again and again.

To build a proper nganga, a mayombero goes with his mentor to a graveyard at night, during the waning of the moon. He soaks the ground over a grave with rum, making the crude form of a cross with the drops. Then the grave is opened.

Working quickly, the mayombero removes from the corpse the tibia, the phalanges of the fingers and toes, the ribs and the head. The mayombero must know whose grave he is robbing, for several reasons. First of all, he must be certain that the corpse, called a kiyumba, has been recently enough buried that he will be able to recover good brain matter from it. The brains are very important.

In the second place, he must know what general type of brain he will be feeding to his nganga. The best kiyumbas most of the time are those of violently psychotic people—valuable for the contribution their souls and power will make to the evil destructive missions of the Tata Nkisi.

But sometimes the nganga is in need of different qualities. A mundele or white person is often very useful, because the soul of a white person is much less wild, much easier to direct, more tractable than the soul of a nonwhite. A mundele is a useful addition for that reason.

The other value of a mundele is that, generally speaking, the spirit of a white person is more effective both in killing other white people and in giving the Tata Nkisi protection from them. If the Tata Nkisi's nganga contains the soul of a white person or white people, then the Tata Nkisi will be safe from the power of white people.

Once the key ingredients have been taken from the grave, they must be taken back to the mayombero's house or secret chapel for ritual taming. The mayombero strips naked and lies flat on his back on the floor, with candles burning all around him. His mentors or, later in life, his followers sit around him in a circle, drinking rum and smoking cigars. The stolen body parts, wrapped in a black bag, are placed next to him.

The mayombero goes through all the typical evidences of spirit possession—grows rigid, experiences convulsions, foams at the mouth, vomits, speaks in strange voices—and then there is some sort of sign. Gunpowder ignites in a dish or a spirit speaks through the mayombero, something to show that the spirit of the kiyumba has been tamed and is now enslaved to the mayombero.

The mayombero then puts coins in the bottom of the nganga or in an accompanying vessel to show that he is paying the price of the kiyumba's soul. He writes the name of the kiyumba on a scrap of paper and places the scrap in the nganga. The brains and other hacked-off parts of the corpse are placed in the nganga. Then there is the business of blood.

The kiyumba must be fed a quantity of blood. The source of the blood and the precise details of this portion of the ritual seem to vary from account to account, perhaps from practice to practice. In some cases, it is at this point that the mentor carves a small tattoo in the arm of the initiate, allowing the blood from the wound to fall into the nganga. In other cases, chickens, goats, reptiles or other animals may be sacrificed at this point in order to give the nganga blood.

The Abakua, about whom much less is known even than is known of the secretive Palo, build ngangas, too. The difference is that the Palo rob graves to supply their needs. The Abakua, it has always been believed, sacrifice living human beings. It is at some point in the Abakua ritual, perhaps at the point of feeding blood to the nganga, that the Abakua are believed to drink the blood of their victim, hoping, if they are extremely fortunate, to drink the blood of the heart. Because of the quickness with which the heart must be seized, and reinforced by beliefs about the passing of the soul into the mouth of the one who drinks the blood of the heart, victims may even still have flickering moments of consciousness as this ultimate violation occurs.

After the cauldron has been fed blood, other ingredients follow, which tend to vary greatly from account to account. Cigar butts are a common element. The smoking of tobacco was a central ingredient in the earliest Indian rituals witnessed by European trappers and explorers in the New World.

Many other things may be sprinkled in—seawater, for the unsleeping tide, mercury, for quickness, candle wax, all sorts of things, each with its own muttered prayer. Dog parts are common, and there is always a variety of herbs. Peppers are a common ingredient, along with all the lizards and bat parts and frog intestines that seem to be universal ingredients in the brew of witches.

Having been properly mixed, the ingredients in the nganga must now be spiritually cooked. To accomplish this end, the nganga is buried back in the same graveyard from which the original ingredients came. After three weeks, by then in a condition that cannot be described, the nganga is removed from the graveyard and returned to the chapel of the mayombero.

In all of this the stench of human rot plays a key role. It is a smell from which human beings recoil instinctively, as if slapped. It is a thing that human beings find more repulsive than almost any other sensory experience. People who experience it for the first time always say that it takes weeks for the stench to leave their nostrils and that, even years later, simple memory can cause it to recur full-force. That stench, so awful and overwhelming for normal people, is something the mayombero must overcome and finally learn to enjoy. When he has taught his own soul to like the smell of human death, it is a powerful sign that he is himself one of the dead, a ruler in their kingdom. Even before he has learned to enjoy it, he must do a fairly convincing job of showing his mentors that it doesn't bother him.

The stink of the nganga is so powerful, however, that it usually must be kept far away from the nose of any errant neighbor. For that reason, a mayombero usually keeps at least two principal places of worship—one an altar in his home and the other a chapel, cave, hiding place or shack of some kind far away from where any uninvited person might wander. There the nganga is kept.

When the completed nganga has been returned to the mayombero's secret chapel, he celebrates by giving it a few drinks of wine or rum. Now it is time for a few test runs.

The testing of the nganga is again a case of varied accounts. Most of the tests are variations on the same theme, which involves burying the covered nganga near a tree or animals and then waiting for the tree to wither or the animal to drop dead. The same rituals often involve some strategic scarring or wounding of the tree or plant with a knife, so it's entirely possible that a well-trained mayombero, eager to convince his followers of the power of his nganga, can help things along with a few skillfully executed nicks and gouges during the marking phase.

Once everyone is satisfied the nganga is working well, the Tata Nkisi may begin to use it in his practice. His practice is well paid. He is one of the most powerful magicians—a last resort, an ultimate remedy. He can charge stiff prices.

One of the chief tasks of a Tata Nkisi is murder. Of course, because he is a Tata Nkisi, it is not considered murder for him to kill someone. He is, after all, death itself. He is the Great Night. He is only doing what he does.

The murderer is the person who goes to the Tata Nkisi —perhaps a jilted lover, a cheated business partner, a betrayed spouse. If a man discovers that his brother has cheated him of his patrimony, for example, and if he decides to hire the Tata Nkisi to even the score, then it is he, the bitter brother, who is committing murder. Not the Tata Nkisi.

The rituals of murder in Palo are similar in many basic aspects to the same rituals in all of the original beliefs. They involve the marking of the intended victim, the taking of personal items from the victim for ritual use and the vicarious torture or wounding of dolls or animals which are intended as spiritual surrogates for the victim himself.

The Tata Nkisi may ask his client for a photograph or a rag of clothing from the victim—items not unlike what a person might be accustomed to carrying to the cathedral when asking the orishas for blessings and help. The Tata Nkisi often digs a symbolic grave for the victim in a nearby cemetery and brings some of the soil back to be sprinkled into the nganga, along with the clothing and photo.

There typically follows some calling of the name of the

victim over the nganga. Then the Tata Nkisi takes a heated pin and runs it through a centipede or other insect, intending for the writhing pain of the insect to be reproduced in the body of the victim.

The mayombero possesses a number of spells and rituals designed to kill different kinds of people in different kinds of ways, including the murder of fetuses still in the womb. To the extent he is successful in seeming to cause the actual death of his victims, his fame and wealth may increase. The mayombero, therefore, has an obvious interest in seeing to it that his victims depart their lives with some reasonable amount of dispatch after his pronouncing of curses on them.

The most common means by which sorcerers and witches through the ages have succeeded in bringing about the demise of their victims is through simple poisoning. Gradual painful poisoning has an especially dramatic effect on the surrounding witnesses.

But killing people is only one manifestation of the mayombero's power. It is far less common, in fact, that a client comes to the mayombero with homicidal wishes than with mortal dread and fear.

If, for example, a person's luck were suddenly to turn bad; if, out of the blue, things began to go wrong; and if, God forbid, the most fundamental certainties of a person's life—his home, his family, his faith—were suddenly and mysteriously to begin coming apart; then it would be reasonable for that person to assume that he himself was the object of a curse, of bad magic, bad luck, the evil eye, a gathering gloom of misfortune. It would even be reasonable for him to assume that a sorcerer was attacking him from some direction, by some means that he was not wise enough to detect.

As these evidences of a poisoned fate mounted, a person would feel compelled to seek more and more powerful remedies and protections. It is at this fulcrum in the affairs of life that the supposed distinctions between white and black magic begin to blur. In order to discover the source of the curse from which a person is suffering, that person must go to a sorcerer at least as powerful as the one attacking him. And in order for the second sorcerer to be as powerful as the first, the second must be capable of all the same magic and then some.

The two sorcerers in this sort of contest, interestingly enough, are not necessarily unhappy or even terribly at odds with each other. Their role is more that of hired advocates, like lawyers.

But in order to protect a client from his enemies, a sorcerer must work more powerful curses and spells on those enemies than the competing sorcerer can work on the client. Hence, the matter of protection becomes much the same sort of business as the original attack.

Protections, for example, involve the same kind of taking from the soul of the enemy. Some piece or leaving of the enemy's person must be brought to the protective sorcerer, so that he may use it to weave a spell.

Most cannibalism has its origin in beliefs about protection from danger. In the Indian traditions of warfare, it was almost universally believed that eating one of the enemy would work to protect a person in battle from the entire enemy tribe.

In general, a very powerful Tata Nkisi should be able to deflect curses and other bad magic directed from the camp of one's enemies and then further should be able to defuse all the powers of the enemies and render person not only safe from but invulnerable to those enemies. Their arrows would fall short each time. Their bullets should not penetrate. Their eyes would not even be able to see.

But of course this magnitude of protection would require extremely powerful magic. Going to a sorcerer capable of that kind of magic always entails the same awe-inspiring risk. In the end, all of the business about white and black magic is trivial and irrelevant at that point. At that point, a person knows to whom he is appealing for help. He is appealing to the Great Night.

For those people who hold these beliefs as devoutly and

The cauldron—the *nganga*—and the lesser vessels. To look into the cauldron is literally to stand on the rim of Hell.

Adolfo de Jesus Constanzo was *El Padrino*, the Godfather, and Sara Aldrete was his high priestess.

After the thirteenth body was found, the federales brought a *curandero* to the ranch to drive out the evil spirits.

PHOTO BY FRANK ORDONEZ

When his exorcism was done, the *curandero* torched the shack that had been Constanzo's temple.

PHOTO BY ANTHONY PADILLA

Mark Kilroy's body was found in a shallow grave midway between the shack and the corral.

PHOTO BY ANTHONY PADILLA

Kilroy's body awaiting transfer to the morgue. He was identified by his dental work.

There were four graves inside the corral. Two of them held more than one body.

Thirteen bodies were dug up before the federales stopped their excavation.

PHOTO BY ANTHONY PADILLA

Inside the cauldron, the federales found human blood, bones, and brains as well as animal organs, a horseshoe, and other offerings.

At the ranch, the federales found Reyes Bustamente, a caretaker who identified Kilroy from a photo and took them to the shack where he had last seen the boy.

In this shack, the federales found Constanzo's bloodstained altar.

Mark Kilroy

The first members of the gang to be captured were *(left to right)* Serafin Hernandez, Jr., Sergio Martinez *(La Mariposa)*, and David Serna Valdez *(El Coqueto)*.

sincerely as any religious European holds his faith, the step of going to this kind of sorcerer for help is almost unimaginably frightening. Of course the sorcerer will say he is going to help. But after saying it, he will take the client by the hand and take him to the nganga. There, in the stench of the shack, by the light of tapers stolen from the church, the client will stare into a cauldron bubbling with blood, human brain matter, turtle parts, cigar butts, wings of bats. Hand in hand with the Great Night, the client will enter the domain of the cauldron to seek his redress and satisfaction.

He can have no idea what the ultimate outcome will be at that point. He can certainly hope. But there is no way for him to know for sure. He is risking the ultimate commodity—his very soul.

He can only hope that his Great Night is better than the other guy's Great Night. And even then, even if his champion does emerge victorious and even if his own fortunes do begin to ascend again, he still has to hope he is paying his Great Night enough.

To all of these mysteries, Adolfo himself was initiated gradually, first by his mother to the lesser, more common and less secret mysteries, then later by the Great Master to the darker and more fiercely held secrets of the nganga. It is not known to what extent Constanzo was instructed in the final and ultimate secret practices to which Mark Kilroy fell victim and to what extent he simply took himself to those secrets of his own volition and under his own power.

But by the time Sara came to him and by the time she brought him Elio, Constanzo already was at the darkest heart of all the secrets. He had become the ultimate mystery and monster of all primitive beliefs. He was truly the Great Night.

Because of the way he himself had been conducted in toward the ultimate mysteries, he knew in great detail and with clear purpose how to bring others in toward the rim. He showed them only the Tarot cards at first, then some of the mysteries of the altar and the taste of animal blood. By the time a human being was kicking and gurgling on the altar before them, it was too late. They were there. They were part of it. Constanzo was very very good at his job.

Keystone. Constanzo wanted half. Half of the profits of a smuggling operation that was moving large amounts of cocaine, between one and two thousand pounds of marijuana and sizable numbers of guns and stolen cars over the border every week. Half.

But Elio never hesitated. Once he had been graduated from Constanzo's little seminary in Mexico City, he never really had a lot of choice. How hard can a man bargain when his soul is in the other man's teeth?

Elio brought the Matamoros branch of the Hernandez family together and informed them that Adolfo de Jesus Constanzo was now a very important part of their operation, along with Sara Aldrete.

Serafin Junior had some inkling of what was coming next, but the others were unprepared. Elio explained to the family that Constanzo possessed terrible and mysterious powers and that he had initiated Elio and Sara into these powers. They would use this vast new power to smite their enemies and to build a new source of inner strength for the family. They would all join the Church of Constanzo.

It was quite a deal for Constanzo. The rich movie stars and high government officials in Mexico City were paying $30,000 to $40,000 for the limpias. One limpia, with the setup and cleanup times included, killed a day. The process was exhausting, and Constanzo was seldom in the mood for more than two or three a week. That amount of income, $60,000 to $100,000 on busy weeks, nothing on off weeks, was not all that much, given the cost of Constanzo's life-style, his retinue, his several homes and his penchant for buying expensive new cars with cash.

At times, and in spite of the great respect the wealthy people in Mexico City seemed to show him, Constanzo still felt as if he worked for them, as if he were merely a very expensive and scary version of a personal trainer or on-call manicurist.

But this money—the money these rubes in Matamoros were handling every week—was in the hundreds of millions of dollars. This was real money—the kind of money a movie star would have.

When word of Constanzo's presence in the inner circle reached the branch of the family on the American side, the split within the family became complete. The American side could not believe its ears. Elio, the spoiled, ignorant half-crazed baby of the family, finally had gone off the end. He was not only trusting an outsider to the family, he was turning over half the profits of the whole operation to some damned Cuban voodoo witch doctor.

Almost as soon as Constanzo had established himself in Matamoros as the corporate repairman who was going to set everything to rights in the Hernandez dope smuggling operation, the Hernandez dope smuggling operation looked as if it were finally ready to collapse and die. Without the help of the branch on the American side, Elio could do nothing. He could grow all the dope in the world on the family's large plantations; he could rip off tons of cocaine from other gangs; but he could do nothing without the other half of the web.

The payoffs, the arrangements, the entire distribution network in the United States had been worked out by Saul and the others on the American side. Now all of that was gone, mainly because nobody on the other side was going to split profits with a witch doctor.

In his profoundly serious and matter-of-fact manner, Constanzo told Elio to stop worrying. Obviously, in addition to the magical assistance he needed from Constanzo, Elio was going to need some practical help, too. Constanzo took him back to Mexico City again, where he put him in touch with some of his own extremely helpful friends in the dope business.

Constanzo always had had such friends. Many of Mexico's most important figures in the narcotics trade had come to him for limpias. Many of the highest police officials had come, too, including some of the most corrupt.

The problem always had been that Adolfo Constanzo, so hungry for money, never had it to offer. Not real money. He made a lot of money, but he spent it as fast as he got it. He didn't have capital before. Now he did.

Little Elio, the hot-blooded rube from the border, was welcome in Mexico City's most sophisticated circles—a thrill for him—and Constanzo, his constant consort, was welcomed with a new level of respect, too. It was one thing to be the famous and fashionable witch doctor. It was quite another to control millions of dollars.

Every inch of the way Constanzo led Elio into these new arrangements was another mile away from everything Elio had been taught from birth to trust and believe. The only thing a smuggler trusts is blood. The only people with whom one does serious ongoing business are the members of one's family.

That was the difference, Saul had told them, between a great smuggling family and the mere criminals of Mexico City, Houston or Detroit. The criminals floated loose and alone in the night, grasping for whatever deals and alliances they could throw together in a pinch and winding up in the slam most of the time because of it. But a family, such as the Hernandez family of Matamoros, could go on forever, because its members never would betray each other.

For all the glitter and chic of the people to whom Constanzo introduced Elio in Mexico City, they were not blood. When it was time to go out into the night with the pickup trucks and the paper plates tacked to stakes, the spiderweb of arrangements would be made with strangers. That went directly against the grain for Little Elio.

But Constanzo, meanwhile, was giving Elio a new family in Mexico City. Most of the retinue of people who hung around Constanzo in Mexico City were obvious homosexuals.

Sexual servitude was an important aspect of membership in Constanzo's inner circle. Of the fluctuating number who were honored to be near him, to share in his wealth and to be protected by his power, only two were important to him emotionally. Both were men. He was passionate in his attentions to Omar Orea Ochoa, whom he called his lady, and to Martin Quintana Rodriquez, whom he called his man.

For Elio, whose dream until quite recently had been to be recognized as the toughest pistolero on the border, some of this business with "his man" and "his lady" was a bit much at first. But Constanzo, whose eye had been trained by a lifetime of practice, missed nothing and saw quickly that Elio needed to be swept into the full circle of horrors, in a place where small anomalies like homosexuality would seem like nothing, would seem almost comfortingly trivial.

Within a short time after his first trip to Mexico City and the positive report on body markings from the Haitian voodoo priest, Elio found himself standing at the altar in Mexico City. The altar was the place from which all the powers of Constanzo over his followers were spun. Elio fell quickly and totally under Constanzo's spell of horror.

Omar and Martin and sometimes another young man would go out into the city to lure a victim. Some of the men they lured were homosexuals who knew Constanzo and were both flattered and too frightened to object when invited back for a free cleaning. Others were lured sexually and had to be beaten and threatened with razors and guns in order to get them to lie down on the altar.

The followers doffed black robes and gathered around the sides and foot of the altar, while the ever-unsmiling Constanzo stood at the head in his spotless white robe, muttering his Bantu hexes and waiting for the spirits to take possession of him. At a key moment, duct tape was slapped across the mouth of the victim to muffle the screams. And then came the blades and the blood.

Constanzo led them into the process carefully, with the knowing and watchful eye of an experienced teacher. At first, he waited until the kicking and tremors had stopped and the geysers of blood had gone flat—until it was plain the victim was dead—and then he ordered one or two of the novices to begin the dismemberment.

The all-important ends of the fingers were taken, the brains, the penis, the ribs and tibia and finally the head, so that the face and some of its underlying bone structure could be hacked off.

All of these things were gathered in a bag to be taken to the nganga. The rest was garbage. They had to do some more hacking and sawing in order to pack the leftovers into the plastic shopping bags they saved in a special drawer in the kitchen. Then they threw the bags in a car, and the younger men were dispatched to dump it all into one of Mexico City's open drains or into the Zumpango River.

But dismembering the victim after death was only an early stage of the process of initiation. In subsequent services at the altar, they would be required to take part in the torture and killing.

When all of the business about spirit possession was finished, when they were sitting quietly on the spotless white furniture Constanzo so loved and listening to soft music on his excellent stereo system, Constanzo explained to them why it was so important for them to take part.

Speaking in his softest and most solemn voice, he explained to them that, in order to acquire power, they needed to penetrate the walls of horror. They needed to overcome all revulsion and fear, and then they would be invulnerable.

It was the most ancient teaching of the most ancient priests. It was the point at which all of the scams and deceptions ceased to be scams and deceptions and worked instead to accomplish precisely what the priest promised. The Aztec priests, high on the pyramid, their hair caked and stinking with blood, eyes wild, flesh at their lips, promised and gave this gift to their followers: beyond this gate of Hell all the fetters of human fear and doubt would fall away in ash and dirt. He or she who mastered these rituals would never again know doubt, fear or vulnerability.

In twentieth-century terms, he or she, at that point, would be totally mad. And not know it. And think that he or she had stumbled on some great secret.

Don Juan, the Yaqui sorcerer in the Carlos Castaneda novels, begins his teaching by showing his student how to control his own dreams, how to mix the worlds of waking consciousness and dream. Assuming it's possible with enough tries and a lot of peyote buttons to pull it off, the outcome would be a situation in which one could make conscious decisions in one's dreams. "I think I'll go walk through that wall." And then do it, in the dream.

Ultimately, the teaching of a Don Juan or a Constanzo is supposed to enable initiates to mix and match elements of madness and sanity, reality and hallucination, at the direction of a calm and self-controlling will. It is the other resolution of the original question that produces all of the original religions.

The question is: "What is this?"

The more common answer—the one most human beings have been able to live with since the first morning of human consciousness, the one that has produced modern religion and civilization—is the one that says: "This is reality. That over there is unreality. The lines that circumscribe reality are the limbs of life."

Constanzo's answer, Don Juan's answer, the answer of all the sorcerers sooner or later is: "This is power. There is no reality. There is no unreality. There is only your power to exert your will in the great black night of madness, sanity, death and life. There are no walls. There is no waking or sleeping, no death or living. There is only power. There is only will."

But if Elio was to be more than a mere follower, if he was to be a priest himself, that would require more. He was to become the Tata Nkisi. He would need to return to Matamoros and prepare his nganga.

Of course, Constanzo also was eager to see Elio return to Matamoros and run his dope business, which was beginning to look worse and worse. In that department, Constanzo's magic was continuing to do no good at all.

The problem with a smuggling operation, after all, was that one bad spider on the web could easily devour all the others. All of the intricate matrix of pay-offs and understandings could be rewired and turned against the smugglers.

Constanzo began to travel with the family on dope business, going along with an especially huge cocaine shipment to Houston in June 1988, to help reassure everyone that the new connections, set up through the heavy guys in Mexico City, would work even better than the old arrangements with the American side of the family. In Houston, Constanzo did a lot of posturing for the group, marching into an expensive car dealership and buying a luxury car with cash and performing other acts of swagger.

But Elio was chewing his fingers, worried to death how on earth they would peddle such an amount of cocaine— 436 pounds of high-grade product at a street value of $20 million—without the help of the old American network.

The initiation of the full family into the rituals was just getting under way. In Houston, Constanzo went through a great rigamarole of setting up an altar in the safe house on Friendship Street in northwest Houston, where the dope was stored, arranging the candles and the orishas, sprinkling herbs and muttering incantations.

He was just topping off his altar with his trademark ceramic Buddha figure when the good-eyes, parked in a car across the street, radioed in that there was suspicious activity in the neighborhood. Everybody in the house, including Constanzo, beat it out the back door in seconds. Half an hour later the Houston P.D. smashed in the front and back doors and seized the largest single cocaine shipment ever captured in the history of Houston.

Police photographers took careful photographs of the voodoo altar and then filed them with all the other evidence of voodoo and Santeria that was showing up in Mexican and Colombian drug busts lately.

In Mexico, things were even worse for Constanzo's new service, if such a thing were possible. There, where bribes and threats were law, the family was being treated with open disrespect—a very serious and dangerous sign in Latin culture that a brutal end is near. If they can sneer at you with impunity, they can kill you.

Constanzo needed to make a showing. Winning over the impressionable young Elio had been one thing. But now Constanzo himself was right where Elio had been—with de facto responsibility for running the drug gang. Especially in his position, having done the things and made the claims he had made, Constanzo could not afford to let his image sag.

Fortunately, there was always a convenient venue available in the drug business for proving one's power. Constanzo quickly took over the ongoing murder activities of the family.

It always had been necessary to kill some people. But the Hernandez family was still doing it the old-fashioned way, the gringo way—taking them out in a field, sticking a 9 mm up their mouths and blowing them off. As a method of terror, that was worthless. Beginning gradually, Constanzo began to show them the proper way to kill.

There was the matter of Cesare Sauceda, the former Matamoros cop who was keeping Elio entirely too much on edge. Even though Saul had never been able to cement a formal relationship with the Matamoros police—the police department's favoritism toward the city's older drug families was a big part of what made Saul so angry at times—Saul nevertheless had maintained certain sources within the department. Sauceda had been one of them.

With Saul gone and this whole business of the federales trying to come in and take over the drug trade, all bets were off. Sauceda had suffered some personal misfortunes, including getting bounced from the Matamoros police department. Now he was looking for new opportunities, and that effort included peddling what small bits of sensitive information he had been able to glean on Saul's operation to other families. Elio didn't give a damn what Sauceda told cops—cops were another matter—but it bothered him greatly that Sauceda was out there telling the other gangs that Elio was the man who was ripping them off.

Constanzo explained to the family that they needed to do much more than merely kill Sauceda. They needed to use his death ritually to evince for themselves a spiritual protection from the Matamoros police and the Matamoros gangs.

Then, with his ever-sensitive eye on the possible issue of mutiny, especially with things going so badly out in the real world, Constanzo decided it was time to turn some of the murdering ever so subtly inward. There was also the question of small-time drug dealer, pistolero and hired hand, Gilbert Sosa, who had expressed an interest in sleeping with Sara.

To the point, Sosa had expressed his interest directly to Sara, skipping the all-important step of checking with Constanzo for permission to have sex with her.

Another very troubling matter was cropping up. It was an especially vexing issue for Constanzo, but it was a problem Saul had faced, too. It was something heads of all drug gangs deal with every day of their lives: drug use.

The dope-smuggling and dope-selling business is an extremely perilous operation, always just on the edge of the razor, demanding extreme wariness, concentration, memory and steely poise. And yet there is always a ton of dope around. No one may be more likely to need some relief once in a while than a dope dealer; nobody has better access; and nobody can afford to use the stuff less.

For Saul, it had been a matter of family, of honor and of culture. He didn't mind people blowing a little grass at a picnic along with a few beers. But members of the Hernandez family were not dopers. They did not do cocaine, ever. Cocaine was God's gift to gringos. Gringos were rich enough, fat enough, surrounded by thick enough walls and buttressed by deep enough pockets that they could afford to walk around with their brains wired upside down half the time. But not Mexican smugglers.

For Constanzo, the problem was even more serious. He was beginning by now to introduce the Matamoros operation to the rituals of torture and dismemberment. These were, for him, an all-important form of brainwashing. In the name of teaching them all perfect courage, he would render them all half crazy but totally under his control. Somewhere in the Gypsy mix of his beliefs, he understood perfectly that the game was off and he would be in great danger from his own adherents if he ever lost his ferocious grip on their minds.

And there was the danger for Constanzo in dope. In his alchemy of terror, dope was a loose cannon, a free agent, an act of God. He could do nothing to control the mind of a person whose mind was controlled by cocaine.

An excellent opportunity to prove the point presented itself. One of the few members of the Matamoros gang who had dared to show open skepticism of this homosexual voodoo doctor and his six-foot witch was Jorge Valente del Fierro Gomez. Del Fierro was older than Elio and had been close to Serafin's father. He regretted all that had happened to the family, and he saw Constanzo as a major obstacle to the possibility of ever healing the wound.

Unfortunately for him, del Fierro was too open in showing his disrespect. In the presence of Constanzo, he snorted cocaine one day. Constanzo told the others to hold him. He calmly picked up a semiautomatic pistol, walked to del Fierro and blew his brains all over the room.

Drenched in blood and brain matter, with the eyeless corpse staring up at them from a corner, the family was subjected to a long quiet lecture on the evils of narcotics.

This killing had a certain effect on the family, to be sure, but it was not precisely the effect Constanzo was seeking. The problem with these Hernandez fellows was that they were border Mexicans—part rube, part conservative old Mexico and part gringo. They understood that tough guys kill people. But Constanzo intended to move them on a much more fundamental level than that. At each step of the way, he felt he was bumping up against a wall of gringo skepticism—a tendency to look down on ancient ways and to trust only what is modern and Yankee.

He did some of his own recruiting in Matamoros, accepting new members into the family and thereby subtly usurping Elio's role as the leader. One of his first recruits was a pistolero the family knew well—Alvaro de Leon Valdez, a fairly well known but quite small-time crime figure in Matamoros. Known as "El Dubi," he had been hiding out for several weeks, working as a laborer on one of the family properties after carrying out a routine contract killing for Elio.

Normally he was the type of dime-a-dozen vato loco thugs the family might hire for a job but would never trust in its councils. Something about the cut of his jib caught Constanzo's fancy, however, and El Dubi was suddenly very much at the center of things.

Constanzo also brought in two local homosexuals who were friends of Sara—David Serna Valdez, twenty-two, who was called El Coqueto or The Flirt, and Sergio Martinez Serna, twenty-three, who was called La Mariposa or The Butterfly.

It was at this point of the process that Sara became so valuable in the training and indoctrination of the gang. She, after all, was one of them—a border person herself, caught in both worlds. She perhaps more than any of them was sensitive to the smug anthropological condescensions of Yankee culture toward these matters. And she happened to have stumbled across the ideal training film. It was a movie that obviously had been sent to Constanzo in this hour of his need by the gods of Hollywood.

Sara was alone with Constanzo in a theater in Miami the

first time they saw *The Believers,* a police-thriller about Santeria cult murders in New York. Already wired to explode by what was happening in her life, she was overwhelmed by the film, which deals with the brutal sacrificial murders of a series of young boys.

In it, Martin Sheen plays a psychiatrist who treats New York City cops for emotional disorders. Jimmy Smits is a Hispanic cop who eventually plunges a knife into his own stomach and kills himself under a voodoo curse.

Again and again in the early development of the film, a dramatic tension is established between the skepticism of Martin Sheen and the terrible fate stalking him. It is easy to see—given her obsessions—how Sara drew a different lesson.

In the movie, there are any number of moments and scenes where Sara may have seen her own image staring back at herself from the high altars of Hollywood. Drugs are an important theme. The good santero, who winds up being Martin Sheen's sidekick in all this, runs a drug rehabilitation program. His beliefs are his shield against the lure of drugs all around him. Parallels are suggested between people who die from overdoses and people who are ritually sacrificed.

In the first interviews after her arrest, when she was still talking fairly loosely, Sara Aldrete told reporters how she had forced members of the Matamoros family to watch *The Believers* over and over again. In talking about it, she said she wanted the members to see how these rituals had been used "to strengthen the families" of the people in the movie.

That conclusion about what happens in the movie is not necessarily obvious or clear. In the film, people use magic to get rich and to get their faces on the cover of *New York* magazine. The business of family does not seem terribly important.

But it was important to Sara, and it was important to Constanzo. The whole challenge within the Hernandez operation was to convince Elio that Constanzo and his rituals could replace what the family had lost in the last two years in its own inner strength. Elio could make the family whole again. He could find the personal power Saul had possessed, the power Saul had used to put it all together in the first place. He could find it in the nganga. In the devil.

Chapter Six

Tamaulipas State Highway 2 runs west from Matamoros to Reynosa. Outside Matamoros it is a typical Mexican state highway—a narrow two-lane affair with soft skinny shoulders. The land is a continuation of the same alluvial plain that runs up to the north on the Texas side; the soil and the weather are the same; and there are major American landholdings on the Mexican side, with the result that the same crops often are cultivated by roughly the same techniques on both sides. Harvest is always a more labor-intensive operation on the Mexican side, where hired hands are still much cheaper than huge machines. But in the spring when the young maize and sorghum plants are budding up green from the sable-colored soil, the land on the Mexican side is identical to the land across the river.

Rancho Santa Elena is twenty miles out from Matamoros. A dirt turnout opens a road that barely turns this way and that as it writhes up into the center of the large plantation. Three-quarters of a mile into the ranch, there is a work station, consisting of a large metal barn, some lean-to structures with tin roofs, and a small frame cottage.

A couple of large tractors and two eighteen-wheelers are parked there most of the time.

Farther down the same soft dirt road, surrounded by carefully plowed fields and rimmed by swiftly running irrigation ditches, was the shack. It was a small simple structure built for storing hay and feed. A few yards away from it was a goat and burro corral made of simple split-rail fence. Hay was piled in loose heaps here and there on the ground.

Constanzo had explained to Elio that the Matamoros nganga—Elio's nganga—would have to be on isolated property somewhere, where neighbors or wandering laborers would be unlikely to happen by. The family owned property in several locations, but Santa Elena seemed best, because it was a relatively easy drive from Matamoros and because it was a cover operation, where legitimate corps were grown, and was thereby less likely to attract unwanted attention.

The shack by the goat corral was fine. The nganga would not be bothered there. It would be safe from men and animals.

A proper pot was obtained, of a type commonly used in Mexican outdoor cooking. The rest was unimportant. Everything else could be improvised. Everything was in order.

The dope operation was still running raggedly. But Constanzo was confident that would change soon. It was a matter of putting power back into the hearts of the family members.

Elio was a slow student. His erratic temperament yanked him back and forth so wildly that it was difficult even for Constanzo, with his stagey manner and practiced technique, to get Elio to concentrate. The killing of Cesare Sauceda, the dirty cop, went very badly and almost made Constanzo look foolish—the one thing a witch doctor cannot afford.

Constanzo had assembled the gang at the shack at two

in the afternoon. He had carefully prepared the altar inside, with all the proper candles and objects.

Three of the younger ones, including Serafin Junior brought Sauceda out into the Chevrolet Suburban—a cross between a truck and a stationwagon. At first when they took his blindfold off, Sauceda must have thought he was in for a dope-trade beating, maybe some minor mutilation, the loss of a finger, something like that. He was quiet but sullen as Elio began to scream an indictment at him, all the things Saul had done for Sauceda, all the ways Sauceda had betrayed the family and the memory of Saul.

Then at some moment Sauceda caught sight of the nganga and of Constanzo and knew suddenly that what lay ahead was worse than the worst he had expected. The horror began then, with Sauceda screaming in a frothing panic and trying to break loose and Elio beating at him with a gun butt, sending spit and blood and teeth flying.

This was not what Constanzo wanted. The killing had to be done calmly. The participants had to be perfectly untouched by the screams and agony of their victim. Constanzo tried to intervene, but by then Elio had gone completely off the deep end. Elio turned his 9 mm around and filled Sauceda with bullets.

The ritual was a bust. The man was already dead. There was nothing to do. Constanzo was angry. He berated Elio, whose wrath rushed out of him like air from a collapsing balloon. Elio was ashamed. He sent the young ones out again and told them to bring him someone else.

Little Jose Garcia Luna had come home from school that day and had eaten a quick meal already prepared for him by his mother. He was in a good mood, because he had a job. His father was headed into Matamoros that evening. Jose asked his father to buy him some music cassettes. He took off his school shirt and slipped on a gray jersey with green sleeves. Then Jose set off down Highway 2 on foot to his job feeding the cows on a neighboring ranch. On his way out the door, he called to his mother, "I'll be back at five."

Serafin and the other two leapt out of the Suburban and threw a feed bag over the boy's head. They hit him hard several times through the sack and then threw him in the back of the truck.

When they got back to Santa Elena, Elio's moment of shame had passed, and he was wild again. They wrestled the bloody kid out of the back with the bag still over his head. The boy staggered around for a moment. Elio came screaming up to him, machete cocked back like a baseball bat, and hacked off the boy's head. It fell, still in the bag.

Elio lifted the bag, proud of himself finally. He dumped out the head and fell back in horror. He had killed his own cousin! The idiots in the truck had been so crazy and panicked by the afternoon's events that they had nabbed the kid without ever looking at his face. The head of his own cousin lay at his feet, black with cakes of blood and dirt, the eyes staring glassily up, the body still pumping blood into the soil.

Constanzo did what he could to salvage what was beginning to be a very bad day for him. There was still good blood in the body. He ordered them to bring the boy to the tarpaulin he had spread before the altar. He lay down next to the body and seemed to sleep. Then his body went rigid and began to quake.

He was on his feet now, muttering and shouting the Bantu incantations. He danced and swayed and rocked around the body, then stooped quickly and hacked open the head, lifted out the brains with both hands and plopped them into the cauldron.

With one great whack of the machete he laid open the chest of the boy like a watermelon. Reaching in to grab with one hand, sawing with the machete in the other, he hacked out the heart, lifted it and smashed it to his sucking mouth. He threw it into the pot with the brains. Reaching and sawing quickly, he hacked off the penis and testicles and threw them in the pot. He chopped away the ends of the fingers and toes, then hacked and sawed on one leg until he had severed it just above the knee. All of this he put into the pot.

While the brew of blood, organs and limbs in the pot bubbled greasily over a low charcoal fire, Constanzo killed goats and chickens and offered their blood, too. He sprinkled herbs and other magical objects into the mix, all the while muttering and singing the incredibly low and threatening sound of the Bantu curses and invocations.

By the end of the evening, things were going well again. They were all in the palm of his hand.

Later, some weeks after her arrest, when Sara was beginning to cut her deal with the federal authorities over what she would blab and what she would keep secret, the authorities began to change their story about her. At times they said that she had never been present for any of the rituals—a vast departure from their detailed early versions of her role in them. At other times, when things were not going well in the negotiations, they returned to the original story.

The original story is the most persuasive. According to what the police said first, before Sara became a larger problem for them, she came to a point in Matamoros where she finally had to put up or shut up. Elio had fed his unintentionally beheaded cousin to the nganga. Now it was time to really gather the body parts and the blood and build the nganga up.

Sara had been full of movies, politics and Constanzo, but that was far from enough.

There was the matter of this Gilbert Sosa. Some of the family members said later she had been having sex with him on the sly. Some said he had only dreamed and bragged of it. The facts of the matter were irrelevant to Constanzo. He needed to demonstrate three things.

Constanzo needed to remind the clan that his control over sex was as important as his control over drug use. Sex, like drugs, was an avenue by which their minds might escape his absolute grip. He needed to shut down that avenue. If they were to have sex, it would be at his behest and direction.

The second thing he needed to do was step up the horror. The rituals following the killings of the cop and the kid had amounted mainly to the butchering of corpses. Constanzo needed them to start listening to the screams and watching the slow death of their victims.

And thirdly, Constanzo needed to see for himself that Sara was really in it. She had made herself too important. She was too much the theoretician already. She needed to get in the middle of it and drench herself in blood, in front of the clan, so that they could believe she too had given her soul to the devil.

According to what the police first said was Sara's story, she directed the death of Gilbert Sosa, while the clan assisted and looked on. She ordered first that he be hanged loosely by the neck, with his arms loose, so that he could just grapple and kick enough to barely keep the rope from killing him.

Then he was lowered slowly into an oil drum filled with water that had been fired to a good rolling boil. While he screamed and slowly boiled to death, half-choking and fighting for his life on the rope, Sara squeezed off his nipples with a pair of scissors.

It was a good show. She had done well. Constanzo genuinely liked Sara. It was after this murder that he began his habit of sitting up late alone with her, sipping brandy, smoking cigars and telling her the long slow story of his life, what he knew, how he knew it, whom he knew, what he knew, always speaking in that soft unsmiling methodical voice, so antithetical to the screaming thing he became when he danced before the nganga.

Again and again the Suburban came bumping down the long barely winding dirt road between the swift running irrigation ditches with another victim. Each time Constanzo swept open the door to the shack, the stench came roaring out and the high fretting shriek of the flies assaulted their ears. And each time Constanzo strode in happily, as if greeting an old friend.

At the end of each ritual, they passed bowls with the soup of cooked and rotten blood, brains and body parts and slopped it into their mouths, spilling down their chins and shirtfronts. They were all convinced that great electric storms of power charged into them at that moment.

They dug shallow graves in the goat corral and buried the remains. Constanzo showed them how to stick wire through the vertebrae and leave an end of the wire protruding from the earth, so that later, when the flesh was beginning to rot off, they could yank on the wire and pull out the spinal bones. The spinal bones made powerful necklaces.

Constanzo never succeeded in truly taming Elio. The fact was that some of the theory and design of Constanzo's whole routine required a level of understanding that was occasionally a little beyond Elio. In particular, Constanzo never was able to slow Elio down enough to get him to be properly calm and solemn while the victims shrieked their unending agonies. Elio was always a little wild.

But that could be handled. Constanzo's training had prepared him for this not so terribly uncommon type of killer.

The thing Elio could do well was wild savagery. And, after all, savagery was really the avenue to the mystery of mysteries. There were some muffed attempts.

But finally, just before Mark Kilroy was taken, Elio succeeded in bringing off the finest climax any ritual could achieve. He and the other members of the clan had already cut off the man's penis, legs and fingers, but had managed to keep him alive and conscious. He could still watch what they were doing to him.

Then with a great whack Elio sliced the man's chest open, seized his heart, yanked it from the cavity without bothering to hack it loose, bit into it and drank while his victim watched.

The business, in the meantime, was finally beginning to improve. Constanzo's Mexico City contacts were working out. The rituals were turning the clan into fearless zombies. Sales were up.

Constanzo explained to them that the Mexicans whose souls they had eaten would protect them in Mexico. But on this occasion, they needed to bring him a gringo—one of the spring-breakers, a boy whose appearance would please him. They would take the gringo's soul, and then they would be safe on the other side of the river, where they had been having so many troubles.

The police were standing not far away. A low roar started up and then became an angry storm of shouting. The master of ceremonies at the Miss Tanline contest on the beach behind the Sheraton was reminding the beautiful coed contestants that there were nudity laws in South Padre and that they would risk arrest if they took off the tops of their swimsuits. But the huge swaying crowd of students was in no mood for rules, not on so perfect a Monday afternoon.

Had they been ten years older and even half so long without decent sleep, the boys would all have been in intensive care by now. But they were slowly winding down after their semesters of hard work and self-denial. When Mark and the others returned from the Miss Tanline Contest and tried to take naps, they could barely sleep.

That evening they drove to a condominium some of Mark's older friends from Tarleton State were renting. The party there was loping along at a decent pace, but they decided they were hungry for something with a little more velocity. At ten-thirty, they left and made the drive again to Brownsville.

In Brownsville they parked the car and did some careful editing of the money, watches and jewelry they intended to carry across, locking the rest in the glove box. They walked across the bridge.

The night before, Matamoros had been coming alive. Tonight it was Bagdad—teeming, thronging, wall to wall, belly to bottom with happy, hard-drinking, hormonal American youth.

Just beyond the edges of the crowd that night, there was automatic-weapons fire. In unrelated incidents, a Mexican truck driver was killed, a student was robbed and beaten, an American girl was robbed and raped.

But in the center of the throng, where Mark and his buddies were, the night was a shimmering bubble of sex, booze and sheer youthful exuberance. They drifted in and out of doors and joked and ogled the girls in the street. For a while they parked themselves in a place called Los Sombreros—the bar where El Dubi had shot a rival gang member whose death had driven him to Constanzo.

But on that night, Los Sombreros had put on its most accommodating and American face. A high voltage sound system blasted the walls with music and a throbbing display of neon pulsed with the fervent beat of the city.

They left Los Sombreros, still looking for the big score in the sky, of course, but by now the booze and the months of fatigue finally were beginning to mark them as human beings. They stopped for a while at a place called the London Pub, which had been renamed The Hard Rock Cafe for the purposes of spring break. After several more drinks, they moved to another place called Garcia's.

Bill Huddleston was beginning to feel the weight of the hours. He looked over and saw Mark alone at a table with four girls, including one from the Miss Tanline contest. Bill went to the bathroom. Finally, a little before 2:00 A.M., Bill told Mark it was time.

By the time Bill announced he wanted to get out of Matamoros, events had folded into a loud fuzzy drunken blur. Bill and Bradley and Brent staggered out of Garcia's into the jammed and throbbing street. The street was thick with flesh. Spring-breakers were walking and stumbling in every direction, whirling in little eddies of activity here and there, surging ahead and falling back in waves, moving slowly toward the bridge.

Little Serafin and three others were parked a few yards

away. Serafin and Mario Ponce Torres were in a pickup on a side street, just at the corner of Avenida Alvaro Obregon. The two others were parked behind them on the side street in the Suburban. Serafin and Mario were in position to watch the mob of gringos passing before their windshield. They surveyed them for one that El Padrino would find pleasing.

Bill and the other two saw Mark behind them in the crowd, leaning against a Volkswagen. He was talking to the girl from the Miss Tanline contest. Bradley and Brent forged ahead toward the bridge, which was only a block ahead down the Avenida Alvaro Obregon. Bill was between them and Mark. Mark called up to him:

"What's wrong with you?"

Bill shook his head. "I'm just tired."

Bill looked back. Mark was still talking to Miss Tanline. Mark had stopped in front of a private home to say good-bye to her. Bill ducked around a corner to urinate. Miss Tanline went her way. For that instant, Mark was alone outside the circle of his friends and family.

They saw him and agreed he was good. Mario Torres got out of the pickup and walked to the edge of the crowd. Serafin was close behind him. Mark was approaching.

Mario Torres spoke: "Hey, man, do you want a ride?"

Bill looked back. Mark looked like he was talking to a Mexican in the crowd. Bill turned and kept stumbling toward the bridge.

And Mark was gone.

In that instant, when Mark Kilroy hesitated and turned toward the young Mexican in the crowd, he lingered for a flickering moment in the familiar world of condo parties and pre-med and loving parents and Padre and drunken nights in Matamoros. And then he plunged through, through a rent in the fabric of time, from the edge of real life to the fly-shrieking stench-blackened bottom of all Hell.

They shoved him into the truck and kept him between them. He was still. Even drunk, he was pausing to size things up. The truck pulled out of its parking place, turned, backed up and ground away from the crowded avenue. The lights of the Suburban behind it came alive.

Serafin was driving. He had to urinate. He stopped and got out of the truck. Mark exploded against the door, blasted it open with his shoulder, rolled out and ran down the dark side street. He was running toward the Suburban.

The Suburban screeched to a halt, the other two flew out, grappled with Mark, hit him hard and threw him in the Suburban with them. They put knives against his skin. At the same time, they spoke to him in English.

"You're going to be all right. Nothing is going to happen."

The two vehicles wound through the old center of Matamoros and then sped through an industrial district on the edge of town. The Suburban bounced roughly over a set of railroad tracks and then picked up speed, flying out onto a two-lane Mexican highway. A thick smoke of fog was just building in the ditches along the highway, blowing out over the road in low places, mirroring the close white clouds that raced along overhead, obscuring and then revealing the waning moon. Abandoned rusting farm machinery and old buses loomed up out of fields on both sides of the road. Here and there, the ever-present blanket campesino sat, half sleeping with his back to the road and his face to the moon.

They hit the dirt turnout at high speed, and the Suburban drifted and skidded a little in the soft surface. They bumped along quickly. A mile into the Rancho Santa Elena, they came to the metal barns and the caretaker's little white frame cottage.

The two men in the Suburban ordered Mark out of it. They pointed to a stand of three scrawny trees nearby. A ratty black rope hammock was hanging between two of the trees. They told Mark to sit in the hammock. Now several men came out of the darkness and gathered around him. They had machine guns.

The gold Mercedes came purring out from behind the

barn. The window whirred down. El Padrino looked at the gringo. He put the window back up, and the Mercedes moved on down the ranch road to the shack.

It was time to prepare the nganga.

Mark sat silently in the hammock until dawn. His parents believe that much of this time would have been taken up with prayer.

Domingo Reyes Bustamente, the aged caretaker of the place, came out of his cabin at dawn and walked over to see who they had this time. He was surprised to see a gringo. The men with the guns weren't paying much attention to their prisoner. Reyes said hello to him. Mark asked him for water and told him that he was hungry.

Reyes asked the guards if it was all right to feed the man. They shrugged. One of them wandered off in the direction of the shack. The shack was another three-quarters of a mile from the hammock where Mark sat. It took the man a long while to return. When he did, he told Reyes it would be all right to feed the prisoner.

The old man made a small fire on the ground. He walked to the back of the work station area, where a crude chicken coop had been thrown together from old pallets and roofing materials. He ducked to go in and found a few eggs that the chickens had laid on the ground near the entry. These he scooped up. He went into his cabin and got a pan and a glass of water.

He gave the water to Mark. Working quickly, he scrambled the eggs over the fire. Mark gobbled them up, eating with his fingers.

Then the hours crawled by. The sun rose up high. In the distance, on the plantations around Rancho Santa Elena, Mark could hear tractors and trucks coming alive. His friends by now would be desperate in their search for him. They would know he had not gone off with some dope dealer or whore. They would be looking frantically. The sun crept up slowly toward noon. The thugs were still around him with the guns. Some of them looked younger than he was. They wore designer jeans and fancy sunglasses. They would only tell him nothing was going to happen to him. They seemed to find his situation amusing. Right out there was the highway, and at the end of it was Matamoros, and in Matamoros was the bridge, and across the bridge was Texas.

He must have thought of everything in those hours. His uncle, Ken Kilroy, a senior special agent for U.S. Customs in Los Angeles, had worked in the Rio Grande Valley and had worked specifically on the issue of Americans who turned up missing in Mexico. These things had been discussed in Mark's home. He was bound to have inklings of the potential seriousness of his situation.

Some time after noon they took him down the road to the shack where the nganga was kept. When they opened the door, the stench of human rot and the surprised angry roar of the flies blasted out at him. Inside, they bound him with rope and closed his mouth with duct tape. He was left kneeling, just inside the door.

Constanzo stood outside, where the tarpaulin had been spread. He muttered and swayed gently. Then he turned to them. Constanzo told them to bring the gringo to him.

Before the Attorney General of the State of Texas would meet with the Kilroys in Austin, he wanted to hear from the mouths of his own staff what they had found. The story of the boy's disappearance had garnered a fair amount of press. The kid's father had been down there in Brownsville and apparently over in Matamoros, handing out fliers and offering rewards. Now the story was dying down. The kid was still missing. The request was that Mattox get involved, ostensibly because he had been involved for a long time in these missing persons problems in Mexico. But Jim Mattox, as always, knew the ostensible score and then he knew the real score. The real score was that they wanted to get him involved in order to get the media going again on it, in order to put some political pressure on Mexico.

Before he could do that, however, he had to know some things. Mainly, he had to know some things about the kid.

Mattox was a Texan. He had grown up on some fairly rough streets. Since Stephen Austin had come to Texas and established the Anglo colony in the early nineteenth century, Texans, especially the rough ones, had been getting in trouble in Mexico. In Mattox's experience, a whole lot of the trouble Texans got into was trouble they deserved.

Of course, all of that is relative to a certain extent. Maybe you can say that an exuberant young man who blows some grass in Mexico, gets drunk and goes to a whore doesn't deserve to be murdered. But in Texas, and among Jim Mattox's kind of people, the same young man also would not deserve a full court press by the state's highest law enforcement official.

The family claimed the kid was a clean liver, did not do any dope at all, was religious, might have had too much to drink over there, but would not have gone to a prostitute. He was an athletic and very handsome lad with a good self-concept, but Jim Mattox always operated on the you-never-know principle. Before he was going to leap into this business, and before he was going to meet with the parents, he wanted to know the score on the kid, the real score, the one he knew the press would dig out eventually if it was there any way.

Mattox had dispatched his best bloodhound to the Valley in the person of Francisco Castillo. At thirty-eight years of age and 6'1" in height, with graying black hair, a salt-and-pepper mustache and a handsome Dick Tracy set of the jaw, Castillo was the kind of man who commanded quick respect on both sides of the border. He had made the rounds. He was ready to report.

Castillo told Mattox that the Kilroy kid probably was an absolute clean case, almost certainly without any drug involvement, probably without any involvement with Mexican whores. The parents, Castillo said, were extremely sympathetic characters. This was an extremely sad story.

The boys had searched Matamoros until dawn. As each fifteen-minute period of their search passed, each time they looked at their watches and realized he was still gone, they grew more panicked. Finally, exhausted, they decided their only hope was that he had hooked a ride back to Padre with Miss Tanline or somebody like that. When they got back to the Sheraton, he was not there. But he might not be there, if he was with Miss Tanline. They crashed.

But when they awoke later that morning, he was still gone, and the sickness of their hangovers gave way to a deeper pit of fear. That day, on March 15, the boys went to the South Padre Island police department and filed a missing persons report. South Padre got a fair number of these during spring break, but they always took each one seriously. No matter how casually the kids themselves took this business of crossing into Mexico to raise hell, no one in law enforcement in South Texas took Mexico cases lightly.

South Padre forwarded this one to Cameron County Sheriff Alex Perez in Brownsville. Perez turned it over to one of his ablest deputies, Lieutenant George Gavito. Gavito went straight to his own man for most of these cases, Deputy Lupe Limas, a former Brownsville city police office whom Sheriff Perez had hired specifically for his expertise on the other side of the border.

Limas immediately set about the business of checking all of the jails on the Matamoros side—federal, state, local and so on. It was a task that needed to be carried out in person and by someone whom the jailers on the other side had some reason to trust or take seriously. The kid was not in jail.

But even before Limas had returned to report in, the Mark Kilroy case had begun to assume a higher than normal profile. Special Agent Kilroy in Los Angeles had contacted Special Agent Oran Neck in Brownsville and had requested him in the most urgent and personal terms to go find Mark.

Agent Kilroy knew Mark was no doper. He knew he was not a kid to go to whores. Mark's father, Agent Kilroy's brother, had explained that the car with all of Mark's valuables had been left on the Brownsville side.

Mark had settled down and was very serious about medical school, was very directed and eager to get on with life. He had not disappeared into Mexico on his own looney-tunes caper. This was serious, and it stank to high heaven of the worst possibilities Mexico could offer. How well Agent Kilroy knew what that could mean. How well Agent Neck knew. From the moment Neck had hung up on Kilroy, he had been burning up the phones, trying to find where this was with the local cops. By the time he got to Gavito, Oran Neck was already way past full tilt.

Neck, Gavito and Limas all knew the problem. In Mexico, you never had any idea whom you were dealing with or what the deal was. Just two weeks earlier, Customs had sent a bunch of agents into Mexico to track the routes by which Central Americans were coming up into South Texas. It was all part of an effort to show they were not the political refugees they claimed to be but just more opportunity seekers.

But Mexico had caught wind of the fact Customs had secret people down there uninvited and unannounced and had cried foul. There had been considerable fireworks over it. The Mexican federal police had been especially jacked out of shape. You never knew why people got mad when they got mad in Mexico. It was unlikely the federal police were especially exercised over the plight of political refugees from Central America. They were much harder on them down there than officials in the States.

The problem was almost always dope. The federales were all tied up in it, the state police, the locals. Everybody down there got extremely paranoid when they thought they heard the big clumsy footsteps of Uncle Sam coming in their direction, because they were never just certain why Sam was coming.

Was it possible that this kid had been nabbed by the federales in retribution? Did it have particularly to do with his being Ken Kilroy's nephew? Anything was possible. To people who had seen photos of Kiki Camarena, nothing was beyond Mexico.

There was the more likely possibility—that it was a random abduction of some kind, but that Mark might blurt out his uncle's position. Once the kidnapers knew they had the nephew of a high official, they might figure it was time to cut their losses and kill him.

By March 16, less than two full days after Mark Kilroy had disappeared, Cameron County had assigned four deputies to work on it full-time, and U.S. Customs had assigned six agents—an absolutely unprecedented commitment of manpower this early in this kind of case.

That same day, the American team went back and closely interviewed Bradley Moore, Brent Martin and Bill Huddleston. Did the boys understand the gravity of this matter? They needed to know there might be factors at play here with which they were not familiar. It was potentially very very serious. They needed to pony up any information they had, a single joint of marijuana shared in an alley, a drunken sex act with a prostitute, a fight, a prank, anything.

There was nothing. Nothing. They went to Mexico. They drank. They flirted with American girls. They did not score. They did not do any dope or try to buy any dope or have anything to do with dope. They saw Mark speaking to a young Mexican man on the edge of the crowd. That was it.

It was decided to put Bill Huddleston under hypnosis. A Texas Department of Human Services counselor agreed to put Huddleston into a trance.

In the trance, Bill Huddleston was drunk again, was back there again, back in front of Garcia's swimming through the fog of night and booze and fatigue. He turned and saw Mark in that final moment. He saw Mario Ponces Torres walking toward Mark, speaking to him, but he could not focus on the man's face. There was a fresh scar on one side. He could not focus. He saw Torres's general body type, size and age correctly, but Torres's face was blurred. It was a face with a scar, a gray blur where the eyes and mouth and nose should have been. The Cameron County sheriff's department decided not to attempt a composite drawing based on Huddleston's eerie recollection.

On the following day, Lieutenant Gavito had another talk with Jim and Helen Kilroy. James Kilroy was forty-five, a chemical engineer. Helen was forty-three, a housewife. They were both extremely composed. It was obvious at the same time they were both desperately worried about their beloved son.

The police were not finding him. They were finding nothing. They had no leads. There were no clues.

Jim Kilroy asked what the Mexican police were finding. Gavito hedged. Kilroy waited and asked the same question again. Gavito explained the best he could. The Mexican police had been informed that the authorities on the American side, including Customs, were urgently interested in finding Mark Kilroy. The problem was there was no way of knowing what that would mean to the authorities on the Mexican side.

In spite of some years of effort at setting up a regular procedure for finding missing Americans on that side, quarterbacked in large part by Texas's own Attorney General Jim Mattox, there still was no regular channel or procedure for handling missing persons cases over there.

It was not a simple matter. The disappearance of people in the Latin American cultures is a social phenomenon with roots deep in those societies. There is great corruption. There is an ongoing level of political violence, much more in Mexico than most Americans believe. The various police agencies often are at war with each other. The way problems are often solved across the border is simply that the person who is closest to the center of the problem disappears. Vanishes.

American authorities had offered lots of computer equipment and so on to the Mexicans, along with a lot of free record-keeping advice. But the fact was that setting up a systematic means of keeping track of people in Mexico would require changing the underlying political basis of the society. So people just disappeared. And nobody could do much about it.

Jim Kilroy weighed this information. He discussed it with his wife. Their son was gone. He had disappeared on the other side of the border, in Mexico. The authorities were doing everything they could to find him. But they could not find him. They had long and complicated reasons why they could not find him, all of which seemed to make sense. Jim Kilroy knew that his brother and his brother's associates at Customs would be giving this case everything they had. He could see that Gavito was a good man. He understood that the Cameron County sheriff's department had assigned much more than the normal complement to this case. But they could not find Mark.

Mark had been what mothers and fathers dream of and hope for when they are young and they learn that a baby is coming. He had been healthy. He had been bright. He had been good to his parents. He had repaid their trust with responsibility. He had treated their beliefs with respect. Jim Kilroy remembered coming into Mark's room when he was supposed to be doing his homework and finding him reading the Bible instead. He wanted Mark to do the homework. But he closed the door without speaking.

They wanted their son back. They wanted to know what had happened to him. They could not let him end. He had come to their lives and had been their baby. They were his parents. They had sheltered him.

They decided that if the police and Customs and this nation and the other nation could not find Mark, then, so be it: they would find him themselves. That very day, on the seventeenth, Jim Kilroy drew up a flier with a picture of Mark, promising a $5,000 reward for information, and he and Helen began walking the streets of Brownsville and Matamoros, handing out thousands and thousands of copies. A sizable press contingent followed them for part of the first day, and the story appeared on evening newscasts in several Texas cities.

On March 28, they walked the streets again and handed

out fliers. The distribution of fliers advertising the name of a missing person was already almost a cottage industry in the region when Mark Kilroy's father took it up. In fact, another family from the Santa Fe area was slowly canvassing the border region with their own fliers at the same time Jim Kilroy was distributing his. The other family's daughter, Rene Richerson, twenty-two, a student at Texas A&M at Galveston, had been missing since October 7, 1988, when she apparently was abducted from her job at a beach-front resort.

The Kilroys were not major news. A few reporters joined the Kilroys during the day on the eighteenth. Helen Kilroy spent most of the day dealing with the usually oblique but stubbornly persistent question of her son's character.

He could not have dropped out of sight on his own, she said. "He's just too responsible a person. He knows we'd be worried about him. Besides, his friends knew to contact someone when he didn't show up. They knew him well enough that if he was going to do something, he would have told them."

He was an honor student in high school—fourteenth in a class of 210 in 1986—who went to his first college, Tarleton State, on a basketball scholarship. He had given up athletics and fraternities in order to work harder at the University of Texas. His grades so far were 3.0 on a 4-point scale.

"He is just a great kid," Helen said again and again. "He put all his energy into school, and when he wasn't doing that, he'd be trying to pick up a game of basketball with friends or playing golf with his father. He was supposed to play in a father-son tournament this weekend."

Jim and Helen were accompanied by Mark's brother Keith, nineteen, a student at Alvin Junior College and the College of the Mainland. Keith tried to explain his brother, too.

"He made me realize how important grades were if you

wanted to go to college," he told the reporters walking along with them. "I thought of him as a friend."

The family walked again the next day. They were alone.

But a curious thing happened on the Matamoros side. Mexican federal police showed up and announced they were going to escort the Kilroys. They explained they were afraid something might happen to them.

In this conversation, there were language problems. The Kilroys thought they might not have understood. They told Neck later the federales seemed to be saying they were concerned that the Kilroys could even come to some harm from the Tamaulipas state police. Of course that made no sense at all and must have been a misunderstanding, they thought.

There seemed to be hints and clues all over in the shadows and swill-running alleys of Matamoros. The *Houston Post* that week quoted a Matamoros merchant who blamed the disappearance on a "college gang" responsible for a wave of violence and voodoo in recent months. But the Matamoros and Tamaulipas police were stony and without words. They shrugged. They knew nothing. They suggested Mark had disappeared in Brownsville, not Mexico.

On March 20, after they had told Neck of the events of the day before, Neck suggested it might be time to regroup. The Kilroys stopped their leafletting activities long enough to have a long serious sit-down with Neck and Gavito.

Gavito and Neck asked the Kilroys to be more specific about what the federales had told them. As they all worked their way through the conversation, hashing out this hint and that veiled suggestion, they came to the conclusion together that the federales were trying to tell the Kilroys that Mark might well have been kidnapped by the Tamaulipas state police. The Kilroys were at an utter loss to understand what that could mean.

In the meantime, the press interest had gone completely dry. No reporters were following the story. None would

even return phone calls. And the bureaucratic pressures
were growing. The commitment of manpower by Cameron
County and Customs was already extraordinary, and yet the
investigation was getting nowhere in terms of leads and
clues—unless there was something in this garbled hint
about the Tamaulipas cops.

Gavito and Neck agreed it was time to get some political help.

The Kilroys were not hopeful in that department. They
already had made a request for help to the office of Texas
governor Bill Clements. Their request had been ignored.

Neck and Gavito had some other ideas. They were a
little more at home on this turf than the Kilroys could be
expected to be.

Neck was ready to do everything he could at the American federal level. This was already beginning to swell like
the Camarena affair—more dope, more damned Mexican
corruption, more nightmares. He was perfectly ready and
prepared, as was Mark's uncle, to start pushing for a travel
advisory. But both Neck and Ken Kilroy knew that a travel
advisory would not be easy. It was pretty much the ultimate
sanction. That would take persuasive evidence and a lot of
luck.

Gavito had some ideas. He suggested that they repair to
the office of former Texas state representative Rene Olivera, who had served in the House when Attorney General
Jim Mattox was a state representative. Olivera listened to
the Kilroys, listened to his friend Gavito and agreed to
place a call to Mattox. He got right through.

Mattox knew of the case. He asked who was present in
Olivera's office. Olivera told him Gavito and Neck were
there and that Jim Kilroy was present, too. In his best
straight-talking Texas way, Mattox warned the people on
the other end—his warning aimed especially at Jim Kilroy
—that he would have to have answers to what might seem
like rough questions. Gavito communicated this message to
Jim Kilroy.

Kilroy was almost expressionless. It was difficult for

Gavito and Neck to know at times how he was taking what was going on around him. Kilroy had turned down the visible flame of his personality to a bare flicker. He nodded to indicate that of course he understood the A.G.'s position and would welcome any and all questions.

Did the kid drink?

Yes.

Could he have been drunk?

Yes.

Was he an alcoholic?

No. He was not.

Did he do dope?

No.

Did he do dope? Any dope? Grass? Pills? Any dope? At all? Ever? Had he ever? Did his friends? Any dope?

No. No. No. No.

Might he have gone to a prostitute?

No.

Was he in trouble? Trouble in school? Trouble with the law? Money trouble? Was he in trouble?

No. No. No.

Did he have any other . . . tendencies? Did he or the other boys, did the other boys have any . . . tendencies?

No. He was straight.

Mattox went through all of it again. He wanted Gavito and Neck to know that he wanted to know. Finally he pushed back from his desk, put the receiver to his chest and muttered to an assistant, "Get Frank in here."

Frank Castillo worked in an office right next to Mattox's own office. He was a right-hand man and a hammer. He often had acted as Mattox's personal emissary and agent. And he would be able to size this stuff up in about twenty-four hours. The people on the other end filled Castillo in. Finally everybody signed off. Jim Mattox still wanted to know the real deal, and he wanted to know it from Francisco Castillo.

Castillo left the office, drove straight home, threw clothes in a carry-on bag and drove to the airport. At 9:00

P.M. on the dot his Southwest Airlines plane touched down in Harlingen. A deputy was there to meet him. As soon as Castillo had jumped in the car, the driver put on the siren and put the pedal to the metal.

Gavito was waiting outside his office. Gavito and Castillo shook hands on the sidewalk, jumped in Gavito's unmarked car and drove straight into downtown Matamoros. In their Stetsons and Tony Lama boots, they were two big typical "ponchos," Mexicans from "the other side," just the kind of guys the tough guys in Matamoros like to test.

Sure enough, they were barely getting ready to park Gavito's car when a Grand Prix with Tamaulipas plates and four extremely thuggy-looking passengers rammed up and tried to nose in ahead of them with its high beams on. Castillo, who didn't know Gavito yet, cringed as Gavito put on his own high beam, threw his door open and started shaking his fist.

"Back up, motherfuckers!" Gavito shouted at them.

The car backed up. Castillo eyed its passengers closely, and they eyed Castillo and Gavito. When Gavito was parked, Castillo turned to him.

"Gavito . . . you're a crazy son of a bitch, aren't you?"

"Fuck these motherfuckers," Gavito said, slamming his fist into the dash. "I'm sick and tired of these goddamn thugs."

Weeks later, when they had met some of them and had seen pictures of the others, Castillo and Gavito would come to the shuddering realization that this little macho set-to over a parking place had been their first and incredibly coincidental encounter with Constanzo and his escorts.

That night they dragged the streets, from Garcia's to the so-called Hard Rock Cafe to Los Sombreros. They knew which clubs were connected to which of Matamoros's eight drug families, new exactly what this crap about the federales and the Tamaulipas state police could mean.

If anything reflected the chaos of the border, it was the relationship between all the various kinds of cops working the border, on both the Mexican and the Texas sides. In

Brownsville itself, the problem was mainly at the level of ongoing petty jealousies. Sheriff Perez and the Brownsville police chief were on opposite sides of some local political fences, nothing more than family disputes for the most part, but it made for rough sledding between the two departments sometimes. Perez delighted in hiring good people like Lupe Limas away from the Brownsville P.D. The Brownsville P.D. retaliated by doing things like stopping sheriff's cars on their way into the sheriff's office in downtown Brownsville and ticketing the deputies for failure to use their seatbelts.

It was small-time stuff when it happened, but it was enough to ensure there would be no eager cooperation when something serious did come down the pike.

The relationship between the American federal agencies on the border always had been troubled. The top people in Customs and in the DEA in Washington were supportive of each other. But out in the field, and especially in the border towns, there was a lot of suspicion and jealousy at the working level.

And then you had the Mexican side. For years, there had been a certain stability—Mexican-style stability—in Matamoros, enforced by the fact that the Tamaulipas state police had a monopoly on the drug corruption. That's how it worked over there. The city police earned practically nothing and were expected to support themselves by shaking down merchants and tourists. If a city policeman wanted to drive a city police car to go carry out an investigation, he literally was expected to go shake down a tourist first in order to get gas money. But the locals had always been shut out of the dope business.

Tamaulipas had always taken care of that. The state police more or less gave their sanction and protection to the established dope families. You always had certain frictions —as with this Hernandez family that had gotten busted up in Grimes County recently and was shooting up the map in Mexico, according to reports. You always had somebody pushing for a bigger slice of the pie. But the role of the state police had been to make sure that action was contained within politically acceptable limits.

Lately, however, it had been very difficult for the American cops—even the really street-wise ones like Lupe Limas—to see into police politics on the other side, mainly because of whatever it was that was going on with the federales. For a long time—a couple years at least—it had been obvious the federales were making some kind of power play to nudge the Tamaulipas cops aside and get the dope corruption away from them. They had sent this guy Morlet—the one who was supposed to be connected to the Camarena killing—in first as a kind of civilian-dress point man.

Then Comandante Guillermo Perez Rodriguez and his top officers in Ciudad Victoria had seemed to be getting directly involved themselves in the dope trade. In Mexico, of course, everything has to be viewed in a seamless fabric, in which local police actions have a connection somewhere to what's going on in national politics. The last president, de la Madrid, had made a lot of noise about cleaning up the dope corruption and then not only had not done diddly but obviously had been in on it himself.

Now there was this brand-new president, Salinas. And he seemed to be serious. There were strong rumors among the border police that Salinas might actually do something real any day now, like arrest the great druglord, Felix Gallardo. You couldn't sniff at a thing like that. If it ever happened.

And closer to home, in Ciudad Victoria, things had really been shaking. Just a month before Mark Kilroy had disappeared, Comandante Perez had been bounced out on his butt along with all of his top people. The attorney general of Tamaulipas had announced Perez was guilty of taking $5 million in bribes in a relatively brief period.

Perez was replaced as Comandante of the Mexican Federal Judicial Police in the Matamoros/Ciudad Victoria region by Juan Benitez Ayala, who seemed a stark contrast indeed to the operatic figure Perez had cut.

Benitez Ayala was a small man, actually middle-aged but of extremely youthful appearance. Half of the time he looked like a street-hip Mexican Indian teenager, in his designer jeans, spotless Beaverskin Stetson and satin Philadelphia Eagles windbreaker. His sunglasses hid huge brown eyes that women found irresistible.

What the American cops noticed, when they were over on Benitez Ayala's side, was that he and his people seemed to be out all day and all night busting dope dealers. Whenever they saw him, he was supervising the confiscation of another huge marijuana or cocaine shipment his people had stopped.

He was an intriguing figure, cosmopolitan in many ways but very Mexican, even very Indian in others as evidenced by his white magic amulets and protective voodoo charms. But everybody in Mexico had that stuff around. He was soft-spoken, almost too nice for a cop. But the Americans noticed that, whenever Benitez Ayala spoke, no matter how softly, people around him seemed to jump out of their skins.

There were some stories about him, of course. In Mexico there were stories about everybody. The Mexican Association of Editors, a neutral journalism association, had said Benitez Ayala was involved in torturing prisoners and extorting money from druglords during his tenure as comandante in the Oaxaca region in southern Mexico. Oscar Trevino, a reporter for El Bravo in Matamoros, had written a story saying the government had kicked Benitez Ayala out of Oaxaca for going too far and stirring things up too much in his attempts to seize control of the drug corruption there. Trevino said that was why Benitez Ayala was shifted to Matamoros. After the story appeared, Benitez Ayala called Trevino to his office and then held him prisoner until Trevino's very angry and desperate publisher had secured his release.

But it was Mexico. You just never knew. These Matamoros newspapers were the same ones that had gotten into a beef with the dead drug guy, Saul Hernandez—the one who was shot to death later by the three guys in a brown Datsun in front of a nightclub. The one who had been with Morlet. Before he was killed, Saul Hernandez had shot and killed a newspaper publisher and one of his editors and nothing was ever done about it. It was all dope. The papers were in on it, too. You just never knew in Mexico. You just never knew.

Gavito and Castillo had been going solid since they hit Matamoros at 10:00 P.M. They had talked and questioned and done everything they could to make their presence known, to let people know there was extraordinary interest in this case, that anybody who came up with useful information about this kid's disappearance would be extremely well received by American authorities, to say nothing of the reward. They finished up the night—by now the early morning—at Garcia's, just a block from the bridge. By the time they left, at 3:30 in the morning, the two American police officers had cut quite a swath through Matamoros.

Fifteen minutes after they walked across the bridge, the Tamaulipas state police engaged "unknown drug smugglers" in an automatic-weapons firefight on that very block, in front of that very bar. Customs officers at the bridge timed it. Seven minutes of unbroken machine-gun fire.

Matamoros had gotten the message.

The very next morning, the federales fanned out over Matamoros in an incredible mobilization, with an even more fantastic mission. Up and down the avenidas, in the unauthorized whorehouses and the authorized gin mills, in the restaurants and at the cab stands, all over every inch of the city, the federales made their message plain and unmistakable. No one, for any reason, under any circumstance, was to pay any mordida to the state or city police—no bribes at all—until further notice from the federales.

From the American side, it was an inscrutable move. How could the federales hope to get any cooperation at all from the state and local coppers if they shut down the mordida? These guys lived on the mordida.

The response from the locals was just what the American cops had feared it would be. Under this kind of extraordinary harassment, the state and local police simply shut down most of their activities, and you could forget any hope of cooperation in the Kilroy case.

There was always a point beyond which it was no longer profitable to spend time sitting over on the American side trying to unravel the Mexican ball of string. There was simply no telling, no way to know what was going on. Maybe it meant the federales were serious. Maybe it meant they knew something and wanted to make sure nothing happened to uncover it.

The problem was Jim Kilroy. His response was always the same. When they tried to tell him these things, when they tried to explain how complicated it was, he just picked up his fliers and went back out on the street. It was almost as impossible to know what was going on in his head as it was to know what was going on in Mexico. But his plan never varied. It was always "Okay, if there are reasons why all of the officials in both nations are unable to find my boy, then I will take my fliers and go out on the street and find him myself."

He really was going to get himself chopped down in a hail of damned machine-gun fire if this kept up.

It was almost time for Jim Mattox to fish or cut bait. Neck and Customs were doing a heroic job of putting the pressure on, but they were nowhere near getting anybody in Washington to cut loose with a Travel Advisory yet. Gavito and Cameron County were really humming by now, running every lead down flat just about the instant it came in. But the situation in Mexico was impossible to read. And, most of the time, the only way to make heads or tails out of a deal like that is just to get somebody else to throw another brick over the wall and see who pops up.

Mattox told his people to bring the Kilroys on up to Austin. He had no idea what to expect or what he would decide. Nothing in the Texas constitution mandates the state attorney general to get involved in criminal matters.

Most of what he is supposed to do is act as the civil lawyer for state agencies.

Still, nothing in the constitution precludes him from getting into criminal cases, and, in fact, he maintains a criminal staff to assist rural D.A.s. In addition, especially because he has Mexico on one of his borders, the Texas A.G. often does get involved in criminal cases. Mexican attorneys general are criminal law enforcement officials, and in their dealings with their counterparts in Texas and the other border states, they often expect and need cooperation in criminal matters.

It so happened that Mattox and his top people, including Frank Castillo, had met at some length and had established personal relationships with the Tamaulipas D.A.—Anibal Perez. Mattox and Perez had talked at great length about the problem of missing persons—usually Mexican nationals who commit crimes in the U.S. and then disappear into Mexico. The real pioneering work in this area had been carried out first by the California A.G., who had supplied Mexican agencies with computers and training to try to assist them in keeping track of their bad guys. Mattox had worked to see that something like the California project would be carried out between Texas and its Mexican neighbors. Nothing substantive had ever been accomplished, but the process had created a working relationship between Mattox and Perez.

So there was a lot of argument for getting involved. The problem was, there was a lot of argument the other way, too. Mattox was preparing to run for Governor of Texas. It is simply in the nature of criminal cases, especially criminal cases involving Mexico, that they hardly ever make anybody look good. The bad guys don't get caught. The good guys turn out not to be good. Somebody cracks the wrong head. For the most part, criminals are idiots and the situations they get into wind up throwing mud and blood all over everybody.

If you want to get involved in something that has a fairly safe political return, you go to a flood or a forest fire

or something like that and vow to help the victims get a
bunch of money from Washington. If you're the A.G., you
might even announce you are going to make divorced dad-
dies pay their child support. You promise something you're
reasonably sure you can deliver.

But this. This was just a huge mess. It was all screwed
up on the Mexican side. It was probably never going to
come out right. The kid had been missing for almost a
month. What was the happy ending supposed to be?

An aide stepped out of Mattox's office and motioned for
them to enter. The Kilroys came in and sat quietly. They
looked bad. It was clear this situation was exerting a cruel
crushing weight on them. Mrs. Kilroy's eyes rimmed with
tears from time to time. But Jim Kilroy behaved just the
way Castillo had described him—so extremely low key,
controlled and businesslike that he was impossible to read.

Jim Kilroy made his flat little monotone speech. When
Mattox finally actually understood what Kilroy was saying,
he was shocked.

Jim Kilroy's message was carefully rehearsed. We do
not understand, he said again and again. Our son has van-
ished without a trace. He was on a main street that was full
of people. Now he is gone, and there is no clue. We do not
understand.

We do not believe there is full cooperation between the
Mexican local, state and federal police. The federal police
have even told us our son may have been kidnapped by the
local or state police. We do not understand that. They say
maybe he stumbled on something illegal and that whatever
it was had gone too far for him to be released. We don't
understand what they mean.

Jim Kilroy droned on in his carefully controlled flat-
eyed way. It is our strong belief that in all probability he is
dead. Mattox sat forward.

We have discovered there are no channels by which people in our position can find loved ones who have disappeared in Mexico. We want to contribute to a process that

would help to establish such a mechanism, so that others to whom this sort of thing may happen will be helped.

We are almost certain he is dead. We want to know. We want this to be resolved. If there is any way you can help. Somebody has got him, and we want them to understand that nothing will happen, no questions will be asked, if we can have him back. We want you to help get that message to someone. Whoever it is.

Jim Kilroy had figured it out. All of the themes whirling around this issue were one huge official and unofficial rat's nest—hundreds, maybe thousands of mean little agendas spinning around each other in a cloud of bullets and blood. And he was going to bore, bore, bore into the middle of that ball and get his son back. Dead or alive. He was telling Mattox, I know I don't know what all of you are up to. I know I don't know what the hell is going on. I am smart enough to see that. But I want my son back. I want my son back. Stop. Tell them to stop. You tell them. Please. Stop the game. I want my son back. I want him out of the game. Please help me. Please give me my son.

Chapter Seven

When the Kilroys left, Mattox was visibly shaken and moved. His top assistants saw him this way only on very rare occasions, usually after executions.

In public, Mattox's persona was always that of the ultimate Texas scrapper, with a bouncy put-em-up roll in his stance and a ready snarl at his lip. Away from the press and behind closed doors, his top aides occasionally had glimpsed another side.

He was an opponent of the death penalty, but under the Texas constitution it was his job to see to it officially that the state's growing number of death-by-injection executions were carried out. Of the twenty-eight that had occurred on his watch, Mattox had been personally present for all but two. If it was his responsibility under the constitution, then he was going to go sit through it with the others who had official reasons.

Before one execution, he learned that one of his aides was going to go along and witness the execution with him for the first time. "You know, if you're like me," he told the aide in a quiet moment before it happened, "for the rest of your life you will not sleep a whole night through without waking up at least once and thinking about it."

Wherever it was that he was touched by the executions, he was touched there even more profoundly by his meeting with the Kilroys. Mrs. Kilroy's grief affected him deeply. And Jim Kilroy had won his admiration and respect.

Every hour of every day, the phones of people like Jim Mattox ring, and on the other end are people with urgent requests for help. Of that lot, Jim Kilroy probably had less idea how anything works in politics or law enforcement or bureaucracy than 90 percent of the people who called. But in his way Jim Kilroy was more effective than all of them.

One light burned before his eyes. It was the vision of his son. He wanted his son back, dead or alive. He knew exactly what he wanted. He wanted Mattox to help him get the message to Mexico. We don't care. This is not about dope or your cops or any of that. Just give us this kid back.

And he wanted Mattox to get into it himself and, with his presence, turn out the media again. To that extent, Jim Kilroy was not naive. Armed with advice from his brother, he knew that getting the media interested again might be the only thing that could mean anything. If they could turn up the heat in terms of news coverage, that would turn up the heat on Washington to get something done, and that might make the threat of a travel advisory more meaningful. Short of that, it was even possible Customs itself could pull off something like the border search action it had used to flush out an ending to the Camarena case. But that would take media, too. And the media were moths. They wouldn't fly in unless somebody turned on a light for them.

Jim Mattox resolved to make a trip to Brownsville that week. Even if it was never resolved, even if it blew up in a big black eye, even if the kid surfaced in California, writing bad checks and staying in plush hotels, Mattox felt the effort would be worth it. He had looked into the eyes of the Kilroys and he had seen grief, desperation and profound personal strength and commitment—too much humanity to ignore. He had to try.

Mattox's top people probably were the most sophisticated media handlers in Texas. Given their boss's penchant for stepping on hot potatoes all the time, they had to be. Elna Christopher was a tough seasoned reporter herself before going to work for Mattox. She knew the Texas and American national press even better than she sometimes wished. Kelly Fero was an experienced reporter and author who had lived in Mexico for twelve years. He understood the rhythms of the Mexican press, which often seemed wildly sensationalistic and macabre to uninitiated foreigners. Ron Dusek was the reigning expert on how to manage and manipulate the often undisciplined Texas press corps. By the time they had put out the word, Mattox's imminent arrival in Brownsville was being anticipated as if he were a cross between Indiana Jones and the ghost of LBJ.

The moment the press clatter started up around Mattox's appearances in Brownsville, Frank Castillo and Cameron County Deputy Lupe Limas got in a car, drove over the bridge and drove out of Matamoros to Ciudad Victoria. There they paid a visit to Tamaulipas Attorney General Anibal Perez, informing him that Attorney General Mattox wished to visit with him and briefing him on what the Texas attorney general would wish to discuss, should the Tamaulipas attorney general agree to meet with him.

There are always some good things about dealing with Mexico. One is that, once you have observed all the elaborate old-European formalities, you don't have to beat around the bush. At all.

Castillo and Limas simply pointed to the obvious. Look, Jim Mattox is over in Brownsville doing everything he can to stir this thing. His people are beating every reporter out of the bushes they can find, from the smallest weekly to the national networks, from Geraldo Rivera of trash TV to Peter Applebome of the *New York Times,* and they intend to keep doing it. We all know what this means. It means heat on Washington at some point, and at some point heat on Washington means more stuff like the border searches during Camarena. And stuff like that eventually means the big T.A. The travel advisory.

Just thought you'd like to know Mr. Mattox's intentions, in a frank, open and spirited exchange of views.

The questions came back just as frank and hard. Why? Some drunk gringo kid gets himself lost in Mexico. This is Mexico. We can't provide around-the-clock baby-sitting protection for every whore-going drug-taking rich brat who comes over here because he thinks our women are sluts and everything in Mexico is free.

Understood. Of course you can't. This is not that. This is a nice kid who did not do one damned thing other than get a little stewed. Somebody nabbed him. Maybe your police. Who knows? Maybe it's tied to the Customs agents who came down into Mexico on the Central American refugee thing. Maybe it's some crazy deal to do with dope.

Whatever it is, the nabbers nabbed the wrong kid. Triple wrong. A, he was innocent. B, he was the nephew of a top guy in Customs. And C, Jim Mattox, who is the biggest media magnet in Texas, has been personally emotionally touched by the kid's parents, and he has one idea and one idea alone on this deal. Stir, stir, stir, until something pops loose—either the kid, or a travel advisory or whatever.

There is this business about the police on your side. The situation is far worse, it appears to us, than a simple lack of coordination. Perhaps, when this does break, the blame will fall with one of the official agencies. You know how these things go. You yourself are responsible for the state police.

You know Mattox. You have met him many times at the Border Attorneys General Reunions. He won't stop. He's angry. He's a vato loco.

Castillo and Limas made their good-byes and left on good terms. Once the polite observances of gentlemen have been made, good frank talk always is enjoyed in

Mexico. Perez said that he would be delighted to meet with his good friend, the honorable Mr. Mattox.

Mattox met with him the next day. Mattox made it plain that he knew he was completely off his own turf and did everything he could to convey his respect for the authority and dignity of his host. He said the only thing he hoped to do in this matter was render whatever assistance he could to the Mexican authorities. He intended to maintain close contact with all of the Mexican authorities, federal, state and local, and it was his solemn pledge that he would immediately share everything he knew with all of them.

After the point had been made enough ways, it was clear what he was saying. Mattox planned to take everything he learned from or about each Mexican police agency and immediately share it with the others. It was also clear he knew exactly what that would accomplish. It would short-circuit all of the walls of secrecy and intrigue between the Mexican agencies and create unending holy Hell. He made his good-byes and parted on the best of terms.

It was one more blind brick over the wall. No telling whose head they had boinked this time. Maybe nobody's. All you could do was wait and watch to see who popped up.

Mattox returned to Austin. Oran Neck and George Gavito and Lupe Limas and Frank Castillo waited and watched, peering across the border every day to see what moved.

It all moved. Suddenly. All of a sudden Comandante Juan Benitez Ayala was everywhere, all over everybody, in everybody's face. The business about the local cops sulking in their corner was over. The mordida was still cut off, but the locals were scurrying anyway, and, wonder of wonders, they seemed to be feeding information to Benitez Ayala and the federales. No telling what kind of information, no telling what it meant.

Heads were being cracked over there. Something very serious was moving. The group in Brownsville got on the phone to Mattox. In the process of deciding to make the call, they had realized a strange thing about themselves. They had become a team. A totally weird and impromptu team—Customs agent, state A.G.'s investigator, sheriff's deputies. Never the kind of team anybody would design on paper. But it was beginning to feel like a good one.

Mattox had barely settled back into his office and the huge stack of work waiting for him in Austin when the call came. He knew instantly what these signs meant. He marched back out to the airport and flew back to Brownsville, back to the streets, back to the press. Stir, stir, stir.

The next day Jim Kilroy received wonderful news. The renewed media glare and the involvement of Mattox and others had attracted the interest of the producers of "America's Most Wanted," a documentary television show based on true stories of unsolved crimes. Produced by Fox Television, "America's Most Wanted" was usually lumped by television critics in the genre of trash TV, because of its often garish scripting and the gory material it usually presented.

But for Jim Kilroy, the call from "America's Most Wanted" had been almost more than he could have hoped for at that point. The show was watched by more than 23 million people. Of the 130 fugitives whose stories it had publicized, over 50 percent had been caught as a direct result of the show.

Normally, the producers steered clear of missing persons stories. Those stories often tended to lack certain essential dramatic elements—like what really happened to the person—and there was always the danger the missing person would show up hiding in the attic over his own garage or something embarrassing like that.

But this Kilroy business was different. There was the incredible drama of the father down there in Mexico every day with his pathetic fliers, trying to find his son. There was the story of the mother and her dear friends back in the little hometown, patching together their homemade network to deal with the international forces of law, intrigue, press, diplomacy and mystery. There was all of this official interest. The producers decided to do this one in spite of their rule on missing persons.

A fair-sized crew—field producer/director Gary Rose and a pickup team of cameraman, soundman and production assistants and an actor to play Mark Kilroy—gathered in Brownsville on March 26 to do the story. Bradley Moore, Brent Martin and Bill Huddleston all had agreed to help by playing themselves.

It became a long grueling exercise in incongruity and awkwardness. With the three boys in tow and accompanied by a sizable contingent of press, the film crew headed into Matamoros toward dusk to try to do its work. The city was jumping—still full of happy American college jocks and nubile American girls looking for fun across the border.

Some of the reporters stopped to talk to the nonstop partyers. Hadn't they heard of the Mark Kilroy case? Did they realize he was still missing? Weren't they worried about continuing to come over here and get so drunk?

Yeah, yeah, yeah, they had heard about it. They had seen it on TV. But that was one guy, you know. Nobody really knows what happened to him. It could have been anything. Maybe he ran away and got married. You never know. You don't give up partying in Matamoros over one incident. Hey, man, it's Mexico. Stuff like that is part of the deal.

With the boys showing them how the evening had gone, the film crew patiently dragged around from Los Sombreros to the Hard Rock Cafe to the street in front of Garcia's, committing a long loopy version of the evening to videotape. Two Customs agents, Robert Garcia and Lupe Alderete, accompanied the entourage to provide security— another reminder to the Mexican police carefully watching this entire phenomenon that the missing boy had connections.

The actor, Todd Roberts, was a Texas kid not at all unlike Mark. Good-looking, a jock, he was eighteen years old and lived in Plano, Texas—a faceless middle- and upper middle-class suburban sprawl north of Dallas near the Los Colinas film production center at Dallas. Roberts had been acting in commercials since he was a kid. He was out on the golf course when he got the call offering this job, and he jumped at it.

The problem that night in Matamoros was that the scenes required a lot of guzzling of beer in the bars of Matamoros. Todd could drink in Mexico, but he was still underage back in Plano. He worried aloud to the crew that some of the drinking might look bad back in Plano.

In the meantime, however, Gary Rose kept plying Bill Huddleston with more beers. Huddleston was too nervous. All three of the boys needed to loosen up and act like the young American sowers of wild oats they had been that night. They were all too nervous and stiff, especially Huddleston. He wouldn't dance. They needed him to dance. He said he could only dance when he was drunk. Rose kept handing him frosty new bottles of Corona.

Todd Roberts was getting more and more put out with the amateur talent. He thought the television news crews following them were the problem. In between every take, the news crews would push in and start interviewing the boys again. How could even professional actors do their work under those circumstances, let alone three guys who were nervous enough just about being in front of a camera and taking direction for the first time?

In the middle of everything, a drunk American girl pushed her face in front of the camera. She had one of Jim Kilroy's fliers wadded in her hand.

"He's dead, you know," she said, sneering and staggering. "They found him shot in the head."

Crew member Kim Davis had just about had it at that point. She exploded at the woman, shooing her away quickly. "We appreciate that, but we're trying to accomplish something here."

They were trying to accomplish a great deal. They were trying to explain the process of acting and dramatics to three rank amateurs. They were trying to function in the wild streets of Matamoros. They were trying to fend off an army of press which Mark Kilroy's family had deliberately alerted to the evening's events. They were trying to do their jobs. And they were trying to help.

Finally Gary Rose couldn't deal with the TV news crews any more. He told them to get out. The Customs agents looked fairly serious about helping in this regard. The TV crews shrugged and left. They were trying to do their jobs, too. Everybody was trying. It was not an easy situation.

Todd Roberts kept at it, trying to build a rapport with Bill Huddleston, trying to help him ease into it. They all drank more beer, visited more joints, rolled more tape. Gary Rose cracked jokes, tried to lighten it up, tried to make it happen. Finally they had enough stuff from the bars, enough material that was at least usable.

It was time for the last scene. They decided to use Juan Garcia, a young Hispanic member of the crew, to play the part of the Mexican stranger who had stepped out of the night and up to the edge of the crowd to speak to Mark. The crowd was more ragged and troublesome than ever, shouting over the director's instructions, bellowing drunken jokes and obscenities. It was going to be hard to wrap.

Bill Huddleston took his post next to a one-story red-and-gray brick house, ahead of where Mark had paused. Bill was just at the point where he had last turned back and glimpsed Mark talking to the Mexican stranger, right after Bill had ducked around the corner to relieve himself.

They were ready to shoot. But Bill balked. He finally was having real trouble with the whole thing. He tried to explain it to Kim Davis. He understood that everybody was doing his job, trying to help. But that didn't help.

"It's really tough being here like this," he said. He gripped the building and shook his head.

Davis approached him. She understood. But they also needed to get finished.

"Don't get me wrong," he said. "I'm not mad at you. But we've been having fun all night, and now this is the point where we lost him." His face crumpled. "Re-creating it is hard."

Finally, Bill composed himself. Everything was ready. Todd Roberts came walking down the Avenida Obregon. Juan Garcia was in the shadow, ready to step out and speak to him.

The crowd suddenly fell silent. It was an unearthly, tense staring quiet. Todd walked on up the street, just barely rolling and reeling. Juan Garcia stepped out of the shadows.

"Hey, don't I know you from somewhere?"

Rose shouted, "Cut!"

The three boys stared at the scene with grim fascination. The crowd roared alive again as the film crew began packing up. In seconds, the boys and the actor and the crew all had disappeared into the whirling beer-smelling must and clamor of the streets of Matamoros.

The tape was rushed immediately to the Fox studios in Washington, where it was edited into a five-minute segment. It aired two days later.

Oran Neck and George Gavito flew to Washington in order to be in the Fox studios when the phone boards lighted up with the expected tips. In the moments after the segment had aired, they took ninety calls. Ultimately they took one hundred fifty calls with tips and information from viewers of the segment.

One caller had seen Mark working in a convenience store in California. A caller from North Carolina wanted to lend Gavito his ten tracking dogs.

The people at Fox made a twenty-second public service announcement in English and Spanish, which they distributed to television stations in the Valley area. Tips were called in from Mexico based on the announcement—reports of an Anglo male drinking with Mexicans and things of that nature.

None of the tips from "America's Most Wanted" led to

any direct break in the case. But the whole phenomenon had two very interesting sidelights, as far as the American team was concerned.

In the first place, it allowed them to see into the Mexican side by tracking what the Mexicans were doing with tips from the show. For the first time, the Americans could see that the Mexicans were seriously running down each tip and that there seemed to be strange signs of cooperation between the Mexican agencies. Comandante Benitez Ayala in particular was out there and definitely on the muscle.

The other was more general. "America's Most Wanted" was big-time American TV, almost Hollywood as far as Mexico was concerned. News crews—that was one thing. But Hollywood! If Mexico had real reverence for any expression of American culture, it was Hollywood. There, in the not so inaccurate Mexican view, was the real center of power in the States.

That this big TV show had come looking for Mark Kilroy and that the story of Mark Kilroy had been broadcast on American national television, in a full Hollywood treatment, with directors and actors and story boards and the pretty girl assistants, was persuasive evidence that the Mark Kilroy case was not destined to fade away soon.

The heat was on. At long last, the heat was really on. Comandante Juan Benitez Ayala was on the horn. He wanted to be on the team, too. And he sounded sincere.

All kinds of things were happening. An anonymous Matamoros businessman hired two nurses to do a room-to-room, bed-by-bed check of all the hospitals and clinics in the Matamoros area. Sometimes people arranged to have patients kept in hospitals and clinics more or less against their will and under sedation, and a rumor had led the un-named benefactor to suspect that Mark Kilroy might be found in this way.

There were certain formalities that still needed to be tended to, in order to make certain that all of the feathers of the Tamaulipas A.G. had been properly smoothed. For one thing, no formal complaint ever had been filed in Mexico. Technically, even though the American team now knew that 250 Mexican police agents of various description were involved in one way or another, there was no official Mexican inquiry under way, because there was no official Mexican complaint, and an official inquiry cannot take place officially under Mexican law without an official complaint.

The other problem was that the Mexican police were being asked to do all of their work based on secondhand information. Yes, their friends the American team told them the boy was this and was not that, that he and his friends had done this and not that. But they themselves had to be content with such information, handed them secondhand by foreign police officials. It was customary in all police work, the world over, to seek the most immediate firsthand testimony and evidence obtainable.

In short, Attorney General Anibal Perez wanted the Kilroys to present themselves to Mexican authorities. And the attorney general wanted the other boys to return to Mexico.

The boys, after all, had been willing to return to Matamoros for the television show. Would it be asking too much for them to come back and answer questions for the Mexican authorities?

This request caused consternation back in Santa Fe, where an entire informal network had sprung up to give whatever help was possible to the Kilroys. Everyone in the town was straining to be useful. There were a million small but unpleasant things. Mark's dental records had to be assembled, so that the team in Brownsville would have them in the event a decomposed body was found.

The Kilroy family's main logistical problem at that point was the press. They had done everything they could to attract the attention of the media. But succeeding in that attempt meant that dozens of editors around the country were now sending dozens and dozens of reporters to the Kilroy story. Each reporter needed to hear the story with his own ears and needed to feel that he or she personally understood something of the Kilroy family and the lost boy, Mark.

The only way to shield the Kilroys from the necessity of going over and over Mark's life, day in and day out, was for other people in the community to stand in for them and tell the reporters what the reporters needed to know. Bill Huddleston's mother, Gwen, had virtually taken a leave of absence from her dance and gymnastics business to handle press inquiries for the besieged Kilroys.

Mary and Eddie de la Houssaye had been friends of the Kilroys for seventeen years. While Eddie was down in Matamoros with Jim handing out fliers, Mary was trying to help Gwen by fielding all of the questions about what the Kilroys were really like and so on.

While Jim was down in Matamoros, Helen was at home. Mark's room was untouched. A laundry basket filled with his neatly folded shirts and underwear stood next to the bed. Over the bed, the seven dusty little baseball caps that marked his career as a Little League All Star hung beneath a shelf crowded with basketball, track and science fair trophies. Every time Helen Kilroy walked through the house, she had to walk by that open door and hold on to her heart.

Friends and people from Our Lady of Lourdes Roman Catholic Church where the Kilroys belonged stopped by the house in an unbroken procession. Each visitor offered to pray with Helen Kilroy. She spent hours on her knees with the vision of Mark dancing in her mind.

At times, the visions were comforting. Mark was being held hostage in those visions, but he was all right. She heard his voice saying, "Mother, I'm all right where I am." She prayed that his captors would not become frightened or panicked by all of the activity whirling around the case now. She prayed they would not harm him.

In one of these moments, she asked the people of Santa Fe to tie yellow ribbons around the trees in their yards—a reference to a corny popular song of several years ago about a man looking for a sign he was welcome home. The people of Santa Fe saw nothing corny in the gesture and never hesitated an instant. They covered the town with yellow ribbons, so that Helen Kilroy could look out and see this sign and hope and pray that Mark could see it, too, somehow.

At other times, her visions of him were disturbing. It was in these moments when her maternal instincts seemed strongest. She was a volunteer paramedic with the Santa Fe Emergency Medical Service and had seen her share of pain and suffering. Even after long agonizing hours of prayer and reading the Bible, she could not hold the dark visions back.

"I've really felt strongly that somehow he's being hurt right now," she said.

The town was pitching in and doing everything it could. But the request to send the three living boys back to Mexico was too much. By now, the Kilroys' suspicions that the Mexican police were somehow involved in Mark's disappearance were well known on the Santa Fe gossip circuit. Certainly the parents of the other boys had been informed. The boys were also all back in school.

The word was no. The boys' parents would not agree for them to return to Mexico and surrender themselves to whatever treatment waited them at the hands of Mexican authorities.

And yet, in order for the last straw of resistance to be broken on the Mexican side, the formal face-saving objections of the Tamaulipas A.G. needed to be satisfied. The solution was for Jim and Helen Kilroy to go themselves.

They had just concluded an especially exhausting and depleting gauntlet of hope and despair which had been kept almost completely secret. On April 4, they had received a call from two men who said they were holding Mark and that they would return him for $10,000. If the Kilroys involved the police in any way, the callers said they would know immediately and would begin cutting off Mark's fingers and sending them in the mail.

The callers were George Miller, Jr., twenty-four, and

Wilton Joseph Smith, twenty-four, both of whom were calling from the Galveston County Jail, where they were inmates. The Kilroys were convinced at first that the calls were genuine.

The $10,000 was staggering. Even though Jim Kilroy was a chemical engineer, the petrochemical industry in Texas had been severely depressed, his own employment had been affected, and he had one boy in pre-med and another getting ready for college in a few years. They pleaded with the callers for some consideration.

In a second call, the voices relented somewhat and told the Kilroys they would be allowed to bring a "down-payment" of $2,000 to an Exxon station in Santa Fe where Helen was to make a call from a pay phone. Helen Kilroy drove to the station with the money at the appointed hour and made the call, but there was no answer.

The Santa Fe police thought they had identified two people who had been waiting around a pay phone elsewhere in town. But a later call from the extortionists claimed they knew she had gone to the police. The first finger would arrive soon. She pleaded for another chance.

In the meantime, the Kilroys were informed that someone had broken into Mark's apartment back in Austin. Eventually police decided it was a simple burglary, probably carried out by someone who had read the many interviews with Mark's college friends and had figured out where his empty and unguarded apartment was. But at the time, the news of the burglary was one more weight of violence and danger to fall on the already burdened shoulders of the family.

The callers told Helen she could meet them one more time. This second time she drove to a meeting at the city cemetery. No one showed up. As it turned out in the end, the police had indeed identified some of the confederates of the callers, and all of the conspirators were arrested and charged. But in the period when they were being asked to go into Mexico, the Kilroys also were expecting to find pieces of their son in the mail any day.

They said they would go. The Mexicans were informed that the school schedules of the three boys would not allow them to return to Mexico. It was hoped this fiction at least would avoid salting whatever official wound was being felt.

Accompanied by their ever-watchful escort of Customs agents, the Kilroys ventured to Ciudad Victoria and officially informed the Mexican government their son was missing.

With this bit of business out of the way, and moving quickly to take advantage of the press flurry stirred by Mattox and the "Most Wanted" show, the Customs people began using every contact with Mexico as an opportunity to talk up their "very grave concern" that a travel advisory was on its way. Considerable lengths were employed and not a little ingenuity invoked in seeing to it that this threat —probably an idle one at that point, given the State Department's intense desire not to embarrass the new Mexican president—was nevertheless conveyed to officials in Mexico City in the most convincing fashion possible.

At this point, there was almost a very bad bump. Everything had reached a moment of extreme delicacy. Whatever was going on among the Mexican police, it was nevertheless obvious that somebody in Mexico City wanted this thing put to rest. President Salinas had caused the arrest of druglord Felix Gallardo, which should have been a major headline story in every American newspaper with more than a passing interest in Mexico. In addition, he was just about to announce he was opening up Mexican businesses to 100 percent foreign ownership.

Both moves—to do something convincing about the drug corruption and also do something dramatic about opening up Mexico's economy to global participation— were designed to win trust abroad, especially in the United States and Europe, where Mexico had serious debt problems.

In order to hold the country together domestically, Salinas absolutely had to cut some slack with the country's foreign creditors. But in order to do that, he had to convince them Mexico wasn't two inches from becoming Panama.

He was taking the most daring steps in those directions any recent Mexican leader had dreamed of. And the only thing anybody wanted to talk about was this damned kid who got lost in Matamoros.

Mexico City wanted it over, done with. If it involved dope, even if it involved corruption, even if it involved police corruption, Mexico City wanted it fixed. The federales in the region were welcome to do the best they could to cover their own asses. But it was to be fixed, the chips were to fall where they might, and the necessary heads were to roll.

The American team could see it about to happen. After tense agonizing for weeks and months, they could feel it in their bones. That's how it was with Mexico. The whole country seemed absolutely immovable, immutable and inscrutable. And then bang! Everything! Their best border instincts told them it was just about to break.

And then Bill Clements noticed it. The Texas governor's office, which had turned down the Kilroys' initial request for a meeting, started calling around, trying to figure out a way to get in. Obviously this was a big story.

For as long as possible, all of the team members in Brownsville either ducked calls or, if caught, mumbled a lot into the phone.

But now the Clements people were suggesting something no one could ignore. They were hinting that they thought a good way for the governor to inject himself into this story would be for him to exercise one of the scant powers available to him under Texas's post-Reconstruction minimalist state constitution. He was going to send in the Texas Rangers.

Anyone who read Larry McMurtry's *Lonesome Dove* or saw the television mini-series will understand how Mexicans and Mexican-Americans feel about the rangers. The

rangers originally were volunteer forces whose mission
was to defend the frontier settlements by clearing the land
of Indians and Mexicans. Their main tool was a Colt six-
gun.

More to the point, the modern rangers had continued to
operate out of a general mission as racial police until too
recently. All along the border, there was folklore and bitter
memory linking the rangers with the very worst of the region's culture of racial and ethnic violence.

The Clements people would not listen to anybody in the
Valley whom they took for a Democrat, which made it
tough, since almost everybody down there who wasn't a
major grower was a Democrat. Fortunately, in this era of
Reagan–Bush hegemony, and given Governor Clements's
famous affection for things tied to federal police or military
agencies of any kind, there were ways of persuading him.

The word found its way to Austin, via Washington,
from a very anxious team in Brownsville. Dear Governor
Bill. Thank you. But no thank you. Please stay home. And
please, whatever you do, do not ever mention the Texas
Rangers in connection with these events again.

A disgruntled but chastened staff in the governor's office bowed to these pressures and agreed to butt out.

With that taken care of, everyone had the feeling that it
just needed one final shove. One push. The Kilroys themselves were drafted for this last bit of strategy. They placed
the call to San Antonio's handsome mayor, Henry Cisneros, whose name was a byword in Latin culture throughout the American continents. Cisneros had gone to Harvard
with the new Mexican president. As a Mexican-American
who had taught the Anglos a thing or two in Texas, he was
viewed in Mexico in the same giddy popular light as Los
Angeles Dodgers pitcher Fernando Valenzuela.

Cisneros had been a star on the national and international political/diplomatic speaker's circuit for years and
kept an incredibly busy schedule. But there was another
aspect of his life and personality working in the interests of
the Kilroys. Henry Cisneros was a father. After the birth of

a child with life-threatening disabilities, Cisneros purpose-
fully had damped down the wick of his own political ambitions and had become a much more private person. He
agreed with alacrity to do whatever he could to help the
Kilroys find their boy. He would go to the Valley the next
weekend.

It might not be easily visible right downtown in Matamoros where the gringos came to spend their money, but
the city was by then almost under federal martial law. Benitez Ayala and his men were conducting heavy-handed
search and seizure operations all over town. The Tamaulipas police, meanwhile, were scurrying around behind the
federales, ostensibly helping them follow up leads, but also
making sure they knew just where and how far Benitez
Ayala was getting.

Everyone in Matamoros knew what it was all about. For
the last week, whenever anyone was stopped by the federales for any reason, the federales always showed Mark
Kilroy's picture. The missing American boy.

Rumors were thick and hot. A woman was reported to
have told Benitez Ayala that the boy had been abducted by
a "gang of students, operating out of a local college." The
rumor had it that the students were devil-worshippers and
had been kidnaping and sacrificing young children for a
year or more. According to the rumor, the police already
knew who these people were but were afraid to move on
them, because the people had too much dirt to hold over
the heads of the police.

Cisneros arrived in Brownsville on Saturday and met
with the Kilroys. They and the American team urged him
to go over to the other side the next day and meet with
Benitez Ayala. The rumors were very strong that Benitez
Ayala already had something. Perhaps Cisneros could dis-
suade him from any temptation he might have to sit on
whatever it was he was finding.

The meeting between Cisneros and Ayala was alter-
nately loose and good-guy and strangely formal and uncomfortable. Cisneros told Benitez Ayala he was very

impressed with all of the activity of the federal judicial police and that he intended to write to his friend, the president of Mexico, and commend the comandante for his efforts.

The comandante was suitably pleased and modest in acknowledging this threat. Cisneros noticed that there were candles and other artifacts—objects whose nature he knew too well—on the comandante's desk. Were these not Santeria objects?

The comandante said that various forms of voodoo and black magic had become common in the drug trade. He mentioned that he had in custody in the building at that very moment a member of a certain family-based Matamoros drug gang rumored to have been connected with black magic sacrifices. The name of the family was Hernandez.

Cisneros had passed Serafin Junior in manacles in the hallway. Little Elio was only a few yards away from him in a cell. Two other gang members and an old man, a caretaker from the ranch, also were under federal lock and key. It was another lead, another possibility. Benitez Ayala said his men would obtain a search warrant and go out to the family's plantation—Rancho Santa Elena—the next morning or the day after, as soon as possible.

It might be nothing, it might be something. They were following every possible path. Cisneros said later he had assumed the voodoo objects on the comandante's desk had been confiscated from the gang. But in fact the ranch had not yet been searched when Cisneros visited Benitez Ayala that Sunday. The objects on the desk were the objects that were always on Benitez Ayala's desk. They were the things he kept at hand specifically to protect himself from the very sort of vileness he now seemed to be investigating.

Under the new Salinas presidency, there were a number of things going on in the area that were not under even Benitez Ayala's anxious control. Since April 5, the army had been joining the federales in carrying out a massive program of nocturnal roadblocks to search for and seize drugs all along the northern border. In that short time, 11,192 pounds of cocaine had been seized, along with 3,005 pounds of marijuana.

Almost from the moment David Serna Valdez ("El Coqueto") had blown through a roadblock the night before in his Chevy Silverado pickup with Texas plates, the Federal Judicial Police had been extremely uneasy, to say the least. First of all, you have to be missing part of your brain to blast through a joint federale–Mexican army roadblock like that. They had chased him to the ranch and arrested him, but throughout the arrest he had acted like he was crazy. Or like he was something else—something the federales didn't even want to think about. He had laughed at them, had told them to go ahead and shoot him, that their bullets couldn't pierce his skin. And he had said that his soul was already dead.

The arrest was a good one. In the metal barns at the work station, midway into the ranch, the federales found 220 pounds of marijuana and four ounces of cocaine, along with three fully automatic weapons, seven rifles and two pistols. They also seized eleven nice new cars, each equipped with the latest cellular phones and radio equipment. They began immediately running the cellular phones through the records to see what fixed addresses were called often from these vehicles. Within hours, they were putting surveillance in place to sweep up Elio, Serafin, and the rest of the group.

When they had originally hit the ranch and taken Serna Valdez, they had found an old caretaker on the place. He had seemed fairly normal. They showed him the picture of the boy. Incredibly enough, he said almost immediately that he recognized the boy, that the boy had been held there on the ranch. That he had given the boy something to eat. That he had last seen the boy in a shack, deeper into the ranch.

Now, back here at the federal jail, it was beginning to come out. This Serna Valdez kept saying he was invulnerable and that his soul was dead, that they could do nothing to him. That could only mean one thing. No one who worked for Benitez Ayala would want to touch it.

And yet here was the handsome, erudite, suave young American pocho mayor, old Harvard buddy to the new president of Mexico, ready to write commendations for the comandante.

This was it. These were the guys. They had taken Kilroy. They had killed him. The damned Cisneros had seen it, had sensed it right away, was already back over there in damned Brownsville blabbing to all the cops about his new lead. There was some kind of curandero, something worse, some horrible Cuban Tata Nkisi in it. It was going to be horrible—a huge horrible international scandal. And there was just no turning away from it, no way to bury it, no matter how numbingly frightening it was for the federales even to contemplate going out there.

Because they believed.

They had been Constanzo's secret all along.

The police believed in the powers of Santeria, Palo Mayombe, Abukua.

All of it.

They were products of the same culture that produced the crooks and all the good honest Mexicans in between. The magic was woven deeply in that culture, much more deeply than the modern overlays of Catholicism, politics and law. The local police, the Tamaulipas police, the federales: they all believed in it, and they were all terrified of it, and therefore it worked. It kept them at bay. Constanzo knew exactly what he was doing.

Up to now. Now there was all the pressure of this other magic, gringo bullshit magic with the TV shows and the bank debts and the Harvard buddies and the press reports and fucking hypnosis—all this other loud and glaring dream. Finally, the other was too much. It pressed in from one side, a clattering glaring mechanical beast, and the Palo Mayombe pressed from the other, dark and febrile, red in tooth and claw. The mechanical monster was about to vanquish the jungle, and there was nothing Benitez Ayala could do but get the hell out from in the middle.

Monday was Serious Day for the subjects. There were two things to do with them. There was what all of the federales wanted to do—let the bastards go and hope they never showed up again. And there was what had to be done instead.

After two centuries of experimentation, the Mexican police had perfected their techniques beyond the dreams of their predecessors. In the past, the extraction of confessions had involved all sorts of blood, time and screaming. Even in recent times, the new technology had worked only imperfectly—the cattle prods, car batteries and so on. All of those techniques left horrible scars and mutilation—an embarrassment for the police in this new era of global media and nosiness.

The trick was to find some mechanism that would not have to work through the external sensory apparati, something that didn't involve cutting or burning or smashing the body but went directly to the pain centers in the brain, instead. There had been much experimentation with drugs, and some of them had worked quite well but often had produced the counterproductive side effect of leaving the victim too crazy to be presentable in court or to the media.

What was needed was something that caused instant and utterly unbearable pain, that left no scars, that allowed at least partial recuperation and that did not require a lot of fancy equipment—dental equipment and the like, which could hardly be toted about in the field.

The answer, as it turned out, was already in their hands every day. A bottle of carbonated mineral water, vigorously shaken and then jammed up the nostril of the victim so that it exploded into his skull, set off all of the panic, pain, drowning, blinding, death and dying alarms in the human brain. You could do it five times in two minutes, never leave a mark, toss the bottle in the trash can and reduce your victim to a mass of quivering jello. The victims almost always lost sphinctral control, the pain was so intense. They sometimes permanently lost their hearing or vision or both. But they could still talk.

Try that for horror, you little bastards. Who rules in Hell now? One by one they brought them in, and one by one they shoved the bottle up their noses, and one by one they told Benitez Ayala the same story, about El Padrino, about La Bruja, about who did what, how they did it, who was present and when and where, all of it in fine and matching detail. When they were done spilling their guts, Benitez Ayala explained to them like a teacher that there would be a large contingent of press around at some point in the next few days, hundreds of reporters, but that at the end of the day there would be Benitez Ayala.

When the Federal Judicial Police arrived at Rancho Santa Elena early on the morning of Tuesday, April 11, 1989, they were armed with the proper warrants, they had a video-camera to record every moment of the search. They were accompanied by Gavito and Neck. And, hovering very discreetly in the background, their own curandero also came with them.

They were beginning to pull in other members of the gang already. They brought the gang along so that they could question them during the search. The effect of the fizz-water nasal treatments had been less than perfect. The gang members were driving them crazy. They were laughing and playing around, joking. The more the gang members laughed, the more they frightened the federales. No one in his right mind laughed at the federales. These people acted as if they were truly protected by the spirits, and, indeed, the more they acted that way, the more they were. After a while, even Neck and Gavito conceded to their Mexican colleagues that the gang members were driving them crazy, too. There was something profoundly irritating and disquieting in the way they minced and giggled, buzzed and mumbled among themselves. They were like happy flies.

Finally it came to a head. Everyone was arrayed at the site of the shack and the goat corral. It was time to begin.

The old man had told them he had last seen Kilroy in the shack. They would have to look there first. The gang members were behaving very strangely about the shack. It stank. Maybe the body was in it. But there was something else. The gang members were all very wired about the shack, which made the police more apprehensive.

The snottiest of them all was this half-pocho kid, Serafin Hernandez, Jr. The rest might just be loco thugs, but he really seemed to be full of it. Benitez Ayala stepped up to Serafin. Like all of his men, he was carrying a machine gun.

"Open the shack," he told him.

Chapter Eight

Serafin grinned at him. He turned and took a few steps to the door of the shack. Then he turned back to face him. At that moment, Serafin began to blow up, to bloat, at first as if holding his breath, then actually, as the video-tape shows, to inflate, his whole body seemed to swell and expand. It was a classic performance of spirit possession —the moment of the spirit rushing into the body—and it scared the piss out of everyone.

It was up to Benitez Ayala. He stepped up to Serafin, right up to him, right in his face. He lifted the machine gun up alongside Serafin's cheek. Serafin glowered back at him with the face of Satan himself. It was going to be now or never. Benitez Ayala squeezed off a staccato burst of bul-lets into the air by Serafin's head.

And that was it. The wind rushed out of Serafin like air deflating from a toy balloon. He slumped. He smirked. And all of a sudden this temple of the devil was a polite, docile little kid from Nimitz High again—the water boy, the joke teller, the one everybody like to have around.

From that moment on, the rest of the gang began to

change, too. There was still a lot of thuggy bravado and swagger in them from time to time, but all crooks act like that. The thing that had terrified the federales—the seeming sense of total personal immunity from harm—was gone. The gang members were even beginning to get a little worried—always a good sign. There began to be some muttered remarks about not being in on this and not having taken part in that—all useful, all important, all going straight into the videotape machine and onto the stenographer's pad.

And now it was time to open the shack. Serafin pushed the door. The stench and the ripping whine of the flies rushed out. Benitez Ayala stared, allowing his eyes to adjust.

They were fedarales. They had seen everything. They had done everything. They felt as if they had touched every horror at least once.

But what they saw in the shack was worse. Far worse. Far more horrible than it would have been to find Mark Kilroy's rotting body.

They saw the thing whose name they would not even pronounce aloud. They could not believe they were seeing it. One heard of this thing. But no one was ever fully certain such a thing existed. Really existed. And here it was before them, in a red cloud of stench and covered with a fury of flies.

Nganga.

They told the gang members to bring it out. Serafin and another one slopped along, holding it by the edges, stooped in their manacles, spilling its slimy contents over the rim.

The federales staggering back. My God! It was the real thing. Hunks of a human brain were swimming in a stew of blood. The long bloody mesquite sticks they used to stir the stuff and paint themselves protruded from the pot like rays of Hell. Turtle parts came to the surface and dipped from view as the thick half-congealed soup slopped from side to side. The stench was incredible. An animal face appeared—the severed head of a goat.

Whose? They pointed to the brain. Whose? Whose?
The gringo.

Finally the federales brought themselves to look inside
the shack. The gang members were enjoying themselves
immensely, thrilled by the sickness and the wobbly knees
of the federales, elbowing each other and giggling whenever another federale rushed off to vomit. Finally they
could not contain themselves and burst into laughter. It was
just as Constanzo always had told them it would be. They
were complete masters of the horror, and these great tough
federales were like old piss-pants women. It was just as El
Padrino had said. They were the complete masters of their
own fates.

Benitez Ayala drew up sharply again when he saw more
of what was inside. Near the door were six unopened crates
of unused votive candles, embossed with the image of the
Virgin of Guadalupe. Near the candles were empty bottles
of the cheapest hooch, an Indian cane liquor called aguar-
diente—rotgut stuff that made people hallucinate before
they even got drunk.

In a semicircle against the wall, made of broken cinder
blocks, was the altar. It was garlanded in green chili peppers and garlic cloves. On the floor before it were shards
from broken liquor bottles and smashed cigar butts. Shot
all over one wall was a huge dark jet of blood—the sort of
stain that could only be made by an explosion of blood
from the heart.

Benitez Ayala ordered the gang members to carry the
other pots and some of the paraphernalia out into the sun-
light. The nganga, thirty inches in diameter, rusted brown,
was two-thirds full. The brain matter, grayish-yellow in
color, floated clear of the charred turtle. There were
twenty-five mesquite sticks in the pot.

Next to the nganga on the little lip of concrete slab in
front of the shack, Serafin dumped a smaller black iron pot
with a trident-shaped pitchfork in it. Grinning, he lifted the
pitchfork to show that a goat's head was impaled on the
end of it. Three small ceramic bowls held beads, small

sticks, and the heads and entrails of goats and roosters. Another pot contained thousands of pennies—the ritual "price" the gang paid for the souls of its victims.

Strewn inside the shack were unlit Palma cigars, liquor bottles, Corona beer bottles, half-burned candles, broken glass, littered candy wrappers and swatches of human scalp and hair.

This place was roaring with the devil. It was the devil's church. Benitez Ayala saw the duct tape they used to stanch their victims' screams and the jagged barbed wire they used to bind their wrists. He saw and understood it all. They had brought Kilroy here and others certainly, and they had sacrificed them all, offered them to the devil, to the orishas, to whoever in Hell they thought would give them power. And it was all still in here, roaring in the corners in the glinting black clouds of angry flies.

It was then that Serafin and the others began their macabre scavenger hunt. Dancing out into the corral, laughing and pointing, they competed to see which one could most accurately locate a body. By noon, beneath a low oppressive bank of humidity and heat, the black stench of death had rolled out over the entire area.

There were nine graves. Four were inside the corral, at opposite ends of the enclosure, which measured twenty-two yards by thirty yards. Two of the graves inside the corral held more than one body. All of the bodies bore marks of savage torture and mutilation. Several had been flayed. Limbs, penises and testicles were hacked off. The body cavities had been sliced open. The gang members freely confessed that some had been dismembered while still alive.

Serafin chatted off-handedly about his role in things, already laying off as much as he thought he could on Constanzo and Sara, his bosses. "They told me to get a white guy, a student who was young. I did it because they told me to do it. If I didn't do it, they'd probably do something to me. We were scared."

He said he had followed Constanzo for practical reasons

at first. He said the rituals had helped him in his life. "Sometimes it worked. Good things would happen and come into your life, like doing well in school and this and that. So I thought maybe it was working."

Mark Kilroy was in a grave midway between the shack and the corral. Three other graves were near his.

At first they dug for Kilroy with shovels. The hard-packed gray-silt earth yielded stubbornly, sending up reek-ing clouds of stench. They had to bring a backhoe over. When the jaw was found, they were able to identify Mark quickly, from the dental records.

He was buried three feet down, approximately where the tarpaulin was spread. He may even have been buried where he finally fell. His body was unclothed. Both legs had been severed above the tibia. His brains had been re-moved. His spinal cord was missing. The phalanges of all of his fingers were missing. His penis and testicles had been cut off.

Two bodies were more recent than Mark Kilroy's.

A federale asked Serafin why they had gouged out Kilroy's brain.

Serafin shrugged. "It was our religion."

Benitez Ayala and his men withdrew briefly from the ranch. Back at his office, he listened to a review of what was known. The cult had a leader, a Cuban-American they called El Padrino. He was their Tata Nkisi. There was a bruja named Sara who lived over on the other side but had people in Matamoros. There was no telling where the Tata Nkisi might be. He was on jets all the time. But he re-turned to the ranch at least once a week to visit with the nganga. He was due back.

And then the other news. The Matamoros police were sorry, terribly sorry. They had become apprised of the situ-ation at the Rancho Santa Elena through their own confi-dential sources and had been attempting diligently to keep what they knew secret, aware, as they were, of the sensi-tivity of the moment, but a hanger-on of the press, one of those people who literally camp at police headquarters, had gotten wind of things.

The story was out. A call came to Ayala from the office of Mexican Customs. An armada of American television satellite dish trucks was forming at the bridge, all of them furious to get across, buzzing and whirring like the flies.

Earlier that morning, Jim Mattox had picked up the phone in his office. It was Oran Neck. They thought they had Mark's body. It was going to be extremely bad. International. Mattox hung up. The phone rang again immediately. Gavito. Can you get down here? There will be hundreds of reporters, we're just about to go dig him up, can you at least send some of your press people? Mattox hung up. The phone rang again. It was Cameron County D.A. Ben Euresti. All Hell is breaking loose down here. They're headed out to some filthy ranch outside of Matamoros, all talking about devil worship, talking about human sacrifice, brains, blood in a kettle, can you get down here?

When Mattox talked to Castillo, he realized this Hernandez family might be the same one his people had been dealing with in Grimes County. He decided to go.

The Kilroys were in Brownsville. They learned there.

Gwen Huddleston and Fred Huddleston were talking almost nonstop to the army of press camped in their house in Santa Fe. The phone in the kitchen beeped nonstop—mainly calls from friends and fellow churchmembers of the Kilroys, asking if the confirmation had come. The Huddlestons explained it was to come at 5:00 P.M.

At a quarter to five, Mary de la Houssaye decided to give Gwen a breather from the calls and went back to the kitchen to catch the one ringing on the line at that moment. She looked up quickly from the receiver. It was Jim Kilroy.

"Hi, Jim," she said.

The people jammed in that end of the kitchen fell instantly silent. Sucking in their stomachs and maneuvering quickly for position, the reporters and photographers in the kitchen slipped in as close as they could get to the phone.

Mary de la Houssaye sobbed. She struggled to compose herself. "Then it was Mark." She listened to a response, tears streaming down her face. "I'm so sorry. I don't know what to say, Jim. Is there anything I can do?"

Fred Huddleston was standing next to her. Behind him, the word had not yet passed. Gwen, his wife, was still out in the other room answering some kind of questions, talking into a TV camera. He turned and faced her with tears in his eyes, and she knew.

Now the story was whirling out over the world, and the people who had been at its center were overwhelmed. Even in this the moment of their most profound grief, even though they had been doing practically nothing other than talking to the media for days, what began to happen in that instant shocked and even stupefied them.

The airplane tires began crunching down on the tarmac at Harlingen International one after another, commercial flights, charter flights, private network jet flights, in and in and in, and out of every plane jumped throngs more reporters and film crews. The press contingent swelled to 100 and then 250 and then 600 and then no one bothered to count. The satellite dish trucks raced back and forth from news tip to news tip in a great caravan of frenzy and titillation, shoving regular traffic into the ditches when they came hurtling down the narrow Mexican highways, the dishes and antennas wobbling and waving in the humid air like the frantic arms of giant beetles.

The search at Santa Elena went on. After the first few bodies had been unearthed, the police began assembling a small amount of farm machinery and backhoe devices with which to continue the digging. The bodies just kept coming up out of the earth, two, and then four, and then ten, all but a few hacked and desecrated in ways that went to an instinctive place of hateful revulsion in the people who saw them come out of the earth.

The Americans wanted more. They were convinced there were more. Searchers had found shoes and clothing of small children thrown in a rubble heap nearby. The

Americans began putting together an armada of heavy earth-moving machinery on flatbed trucks in Brownsville. Benitez Ayala and the Tamaulipas A.G. for once were in perfect unanimity. The Americans should keep their equipment the hell out of Matamoros. The Mexicans would direct this dig, spade by careful spade.

The blood libel was loose on the land. And no one knew if it was a libel. As driven as Benitez Ayala had been to solve this case, going largely sleepless in the last week, he knew he needed to get a grip on this story. Reporters were coming in from all over the world, and the blood libel was loose on the land. Mexican people taking children, sacrificing them, eating them. Benitez Ayala had seen the body of Mark Kilroy. He had seen the nganga. He knew that anything was possible. He was trying desperately to get ahead of the story, to control the flow of information.

But it was impossible. Even his own normally disciplined and tight-lipped troops could not control their tongues. Tuesday, while the bodies were still coming out of the graves, a detachment of federales surrounded the little house on the Street of the Beheaded Saint. A bewildered Israel Aldrete came to the wrought-iron gate at the outside wall and opened it. They rushed past him and went room to room with automatic weapons at the ready.

They found nothing. The one the gang members were calling La Bruja was not there. A federale shoved the snout of the machine gun up Aldrete's crotch and yanked him forward by the hair of his head. He pleaded that she was not there, that they had not seen her, that she had rushed in the previous Saturday, went to her apartment in the back and rushed out with some clothes. She had not spoken to her parents.

The federales told him to lead them to the apartment. The door swung open, and it was Israel Aldrete who gasped loudest. There, in the back of the little living room area, was a voodoo altar, splattered with blood. The candles with the pictures of the orishas were arranged in a semicircle. Saint Barbara—Shango—was there. At the top of the altar was Constanzo's little Buddha. There were bloodstains on the floor and wall around the altar.

Israel Aldrete began sobbing that he had never known of this altar, that he had no idea, that his daughter was a good girl, that he and his wife were good Catholics. A federale stalked to the far corner of the room and began poking through a pile of something on the floor with his gun. He whirled around suddenly and told Aldrete to shut up. He motioned for his superior to come quickly. His superior peered into the pile for a long moment, apparently not understanding what he was looking at. Then there was a muttered stream of Spanish curses.

The two men began to lift them one after another: items of children's clothing, dark and stiff with blood.

The reporters were already outside when the federales came out. They were everywhere, asking. The federales were beside themselves, unable to maintain their composure. Word of it got out. The reporters were asking about the blood.

And the word raced across the Valley, in both Mexico and the United States. According to the rumor, the narcosatanistos, as they already were being called in a freshly minted Mexican media word, had been cannibalizing small children and had vowed to take more in retribution for the arrests. Parents rushed into the streets of Matamoros and clutched up their children. Outside the public schools in Brownsville, cars were lined up and drivers were angrily honking their horns, fighting to get up to the door and rush in to take their children home. There was heart-stopping panic in the land. A rumor spread that a certain rural church had been used by such people: it was burned within an hour of the first spread of the rumor.

An army of press was present by the time the final disinterring took place. After twelve bodies had been produced, Benitez Ayala had tried to call it off, announcing that everything had been found and that the Rancho was now off limits. But no one listened to him; reporters continued to flow over the ranch in droves: his own men were far too busy to do anything about it; the Tamaulipas police suddenly had made themselves scarce; and now the little bastards back at the jail were telling people there were more bodies.

In a foul mood, the federales brought Sergio Martinez back out. He was twenty-three years old—the one the gang called "La Mariposa." He seemed to resent all the attention the others had gotten. He said he too knew how to find a body. The press, which by now included crews from Japan and Norway, crowded in around him. The federales shoved a spade in his hand and told him to have at it. The backhoes, for some reason, had disappeared. The weather was hot and humid and the clouds were scudding low over the sorghum fields as Martinez's shovel began clinking at the hard dirt.

He dug and sweated. When he had dug for half an hour, down only about two feet, a fetid stink began to rise from the ground. He reeled back, and the film crews moved in closer. One of the federales barked at the crews not to get between Martinez and the ready machine guns of the federales. They were taking no chances with this bastard. And they had no idea what to expect from that hole he was digging. But the press, as always, did not like being ordered around by people in uniforms.

Martinez was bathed in sweat and dirt, and the flies, attracted to the smell of rot, were beginning to bite him. His cockiness was gone. He asked the federales for water. They shrugged. The press asked the federales what the "boy" had said to them. The federales said he had asked for water. The people in the press canvassed themselves and found that they had no water, either. The federales watched this process warily.

Martinez said he could no longer stand the stink, that he could not go on. The federales simply pointed their guns at his face, but a member of a very well equipped Japanese film crew took off his own surgical mask and gave it to Martinez.

Then Martinez said he could not complete the digging

with a shovel. The federales had had it. One of them stepped up to him and spat out: "You will dig it up if you have to dig it up with your hands!"

Martinez went back to his digging in earnest. It took him over an hour to complete his work. The hole was four feet deep and two feet wide. A Mexican reporter helped Martinez pull the body up to level earth. Martinez surveyed the faces of the press eagerly as they squinted down trying to make out what had happened to the body. One of the federales crossed himself, then several did.

The head was severed. The heart was missing. The chest cavity had been slashed open. The rib cage was smashed and protruding, the bones wrenched upward. The press still didn't get it. One of the federales explained. Another of the bodies had been like this. The heart had been violently torn from the chest.

The mincing truculent Butterfly had unearthed a piece of his own special handiwork—little Jose Garcia Luna, the fourteen-year-old cowherd, whose head had so surprised and enraged cousin Elio when it had plopped staring and unexpected from a feed sack.

The reporters turned and stared at Martinez. In the background, a Mexican Protestant evangelist minister was reading from a Bible, mumbling into the low foul-smelling breeze from the grave. Martinez muttered some feeble excuses. He said he only delivered chickens to the ranch. He said he had also delivered some candles. He said he had helped bury some of the bodies. He said yes, that he did "have shame."

There was an eerie and protracted silence as the reporters and the film crews and the federales packed up. The penchant of the press corps for wisecracking and putting on a brave face had left them. No one had the slightest idea what to make of this. The stink was up everyone's nose and deep in the lungs. The bones sticking up where they had ripped out the heart looked like sticks protruding from this thing the federales kept calling, in hushed almost reverent tones, the "nganga," which still stood where Serafin and his friend had slopped it to the earth, still full of rotting brains and blood.

Gavito and Neck were racing to keep up with Benitez Ayala. The public panic over the children had created a whole new political dimension to the situation. Mexico City had demanded that the thing be cleared up, but no one could have guessed all this was coming. After the thirteenth body came out, the word initially was that Benitez Ayala would bring in his own earth-moving equipment and scrape the ranch for more bodies. Now suddenly that was off. There would be no more digging. Benitez Ayala said all the bodies had been found.

Late in the afternoon of the same day when he announced the digging was over, Benitez Ayala headed back out to the ranch with a contingent. Gavito caught wind of it and raced out there behind them, arriving just a few minutes later. The federales all stood around, surveying the place silently. Gavito watched. Nothing was happening.

Then it came clear. A man stepped around from behind the shack. It was the curandero. They had brought him out here to do something for them. The sun was beginning to set. The federales were extremely jumpy, sweeping around with their machine guns and twitching at every sound. They poured sweat and scowled, obviously very unhappy to be there.

The curandero motioned. A young assistant appeared from a pickup truck. He was carrying a white dove and a cardboard box. He placed the dove under the box and then kneeled over the box, so that he could watch the dove through a hole.

The curandero circled the building, muttering incantations and sprinkling holy water stolen from the cathedral in Matamoros. All of the federales stared at the assistant, who stared down into the box and watched the dove.

Finally the curandero doused the shack with gasoline and lighted it. It went up with a great *whoomp*. A black greasy smoke shot up and then spread out low.

The federales stared at the assistant. Some of them were

literally shivering with fear. He looked up into the box, then lifted it and held up the dove. It flapped its wings. It was alive. Several of the federales had tears of relief in their eyes.

The outlines of the story were beginning to form in the press. Mark Kilroy had been the victim of a voodoo cult and twelve other bodies had been found. It was just beginning to be understood that the cult members were major drug dealers. And it was known they had two leaders, one they called El Padrino and one they called El Madrina or La Bruja, both of whom were at large along with several of their followers. A wispy outline of Constanzo was beginning to emerge in the stories, in which he was described variously as a Cuban drug dealer, a Marielisto and an American playboy.

There was a general rush to the experts for any kind of explanation they could give for the altar, the mutilated bodies and the cauldron. The academics and the medical people, working from descriptions of voodoo that were, for the most part, at least half a century out of date, said they doubted the grisly affair in Matamoros had anything to do with real voodoo.

The altar in the shack was a confusion of religious symbols—a Buddha-like figurine, Santeria candles, Roman Catholic candles, symbols associated with Haitian voodoo and other symbols associated with the Afro-Cuban cults of Palo Mayombe and Abakua. Already the boys in custody were blabbing about the movie, about how La Bruja had made them watch the thing over and over. The conclusion most of the experts drew from the sketchy information reporters could give them was that the people in Matamoros were druggies who had invented their own cornball version of voodoo from things they had learned in movies.

"Some groups use these sorts of things to cover their psycopathic behavior," said Dr. Peter Olsson, a Houston psychiatrist who was an expert on cults. "It sounds to me like this is not a classic satanic group but a psychotic pathological group with superstitions."

But that sort of talk only whetted the reporters' appetites. What was a "classic satanic group," for that matter?

A church of Santeria had been formed in Hialeah outside Miami. The Hialeah city council was passing ordinances against animal sacrifices left and right; the neighbors were trying to get the church on zoning complaints; the humane society was after them for cruelty to animals; and the health department was all over them for improper disposal of animal parts; but the church was still covered by the First Amendment.

As strange as all of that may have been to people who had never lived near a large Haitian or Cuban population, it still didn't come close to explaining Matamoros. Even the scholars were confounded. "If this is really an offshoot of Santeria," said Dr. Ed Foulke, an anthropologist with the New Orleans Psychoanalytic Institute, "it is a very bizarre one."

Mercedes Sandoval, an adjunct professor of psychiatry at the University of Miami, said: "To me it sounds like these people are using the drugs themselves. More than any type of religion, I'd say these are gangsters."

But who said gangsters don't have religion? The reporters were looking in the wrong direction, asking the wrong people. Perhaps the things being found in Matamoros did not line up perfectly with what scholars knew of the various cults. But not a lot was ever known in the first place. And cults are like everything else. They change. When the reporters got back over to the cops, they began to hear a different story. The cops—the dope cops especially—were out there all the time. They knew what was happening in the here and now.

Jaime Escalante, an investigator with the Houston police department, said there was not a lot that was terribly unusual about this group. The bodies, yes, the extent to which they had gone, yes, that was unusual. The fact they had gotten caught. But the religion? It was a commonplace in the drug business today.

"It's just like guns are a part of the drug trade," he said.

"Cocaine dealers carry weapons—it's part of the business. These cults have evolved as part of the drug traffic world, too."

He reminded reporters that even if a guy in the drug trade is wearing thousand-dollar Via Veneto suits and flying around the world on his own jet, it doesn't change what the hell he is or what he was when he went into the drug business in the first place.

"These guys are very superstitious, many are illiterate. This [voodoo] has been passed on from generation to generation in South American and Caribbean countries and in Mexico too," he said.

One scholar, whose view was broader than the study of cults alone, said she thought the general movement toward voodoo cults was growing in the Third World. Hazel Wideman, a professor of social anthropology at the University of Miami, said the use of voodoo in criminal gangs was not at all uncommon in many countries.

"The priest of the cult house is a powerful individual, and the initiated member becomes a member of a family and will do what he is told."

Armando Ramirez, a DEA agent in Brownsville, said it was all over the border. "Every arrest we make on the border, the suspect has some kind of black magic pouch on his person. It's about as common as driver's licenses.

"Black magic is a big part of the Mexican culture," he said. "I don't think it's so much that drugs and black magic go together as that people with sick minds might be attracted to both."

He said the most common artifacts found on the persons of drug criminals were pouches of sacred dirt and the seven ribbons that represent the seven African powers.

Tony Zavaleta, the anthropology professor who had taught both Serafin and Sara at Southmost College, was profoundly shaken. He admitted candidly he was afraid of his own students. And more than that, his heart was reeling with what all of this meant for his beloved Brownsville.

"We love our community. We're struggling for it to survive and do well. Of all the places you'd think they might be sacrificing people, they're doing it right here in my home.

"My God, what infamy."

Chapter Nine

By Tuesday evening, the concern of the Kilroys had turned entirely to getting Mark's body out of Mexico. Gavito and Neck were racing to keep up with the Mexican police and were dodging an army of a thousand reporters, few of whom spoke Spanish and all of whom wanted the American cops' version.

Mexican law said a body could not be removed from Mexico until three days after being discovered. Mattox went to work trying to put pressure on the Mexicans to break their own rule and let the body out faster. Mattox's press people told Gavito and Neck to stop running from the press, hold an organized news conference, let everybody have at them at the same time and then go back on about their business. They agreed. Gavito and Neck pointed out the pressure on the Kilroys was even worse. They all agreed the Kilroys should be included in the conference, that it was the only way they would ever be able to clear a path through the horde of media still converging on the Valley. The Mattox people set it up.

On Tuesday night, the Kilroys, Gavito and Neck surrendered to the media. It went off almost too smoothly. Gavito and Neck answered all of the cop questions efficiently. Mattox was present, because his people had set the thing up and it would have seemed odd for him not to be there, but he didn't say much.

The steely self-control of the Kilroys was never more in evidence. It fell to Jim Kilroy to relate the basic story. "We feel like Mark was killed twelve hours after he was captured," he said in his measured, flat, businesslike tone. He paused.

"He had twelve hours to pray."

Jim Kilroy half muttered his thoughts, showing only the outer peaks and rims of what he was feeling within. The reporters listened quietly, understanding that this was a man trying to tell the world of the twentieth century what had happened to this boy.

"Mark's with God—no problem. We can accept that. If he had died of drug overdose or in a robbery, we couldn't have accepted that.

"They said he was killed suddenly. With a machete. He was tied up for twelve hours. Then they executed him."

He said Gavito had told him Mark had been killed "for satanic reasons. The devil told them to kill an Anglo. He was the unfortunate one they picked up."

The reporters had been quiet long enough. Gingerly at first, they probed. Then they moved toward the more obvious questions of wrath and revenge. How did Helen Kilroy feel toward the people who had done this to her son?

"I will pray for them," she said quietly, "so they will realize how wrong all this is."

Jim Kilroy listened to his wife and surveyed the forest fire of strobes and TV lights before him. His mind was flitting to the afterlife. But as always, he spoke in the fiercely toned-down mundane language of the businesslike, churchgoing, kids-and-housework middle class. He said: "I think that their emotions were so bad—that they were so bad off, that I think they will never really ask for forgiveness for what they did. Someday I would like them to go up and apologize to Mark."

He said he wanted the people who did this to be "kept away from society. I think it is very important that they never be allowed to do this again."

Then, fretting inwardly again over the realm beyond life, he said, "We're not worried about Mark, because he was a good young fellow. He made us proud. We loved him a lot. We feel that the Father in Heaven loves him more than we ever did, and he's taking care of him."

The press conference closed.

The next day, Texas Governor Bill Clements hit the fan. He could stand it no longer. Every time he saw footage from the Valley, there was that damned Mattox and his big sorry mug. Clements used a press conference on an unrelated topic as a forum from which to go on the attack.

"I know he has no authority whatsoever," Clements told reporters. "He has no purpose in being down there except to get in front of a television camera."

It seemed like an almost unimaginably petty and self-serving attack under the circumstances, but Texas is a strange place politically, and Jim Mattox, because of his maverick role, is a lightning rod. Within two days, the state's conservative press had launched a major assault on Mattox, accusing him of ghoulishness for injecting himself into something that was really only another Mexican deal in the first place. Mattox, with lots waiting for him to do on the desk back in his office, pulled in his people and left the Valley. From Austin, he attended quietly to what he considered his final chores—setting up a trust fund to help the financially beleaguered family and trying to get the body out of Matamoros.

Benitez Ayala, meanwhile, had his own media relations problems to worry about. In Mexico, as in most of Latin America, the only way the public will believe a prisoner is still alive is if the authorities present the prisoner for television interviews. In that sense, television has set a new bottom line for the rule of law: it is now at least possible for the general public to know whether someone has been executed or badly maimed through torture.

On Wednesday, just a day after the big dig, Benitez Ayala invited the press to an open-air showing of his prisoners in a courtyard at the back of federale headquarters in Matamoros. Assurances were made that there would be full and cheerful confessions.

Over 350 reporters jammed into the courtyard while many more milled in a disconsolate mob outside. Benitez Ayala presented his four performers on a balcony over the heads of the reporters. All four confessed with childlike candor. The federales stripped back Elio's shirt and had him show the tattoos Constanzo had cut into him. Elio explained it meant he was a priest and that he was specifically qualified to do the killing. The others gave details of how the cult was organized. They spoke reverentially of Constanzo and Aldrete. Benitez Ayala was extremely proud.

His success, however, was not meeting with universal approbation in Mexico. The tourism trade in Matamoros was instantly dead. It simply stopped, like a great river that suddenly sank into a raw new hissing crevice and went dry. The vendors and the bar owners and the restaurateurs whose families depended on the great crowds of Americans who came over every evening to be entertained found themselves standing on silent streets, wringing their hands in clean aprons and staring at each other.

The inner nature of the inevitable questions about Mexico was beginning to grate, at least at the official level. The Mexican consulate in Houston issued a stiff-necked formal response in the form of a sort of policy statement on the nature of Mexican society. Mexico, the consulate said, is not a "Dislandia."

"If you are planning on going down there to be a rebel, don't," the consulate said. "Conduct yourself as if you were at home."

Within Mexico, responsible leaders and observers were much less defensive and much more despairing in their assessments. They laid the blame on the hopelessly corrupt national, state and local governments of Mexico.

"What worries me most," said Teresa Jardi, a Mexican human rights activist, "is that we are resembling Colombia more and more. There does not seem to be any will to combat narcotics trafficking. The government has allowed it to grow in a major way."

Carlos Quintero Ace, Roman Catholic Archbishop of Sonora, said: "Sonora is in the hands of drug traffickers and criminals. Names are well known of persons in public posts who have used their influence to trade in drugs."

The reaction in Matamoros was infinitely more poignant and bitter. A de facto alliance of business and political groups set the tone in a statement which said, "The impunity that reigns in this city and that caused a horrifying case like the current one should end immediately."

On Friday a crowd of over 100 citizens, including many members of the families of the victims, packed themselves into Matamoros city hall to confront Major Fernando Montemayor Lozano and Tamaulipas Attorney General Anibal Perez Varga.

Their major complaint was the obvious: when it was only their own Mexican loved ones who were missing, when it was only citizens of Mexico, the Mexican authorities didn't lift a damned finger. A brazen young reporter for *El Bravo,* a Matamoros newspaper, stood up, pointed his finger at Perez Varga, and said everyone knew the Tamaulipas officials regularly took bribes from the druggers, let them out of jail all the time in exchange for money and were even partners in their business.

"That's your opinion," Perez Varga said lamely. But Tamaulipas police officials on the edge of the room stared hard at the young man and exchanged meaningful looks with each other.

That day, *El Bravo* had carried a story quoting a well-known local official as saying, "It is well known there are untouchable groups in this city, composed of students, narcotics officers and prominent city persons.

"If it had not been for the death of a gringo, the police would not have solved anything," the official said.

A spokesman for an alliance of small farmers in the area rose at the meeting and said: "We have seen the indifference of the authorities against drug traffickers. Now we want this city to be cleaned up of these evil elements. We regret those boys who were poisoned to act in this manner."

When he had finished, several reporters, Mexican and foreign, began to press Perez Varga on why more had not been done to solve the other disappearances before Jim Kilroy had started coming over every day with his fliers. Perez Varga and the police officials in the room exchanged irritated commiserating glances. Suddenly the attorney general put up his hand and said he had just remembered a pressing appointment in Monterrey. Monterrey is 150 miles from Matamoros. When Perez Varga wheeled and stalked from the room, the police officials guffawed appreciatively.

The next morning, Saturday, 1,500 people came to Our Lady of Lourdes Catholic Church in Santa Fe for the ninety-minute Mass of Resurrection. Jim Mattox had succeeded in getting Mark's body out of Matamoros. It had been cremated in Brownsville.

Seven hundred people packed the church. Eight hundred sat outside under six tents, erected because the weather had been rainy and dark all week. But even as the service began, the skies cleared, and the day grew bright and strong.

"Don't be sad for Mark," Jim Kilory told the silently attentive assemblage. "Be sad for us and yourself, because the world is going to be missing another great man.

"We are proud of Mark, and we thank God for the way he was when he was with us."

Helen Kilroy rose. "I especially want to thank my mom and dad and Jim's mom and dad for giving us our belief in God. That's what's gotten us through all this."

Their pastor, the Reverend John DeForke, faced the

Kilroys and said: "You have taught us how to face adversity of the worst kind with dignity and faith. The Kilroys have been evangelizing us while they have been enduring."

After the service, all 1,500 people gathered around a traditional Texas barbecue and covered dish dinner, all provided by the community.

Max Tully, a Santa Fe pharmacist whose son graduated with Mark, helped serve the ten briskets his son had barbecued the night before. "It is so gratifying to see so many people coming together," he said. "And it's not just the Catholic community, either. It's people from different faiths all coming together. But then again, that's a special family."

On the morning of that same day, the poor campesino parents of Jose Garcia Luna presented themselves at one of the two funeral homes in Matamoros where most of the bodies were being kept. Flanked by sobbing relatives, Herlinda Luna de Garcia, forty-five, explained she had heard her son might be there. She had given her only pictures of him to the police, who were to have forwarded them to the funeral homes. Did they have these pictures?

No. There were no pictures. All lost. What did he look like?

Meekly, the mother of twelve children described her missing fourteen-year-old. A mild boy, very gentle and "very Christian," which, in the language of Mexico means, "Protestant." The father, Isidro Garcia Benavides, explained they had not seen their fourteen-year-old son since he had set off to do his job, feeding animals on a neighboring ranch. He was a slight boy, with a sweet grinning smile and large brown eyes. He had been wearing a gray jersey with green sleeves. He wore his hair like this (the father showed the bored mortician's assistant with his hand). They wondered if their son could be one of the dead. A minister had seen one of the bodies when it was unearthed. It could have been he. He was a cousin of the gang, but he had no connection with them. He was a good boy. The last thing his father had done for him was to buy him some music cassettes in Matamoros, but he never was able to give them to him, because...

The assistant put up a hand for them to be quiet. He shoved a piece of paper at them to sign. They could not sign it. They were illiterate. The assistant shrugged, asked them their names and wrote the names down.

"They were my only pictures of him," she said.

No pictures. All lost. Come this way. He took them to the back.

I gave the pictures to the police.

The pictures are lost! Forget the pictures! Here. He knew which one it was, because of the description of the shirt. He pulled the sheet back. The body was lying in a congealed pool of blood and dirt. The head was lying next to it.

The parents looked at the head. Yes. It was their son. They followed the assistant back out to the front of the mortuary. The assistant asked what they wanted to do with the body. He assumed they would take it. They obviously couldn't afford a cemetery plot. They would take the body off somewhere themselves, to their place, if they had one, or some wooded spot they liked, and bury it.

Yes, they would take the body. The father had an old pickup parked outside. He would take the body to his farm. So. He was not so penniless after all. He had a truck. And a farm.

The assistant told the father it would be seventy-five dollars.

For what?

For the body bag.

The old man shook his head. He muttered privately to his wife. They both shook their heads. No. The government is supposed to pay for that. It is the law. We know that. We are not fools. We are poor campesinos, but we are not fools.

The assistant shrugged at them. Pay the money, or all you get is the body and head. We'll dump it in your truck for you for free.

An American reporter and photographer were sitting nearby. They had stationed themselves in the funeral home to watch for families like this one. It was evening. They spoke about it to each other in whispers. They dug into their pockets.

Here. We have seventy-five dollars. Please take it. It will pay for the body bag.

The father stepped back, offended. No. You do not understand. He is cheating us. The government pays him for this. He thinks we are fools. It's the principle. We have suffered enough. We will not be made fools. My truck is backed up to the door.

Give me my son.

Chapter Ten

Sara and Constanzo had been in Mexico City and Miami over the weekend. They returned to Brownsville on Monday. Constanzo retired to his room at the Holiday Inn for a nap, and Sara went to school. It was there she heard. They had Serafin. They had Elio. They were going to the ranch. They were going to find the nganga.

She called Constanzo and alerted him. She raced across the bridge to her parents' home in Matamoros, threw together some clothes, got rid of some of the evidence in her room, and headed back across to Brownsville. He was waiting for her. They got into the gold Mercedes and went into Brownsville to look for some of the others. They drove straight from Brownsville to McAllen. From McAllen, they flew on a commercial flight to Mexico City.

There was a new vibration coming from him—a low growl that never stopped. He knew immediately what this was. He knew they were closing in on him. He knew this was life and death. His black world of shadow and rot and sexual perversion was being invaded by one force he could not conquer—the blasting light-field of intense publicity.

The police in Mexico City were smarting under the words of the so-called gringo experts who said this was no real curandero, that these were mere druggies like the confused American children who drop acid, listen to heavy metal music and use spray-paint to draw Satanic symbols on freeway bridge abutments. The whole American attitude toward the power of the curanderos was derisive and dismissive, like their attitude toward Mexico itself.

The Mexican police, meanwhile, were treating their search for Constanzo and his followers as a full-scale military operation. The Mexico City police department alone had 300 cops out looking full-time for him—an incredible deployment. But Federal Judicial Police may have had even more people looking. Other federal agencies, especially the Federal Security Directorate (Tomas Morlet's old outfit) had made the search for Constanzo almost their sole occupation.

Of course, the Mexican police agencies had their own internal and intra-agency agendas to pursue. Early in the hunt, through some unexpected blurting of things at a news conference, the press had gotten its hands on the name of Florentine Ventura, the chief of Mexican Interpol who had killed himself and his family a year earlier after visiting Constanzo and the group several times to take part in certain rituals. The fact was that the arrested suspects were spilling out other names of high police officials. Each of the Mexican agencies had its own reasons for wanting to get to him first.

But it was also insulting to have this very dangerous man equated with teenaged American slobs—spoiled bourgeois drug addicts who listened to too much bad music. With information from the suspects, the federales had been able to make his apartment quickly, ahead of the other agencies.

There they found Constanzo's notebook. With some quick rip-and-tear editing, they pared from it the information they could not afford to lose to the press and Xeroxed the things they wanted the press to see—especially the

Bantu notations following each of the careful entries Constanzo had made to record his rituals. There was some proof that would put the lie to the so-called experts.

And there it was, indeed. In Constanzo's handwritten characters—pressed too hard and compulsively neat—were the names of his clients, many of them famous and powerful, and the names of the rites he had performed for them. As soon as the Xeroxes of the edited pages from the notebook were out, the experts began to recant.

With a curious tone of respect, Miami anthropologist Rafael Martinez said: "He really knows his Palo Mavombe."

That statement was, if anything, the grudging understatement of the year. The description of ritual in the journal was in Bantu terms and pidgin terms that many of the experts had not seen before. The journal itself was, in fact, a scholarly event on a par with Lydia Cabrera's rediscovery of practicing naniguismo cults in Cuba in the 1950s.

Constanzo's journal showed him to be a thing which had been believed extinct. He was a direct link with the most ancient, fearsome time-shrouded memories of man.

The massive dimension of the Mexican police mobilization was not merely an overreaction to a gang of drug-running murderers. It was not only a response to President Salinas's impatience with this story, which kept spoiling all of his best announcements. The problem was not only that Constanzo, once arrested, would implicate high police officials. It was all of that. And it was the horrible fact of what he in fact was himself.

He was the blood libel incarnate. The real thing. The Tata Nkisi. The Great Night.

Americans and Europeans, meanwhile, were having enough trouble understanding what any of that really meant. The fact that something so bizarre actually was a fairly integral and even normal part of everyday life in Mexican culture was beyond them. While police squadrons combed the alleys and bistros of La Zona Rosa searching for him, ordinary residents of Mexico City who had dealt with Constanzo tried to explain the homely events that had brought them into his sphere.

One woman whose name had appeared in the journal, speaking on the condition that her name not be published, explained that it had involved the taxi she and her husband drove for years. It was their sole source of income, she said. They had worked for years to get it. Without it, they were ruined, destitute, faced with homelessness and starvation.

It was a case of cheating, she said. A wicked man had cheated them of the title to the cab and had taken it for himself. The police could do nothing for them. The police were not interested. The man had made it look good on paper.

In a city where thousands starved slowly, sickened and died from want of money all the time, the taxi had been the one and only shelter they had been able to provide for their children and themselves. Now bad luck and wickedness had taken it from them.

A young woman who lived near them was a friend of Omar Orea Ochoa (Constanzo's "lady"). The young woman knew of Constanzo through Omar. She was deeply moved by the woman's story about the taxi. It was the kind of injustice the decent working poor of the city seemed to suffer all the time, and no one in a position of official power ever cared. She told the woman that this Constanzo was supposed to be a great santero, an extremely powerful curandero. He might be able to help with the cab.

The woman was ushered into the obsessively neat apartment, with its white leather furnishings and spotless white carpets. Constanzo appeared and nodded in his very formal and serious manner. Speaking in a soft polite voice, he said, "This is the house of the devil."

The words struck an instant and profound horror in her breast. She mumbled an involuntary "Ave Maria." But she stayed to see if this man could help her.

He would do psychic readings and limpias—the cleansings. It would cost a great deal of money—a fortune to the woman. He toured her around the apartment a bit and managed to give her a glimpse of the large and elaborate Santeria altar set up in the back. She still did not fully understand what he intended to do with or for her, in terms of the precise rituals he would perform. Rather than press the point, she told him she would consult with her husband and return.

Instead, she decided to keep the whole business from her husband. She went back to the young woman on the street and asked her to find out what this handsome young curandero in the fancy white apartment intended to do.

The young woman consulted with Omar, who spoke to Constanzo. The young woman returned to her neighbor and explained: "He says if you want to be cleansed, when you leave here, you will no longer have God, but you will have other forces to call upon for inner strength."

The woman instantly understood what deal was being offered. "I said no! My protector is Michael the Archangel!"

The neighbor explained patiently that, under this arrangement, Michael the Archangel would be history. She would no longer need him.

"They told me I would have other powers to call upon. But the truth is, I only love God. He is my only source of strength. I didn't want to have anything to do with them."

In a culture where Christianity still strives daily and uncertainly with the gods that went before, the sort of commerce in which Constanzo was dealing made perfect and ordinary sense. The appeal was persuasive. "Look. Look what God and Jesus and Mary have brought you. Ruin. Hunger. Danger. Your children will die, and no one will care. You will die alone on the street. Jesus and God are gringo gods.

"Here—the one they call the devil. I offer him to you, as I offer you to him. You know why they are so eager for you to eschew him. Of course you know. It is because they don't want some round little Indian-faced woman to have power. Be smart. Come this way. I can arrange it."

Even in professing her revulsion and in telling again and again how loyal she was to God, the woman who lost her taxi could not resist mentioning that Constanzo's prices also had been a little steep. She remembered thinking, in the moment when she was finally deciding against it: "He wants two things that I don't want to give up. Money and God."

The fierce publicity focused on the case was flooding the earth around him with a scouring light in which he could ill afford to dally. Once Sara had joined him at the Holiday Inn, he made his break for the border. The others would have to follow and join him later. He had homes in both Miami and Mexico City, but the better rallying point would be in Mexico, where his connections and his powers were strongest.

No passports or visas are ordinarily necessary for travel between the United States and Mexico. It's a matter of telling the clerk at the ticket counter who you are, and Constanzo had a way of telling people things that seemed to preclude further questioning.

They bought tickets to Miami in their own names. Then they flew to Mexico City under false names. As soon as they were in the Benz that they kept at the airport in Mexico City, they began contacting people. He drove, and she worked the cellular phone.

There were actually several places in Mexico City—the Zona Rosa apartment, Omar's condo, the house. Constanzo thought the house would be safest. It was in the Las Alamedas section of Atizapan, a middle-class suburb fifteen miles north of Mexico City. It was the neatest house on the block, a semi-detached two-story structure, always with a fresh coat of white paint on the stucco, obsessively tidy walks and gardens in front, satellite dish on the roof. The perimeter bristled with security devices, television cameras, motion detectors and so on, none of which were unusual in a Mexican neighborhood where people had things worth stealing.

The gathering at the house was a little bumpy, in comparison with the normally pompous, almost funereal tone of the clan's meetings. By now it was on the news—the federales were digging up bodies on the ranch. That was not supposed to have happened. It was not supposed to be possible. The ranch was the home of the nganga. The nganga was the ultimate center of Constanzo's power. It was his hand-made Hell, his private universe in miniature, prison of the souls he had captured, garrison of his horrible slaves. Now the federales were all over the place with backhoes. The damned Texas attorney general was on TV staring into the nganga with all the respect and horror of someone who had just found something untoward on his shoe.

The Mexico City arm of the group had been worried from the beginning about the Matamoros people—these Hernandezes. For all their money and their big dope business, they were hicks. You never knew what they would do.

This business of the search for Kilroy had been building for two months, and during that whole time, the question in the minds of the family had been whether taking the gringo had been a mistake. Constanzo's power was one thing in Mexico, where there was the advantage of everyone believing in such things anyway. But the United States was another matter. The United States was always another matter, with its simple-minded literalism, its wealth, arrogance and smugness.

Sara had forced them to watch the movie again and again, because she said it was proof of Constanzo's most important claim—that his powers could sway events and people on the gringo side just as they could in Mexico. Indeed, the movie was very convincing. The movie was made by someone who obviously knew much of what Constanzo knew—even some of the incantations—and it was made in Hollywood, the center of the gringo universe. Therefore, it would seem to follow that the gringos, for all their hypocritical protestations, believed in the seven powers and were affected by them just as Mexicans were.

But now all of this fabric seemed to be unraveling, and the gathering in the house north of Mexico City had too much the feeling about it of an ordinary criminal rout—a process most of them had taken part in at one time or another. They thought they recognized the smell of these events, and it made them a little less reverential than they were ordinarily in these gatherings.

Sara, meanwhile, was the most inwardly anguished of them all. She lacked the conditioning experiences most of the rest of them had as small-time crooks. She not only had believed more intensely and fanatically than the rest, she had constantly informed Constanzo of their lapses in faith and had taken it upon herself to become El Padrino's special assistant in all matters, including the rituals. Now it all seemed very ragged indeed, and she didn't even know how to hide out.

Constanzo was in no mood for mutiny. The course of action open to him was plain and straightforward, but he would have to keep the others in line in order to pull it off. He spoke to them with the new low growling intensity that had crept into the lower timbres of his normally glove-soft voice. They would shut up. They would do exactly as he said. He would protect all of them. But they would shut up, and they would obey—leap when he ordered them and sit silently when he did not need them.

Beginning even that evening, even before they piled in their caravan of expensive cars and headed for Cuernavaca, Constanzo began working his real magic—the tough stuff, that went deeper and harder even than Palo Mayombe or Abakua. He began calling people he knew to tell them that they were going to help him. If they were rich and powerful, they would help him or he would ruin them by exposing his connection to them and their role in the rituals. If they were little people, he wouldn't bother with all that. He would simply kill them and their families horribly. Everyone believed him.

Suitcases of cash, gathered from the Mexico City addresses, were loaded into the cars. He told them all to get rid of their IDs. Sara balked, and he threw her purse and all of its contents on the floor in a quick little shuddering rage.

They threaded their way out of the city by night, headed to the resort area fifty miles south where people were expecting them.

For three weeks, they spent their time almost constantly on the move while Constanzo worked his complicated arithmetic of bluff and threat with the Mexican authorities. During that entire period, speaking through intermediaries, Constanzo and the Mexican police were dickering for his surrender and/or escape. There was a problem, however, with Constanzo's math. He was confident he had enough on the authorities to blackmail them into cutting a favorable deal with him. But he was not able to see the real bottom line.

The problem was simply too huge. The outrage over the death of the gringo had become a factor in Salinas's public relations campaign to allay uneasiness over the Mexican economy and society. Even worse, the horror of the Americans and the Europeans over the details of the cult's practices—now coming out in gruesome detail—was working to excite and increase old anti-Mexican bigotries, the view that Mexico was little more than a savage Indian culture barely clothed in the flimsiest gauze of civilizing influence.

The point was that, whatever Constanzo had and no matter on whom he had it, he had to be brought to ground. If it meant sacrificing some high officials on whom he had dirt, then so it would have to be. Mexico had to rise above this man and crush him. In the end, the money flowed according to the gringo magic, and that meant the gringo magic would win.

Whenever he could, Constanzo called his mother. To her alone he confided his fear of the police. She encouraged him as much as she could. She was having some problems of her own. She was about to be sentenced to two years in a Florida prison for stealing a refrigerator from a house where she had been working as a caretaker. She wouldn't have to stoop to such things if she only had a bit of money to rely on. "I have to run, Mom," he said.

During the same period, while Constanzo and his followers were shuttling from address to address every two or three days, El Padrino was being betrayed. He was not the only member of the group involved in negotiations. For one, Sara, the true believer, was hedging her bets, too, presenting the police with a delicious possibility. The best of all possible worlds, after all, would be to take a very credible prisoner, who could help to exorcise the whole matter with a detailed and convincing confession, but who would also, in the process, make it possible for the police to blow Constanzo's brains out.

After three weeks of running, something clicked in Constanzo's uncanny eye. He perceived somehow that things were coming apart within the group. He could no longer afford to give them even the brief respites from himself that driving from city to city involved. He needed them all under his own watchful eye, and under lock and key.

Fortunately, Maria del Rocios Cuevas Guerra had completed her task. The forty-three-year-old former fashion model had balked at first when Constanzo called to tell her to find him an apartment in Mexico City. She had made the mistake of believing that her relationship with him and the group had ended.

Maria Cuevas went to him for the same reason everyone did. She had bad luck. She was beautiful. She felt she should have been more than a model. She should have been a movie star. But she was neither. Constanzo was the perfect doctor. He understood these things. He had friends who could help her. And he had his powers.

He performed some rituals, and her luck improved. She began to be called for work as a model. She thought that was it. But Constanzo had called her back. He performed additional rituals for her, which she paid for. Eventually, she played the role of worshipper at rituals Constanzo performed for others. And eventually she saw things too horrible to believe or to escape.

But even that was not the final price. Now he had called her and told her that she would find an apartment for him

and his band and would help stock it with provisions, or he
and his people would hunt down her and her family and
torture them to death. It had taken her a while to come up
with something suitable. Now, just when he needed it, she
had found a serviceable place in a four-story building in
one of Mexico City's better residential areas.

They swept in late one night. While Constanzo worked
the telephone, the rest of them set about their busy little
housekeeping tasks, hanging up his clothes and preparing
yet another new altar. They gave a wad of cash to Cuevas
and sent her out to buy groceries. She realized then that
they were going to hold her by the throat until they were all
dead and had taken her with them. During that first grocery
run, she made her own first very tentative phone call, providing the second rip in the Tata Nkisi's long black robe.

It was impossible now for Sara to get any word out by
telephone at all. The fate awaiting someone caught making
calls from Constanzo's phone was unthinkable. Sara, the
health nut, resorted to the prisoner's time-honored ploy—
the fake illness. She began slowly to complain of cramps,
then severe stomach pain. She threw several purple-faced
fits until finally she had fooled even the microscopically
searching eye of El Padrino. He called upon a doctor who
was within his power.

The doctor, Maria de Lourdes Guero Lopez, twenty-
nine, visited Sara several times and left with messages
from her each time.

The business of bringing the gang to earth was excru-
ciatingly complex. Several agencies had their own reasons
to want to control the process themselves, and no one knew
exactly what anybody else's agenda was. In spite of the big
names in his journal, Constanzo's day-to-day criminal activities had been carried out at the level of local law enforcement interest. Therefore, he and the Hernandez family
had much more on local cops in Mexico City, Monterrey
and elsewhere than they did on the federales. Therefore,
the gang was in much more danger from the locals than
from the federales, because the locals had more reason to

want to stop their mouths. But they had some things on the federales too.

The information coming to the authorities from Cuevas, Aldrete and Constanzo himself was coming through several different agencies. No one had the address or even a near fix on the address where the gang was hiding out, until after Aldrete's second message through the doctor.

On the same day, April 18, the American federal authorities and the Mexican federales landed prime informants for themselves. With significant help from Jim Mattox and the Texas Department of Public Safety, federal agents in Texas were able to whip together a sufficiently credible rap on Serafin Hernandez Senior to persuade a judge to let them dump him back in jail, in spite of his bond and the shaky nature of the original charges against him in Grimes County.

The beauty of the American prison system, from the point of view of some law enforcement officials, is that the system is so overcrowded and smelly, especially in Texas, that law enforcers don't need to go around squirting cola up people's noses. All they have to do is toss them in a screaming sinkhole like Houston's Harris County jail, which is exactly what they did with Serafin Senior even though the charges against him were federal.

No one knew how much Serafin knew about the Mexican side of the family now or how much he knew about Constanzo or whether Serafin Junior might have been in touch with his father. But the point was that Mexican authorities had to worry that the American federal drug people might find out a lot and fast, now that Serafin was back on the burner.

On that same day, a surveillance of Constanzo's Mexico City house turned up one Maria Teresa Quintana, twenty, who was the little sister of Constanzo's lover, Martin. Little Maria, frightened to death, led to the cult by her brother, in it up to her youthful ears, drenched in the blood and bestiality of the rituals, began spilling and spilling and spilling her guts the minute the federales put the bottle to her nose.

Suddenly all of the regularly frequented addresses of the gang were known to the federales, all were searched, more arrests were made and major caches of arms and money and dope were seized, cutting off the gang's supply column behind them as they ran.

Even more tantalizing, Martin's little sister was providing the police with a flood of detail that closely corroborated the immediate round of confessions the federales had extracted from the gang members arrested in Matamoros. In particular, her description of the role of La Bruja exactly matched the damning evidence provided by the others. According to both versions, she had stood at Constanzo's side during the tortures, suggesting additional embellishments from time to time.

Meanwhile back in Matamoros, the boys in jail there were still spilling more and more detail, especially about Sara. The only subject on which they remained absolutely silent, all of them, no matter what the torture, was El Padrino himself. About him they would say nothing.

At this late point in the process, Benitez Ayala and the Americans were still sharing a remarkable amount of information, in part because they had come to trust each other, at least for the short run, and in part because they had to share in order to barter back and forth and so that each side could keep tabs on the other.

But it was at the point that Maria Quintana came into the fold that Ayala began to subtly back-peddle from this uncharacteristically cozy relationship with the gringos. He disclosed first that Quintana had implicated a very major Mexican drug dealer, who had implicated some people at the pinnacle of the Mexican film and entertainment world. At least one of these "famous actors" was found to have one of Constanzo's trademark altars all set up in his palatial home, ceramic Buddha, blood smears and all.

At the same time it was revealed, probably accidentally,

that some of the Mexico City searches were turning up more bloody children's clothing.

If it were possible for such a horrible story to take on an even greater dimension of horror, this was that possibility looming large. If the cult had been snatching children and torturing them to death; and if the cult, especially that aspect of the cult, involved people at the top of Mexico's popular culture, then it was possible for this horrible tale to become much more awful. It was possible for this story to turn Mexico into a pariah nation in the opinion of civilized people everywhere. Always privately torn between its primeval heart and its European brain, Mexico could not bear for this unresolved tension to become international public fodder.

It was at this point that even the possibility of further digging at Rancho Santa Elena was slammed shut. Even though nothing had been touched at the ranch since the exorcism, Benitez Ayala said new evidence coming from the ranch indicated that very few of the victims there had been innocent.

Instead, Benitez Ayala argued, they were almost all dope dealers, and this whole business had little to do with Palo Mayombe, much to do with dope. It was at this point that Benitez Ayala began suddenly and dissonantly to speak of Sara in kinder tones, suggesting to the press that he thought she might not really have known all about the rituals and that sort of thing. What it meant to close observers of the hunt was that some new kind of deal was being tested out in the echo chamber of media reports.

The very next day after Benitez Ayala's turn-around on Sara, the prisoners in Matamoros finally were indicted. Vehicular and pedestrian traffic was banished from the streets for a block in every direction around the Federal Judicial Courthouse. Shotgun-wielding federales scoured the streets and rimmed the courthouse until it was over.

Meanwhile, the incredible number of cops who were out there looking for Sara and company finally started to get lucky. On the same day the second Aldrete message reached the federales, an informant of the Mexico City police called them to say that the woman who made large grocery purchases in cash had returned. Detectives were dispatched immediately, in the hope this was the same woman who had been calling, trying to tell them she had been pressed into service somehow.

It was all within hours of ending. The others in the group were gifted with the criminal's most useful mental attribute—the ability to feel nothing. Their numbness was their armor.

Sara was not so blessed. She knew better than any of them what was ahead. She knew that Constanzo wondered. She could feel his eyes scouring all of them every second. And she lacked the numbness. All of this had been a matter of deep belief on her part. Now if it came apart, and if she helped bring it down, then what had it been? The screaming and the blood and horror: what had it all been? What was she? Sara had to live with her conscience and her terror and keep up a very good front, all at once. It was a demanding performance.

But none of their problems approached the level of what the Tata Nkisi faced. He was a great power. A movie star. The Great Night. The only thing that could defeat him was another even greater power. The only way he could avoid defeat was to summon every ounce of his power, every shred of his concentration and use it to push back this contending force, this other Tata Nkisi.

The precise nature of the final negotiations probably never will be known publicly in detail. By the morning of Saturday, May 6, it had been decided that the Mexico City police would make the arrest. There were several reasons to let them have it.

The Mexico City police department had made a huge commitment to the search in terms of very visible manpower mobilization. The department might appear foolish if some other agency came swooping in and nabbed the cult.

Most of the immediate traffic with the group, especially

Sara's missives, had wound up in the hands of the Mexico City police. They could make a plausible claim that theirs had been the most effective investigation, during the phase of the cult's flight from Matamoros.

More to the point, the Mexico City police had more to lose by letting this get out into the press. It was true enough that the Tamaulipas state police had their worries about public disclosure. But this was not Tamaulipas, and that was their problem. It was true that the federales might suffer some embarrassment, but the federales basically were above embarrassment anyway.

But Constanzo's own principal dealings in Mexico City had been with the Mexico City police. That's why they had some serious things to worry about. They needed to make sure that, when the arrest happened, it happened right. The other police agencies trusted them to see to it. They all knew the Mexico City police could ill afford to botch it. When the arrest was over, Constanzo would be dead.

Though the apartment itself was in disrepair, the area around it was one of Mexico City's better neighborhoods, Colonia Cuauhtemoc. The apartment was Number 13, on the fourth floor of a building at the intersection of Rio Balsas and Rio Sena, only a handful of blocks from the American Embassy on Paseo De La Reforma.

Originally, the operation was not supposed to require a large number of police or much gunplay in the streets. Sara knew it was coming, and at least one or more others of the five in the apartment at the time knew the arrest would come soon and had agreed to a certain preordained choreography.

What the choreographers had failed to take fully into account was Constanzo himself. Normally and outwardly a steely-fisted mountain of reserve, Constanzo by the last morning was visibly coming apart. His eyes had changed, they were cavernous and dark; and he had developed a curious quaver in his voice. It was as if he knew exactly what was coming and when it would come.

Sara was especially terrified by the changes that were

coming over him. In the last week of smuggled messages and double agendas, she had indulged herself in the hope she had achieved a certain kind of mastery over him for the first time.

But now he was not the same man, and she had no idea what to expect of this new monster. He could go any way, do anything at any moment.

At midmorning, Constanzo made a strange speech to them, still trying to maintain his posture of quiet solemnity. They must vow that, if the police actually were about to overtake them, they would all help kill each other. In spite of his best efforts to conceal them, cracks were showing in the veneer of his priestly personality—flashes of wrath and craziness that leaked through the dark facade like fire inside a building. They all nodded sanctimoniously and assured him they would act eagerly in this murder-suicide pact.

The other one Sara had to worry about was El Dubi. El Dubi was a thug anyway and this was just the kind of situation he lived for. El Dubi was almost quivering, vibrating, sensing that something big and bad was in the air. Finally he went to the bedroom, lay down and dozed off in the peaceful sleep of a child.

Constanzo kept sending out good-eyes to check the neighborhood. Shortly after noon, one of them spotted the plainclothes cops nearby. The police were parked in several unmarked cars, talking on the cellulars, waiting for other units to arrive. The lookout headed back to Apartment 13. The police saw him and figured out they probably had been made. They sent two officers after him. The rest stayed behind and loaded the AK47s out of the trunks of the cars.

When it was ready to happen, Constanzo already had been fully alerted by the lookout. He was standing at the window, peering through the curtains, when the heavily armed police began to slip around the corner and mass in an alley and behind parked cars.

They had come. They had brought assault weapons with them. None of his clever phone calls or eerie threats had amounted to a thing. They were here, and obviously they would kill him. That was why they were here. They were not here to parade him in front of the press and ask him to sing his little heart out. They were here to exterminate him. They probably already had a deal. Maybe one of his own would blow the back off his head at any instant now.

He shouted, "They are here!" El Dubi came sprinting from the other room. Constanzo made a wild cursing speech. He had failed. His magic had failed. Another magician somewhere had vanquished him. He told the others that one of the people he had threatened had hired an even greater priest than he and that this priest had defeated him, had overwhelmed his powers, that it was all over. In telling it, he began to rave and quiver. His eyes were wild and his mouth was flecked with white spit.

He was humiliated and that made him furious. He was coming apart. In Constanzo's mind, the most important thing for him to do at this moment was to deny his victor the satisfaction of taking his power. He may or may not have known who his victor was. But he knew, by all the assumptions and credos of his life, that whoever it was would want to consume Constanzo's power, eat it, ingest it and weld it to his own.

El Dubi, meanwhile, was high, vibrating, shimmering with excitement. He had checked out the building. He had a plan.

Constanzo's rage infected El Dubi. El Dubi disappeared into the bedroom, reappeared with an AK47, walked to the window and squeezed off a burst at the police outside.

Now the police had the beginnings of a real mess on their hands. This was not at all the way it was supposed to happen. They hit the decks behind parked cars and around corners. Then they opened up on the apartment with machine-gun fire.

Inside Sara screamed. The others shouted and flattened themselves on the floor. The walls exploded in pocks and geysers of plaster dust all around them; glass shattered, wood splintered, plastic appliances and dishes blew up.

There was silence while the police waited. Constanzo was still standing. He was incoherent. They couldn't understand what he was screaming, then realized half of it was in Bantu. He lurched into the bedroom, dragged out the suitcase full of American money—twenties, fifties and hundred-dollar bills—and threw it onto the floor in the kitchen.

He wrenched the suitcase open and began piling fistfuls of cash on top of the stove. "They can't have it! They can't have it!" he said over and over again in a high-pitched shriek. He turned on the gas, and the money caught fire and began blazing.

The police outside opened up again and this time their bullets came into the apartment in a driving rain, smashing and ripping the floor and walls and ceiling. The others looked up from where they had been rolled in quivering balls on the floor. El Padrino was still standing and unmarked, burning his money. None of them had been hit!

Constanzo whirled on the rest of them as if thunderstruck by a wonderful idea. "Let's all die!" he shouted.

Sara half rose, sobbing and shaking her head. "No. Adolfo! No! I don't want to die!"

He pondered her words curiously, with his head cocked half-up like a bird, then seemed to forget this notion. He grabbed some more money from the suitcase and raced to the window. He threw the money at the police and shouted at them in Spanish and Bantu. El Dubi appeared at the window next to him and began spraying the street with bullets.

Suddenly Constanzo stopped raving. He seemed to shake himself free of his fit. He recaptured at least some of his customary composure. He stared at El Dubi. Then he turned and stared at Martin Quintana, his lover. The Great Night had decided to make his retreat into the realm of his own dreams—the blackest stink of Hell where he knew he was destined to be received with open and horrible arms by The Creature himself.

He strode over to where Martin was lying in a ball on

the floor. He reached down with a delicate finger. Martin lifted up one hand and took Constanzo's finger. Constanzo lifted him from the floor and led him toward a small closet.

He told El Dubi that he was to lift his gun and kill him and Martin. El Dubi balked. Constanzo pleaded first, then reached out and slapped El Dubi hard in the face twice. "It will go bad for you in Hell if you do not obey."

Constanzo pushed the wide-eyed Martin into the closet, stepped inside, sat on a stool next to him, and pulled Martin to him in a tender embrace.

Still El Dubi hesitated, paralyzed by his fear of the man commanding him.

Suddenly, from somewhere, from wherever she had been crouched, Sara appeared. She was clawing the air and shrieking at El Dubi: "Do it! Do it! Do it!"

El Dubi lifted his weapon, pointed it back and forth between Constanzo's face and Martin's face. He squeezed the trigger and filled both of them full of lead. Gushing black spouts of blood exploded from their faces, necks, chests and arms, splatting against El Dubi's own face and chest. When El Dubi took his finger off the trigger, the bodies stopped jumping. Constanzo and Martin slumped down into the closet floor and deeper into each other's bloody embrace.

El Dubi, wild and surging now, raced back to the window and began blindly spraying the street with bullets. He kept it up until the clip was empty and then went for another. The moment he stopped firing, the police opened up like World War III. By now it had gone on for almost forty minutes. Everyone except the gang had long since fled the building.

The police broke for the front door of the apartment building. They came up the stairs laying down an unbroken blanket of machine-gun fire ahead of them, ripping the walls and ceilings apart as they moved up the stairs. They shot out the door, kicked through it, leapt into the apartment. It was empty.

Other policemen by then already had raced ahead to the

roof. Sara, El Dubi and Omar were standing at the far edge, getting up their nerve for a long jump to the adjoining building. A police officer lifted his machine gun and fired a single burst into the air. El Dubi dropped his own weapon. The three turned and faced the police. They were docile.

The police approached them slowly, weapons at the ready. When the first officer was close enough, he reached out, grabbed El Dubi by the hair, wrenched him flat on the roof, yanked his face up and to one side and shoved the barrel of his machine gun into his mouth. Another officer grabbed Sara, threw her down hard and put a gun in her face. Omar lay down on his own. The police made quick but effective searches of them, then reached down to the hair again and yanked them to their feet. Hauling them along quickly and jabbing and poking their guns all over them every instant of the way, they hustled them back down to the apartment.

In those few seconds. Sara already had begun screaming that Constanzo was dead and in the closet downstairs. The police hauled the three back down into the apartment. She pointed to the closet and tried to hang back, but the police threw her ahead in front of them as a shield.

An officer threw open the door and stabbed at the space inside with his gun. He drew back, staring hard at the bodies. The others watched him. He looked up, nodded affirmatively.

By now the police photographer already was up the stairs and, with him, some of the Mexico City paparazzi favored by the police department. Within a few minutes of the storming of the building, a photograph of Constanzo dead in the arms of his lover, full of little black holes like a Dick Tracy character, was on its way to the lab and to the hungry newspapers and television stations of the world.

The second press conference was easier to arrange than the one in Matamoros had been.

The Mexico City police had arranged visuals before-hand, in the form of a three-by-six table bearing the black robes that had been confiscated from Constanzo's house, some jagged swords and votive candles, which were already lighted when the press was allowed to enter the room.

When all of the reporters were well situated, the police brought in the three from the shootout—Sara, El Dubi and Omar—along with the two turncoats, Maria Cuevas and Maria de Lourdes Guero. At first they stood in a sullen gaggle in the corner, but as soon as photographers began calling on them for poses, they voluntarily lined up behind the table.

In response to questions, El Dubi spoke in a matter-of-fact manner about how and why he had killed the godfather.

Constanzo, he said, went, "crazy, crazy.

"He said everything was lost. He grabbed a bundle of money and threw it and began shooting out the window. No one's going to have this money."

"He told me to kill him. He said that if I didn't, I would have a tough time in Hell. He pleaded with me.

"He slapped me twice in the face. We could hear the cops outside shooting. A lot of shots could be heard. They sat down in the closet, Constanzo on a stool and Martin beside him. I just stood there in front of them and pressed the trigger. That was it."

Constanzo, he said, "used to kill with easiness. He said all Christians were animals."

He shrugged off his own role in the killing of Mark Kilroy. He said matter-of-factly that he might have cut off one of Kilroy's fingers but nothing more than that.

Then it was Sara's turn. In a meek voice, she corroborated El Dubi's version of Constanzo's death. "He ordered him to kill him, because it was the end, and he wanted to die with Martin."

The reporters and cameras closed in on her. Here finally was the one they had all come to see. La Bruja. The witch doctor's special assistant, the one the police said had specially supervised the torture and mutilation of victims, had boiled and hanged a man at the same time and torn off his nipples with blood-rusted shears while he screamed in his final agony.

For those who had been there when the bodies came out of the earth—only a handful were present for the Mexico City press conference who had seen it all—it was an especially keen and wincing moment. Images of Mark Kilroy's body coming up from the earth floated in their minds.

When the backhoes first touched it and the dirt began to fall away, the body had looked strangely like that of a baby. Or a dwarf. The dirt fell off in clods, and the stench was so powerful at first that it stopped the eyes of the witnesses from focusing. No one had known at all what to expect.

Then slowly the witnesses had assimilated what they were seeing. The arms of the body were tied behind it at the wrists. The fingers had been chopped off. The body was short because the legs had been hacked off above the knees.

The gaping holes in the chest with the rib-ends sticking up like the prayer sticks in the nganga were the openings from which the heart had been torn. The penis and testicles were missing.

But it was the head. It was the head that stayed in the mind, because at first it had appeared as if the head was still there. It looked like a tiny head, turned to one side. It took a long time for the eyes to recognize that it was the stump of a head.

How would she speak? With what low guttural Bantu curse would she announce the actual tenant of her being?

Sara rolled her eyes upward, tilted her head back and spoke girlishly, with only the very farthest most distant hint of defensiveness.

She said that she had been held prisoner by Constanzo since the escape from Matamoros. It was only during the period of flight, she said, that she learned of the human sacrifices, by watching news reports on television.

Up until then, she said, Constanzo had been her spiritual leader, had told her fortune and so on, had been "like a father" to her, but she had never had any inkling of the sacrifices until she saw the bodies on Mexican television.

"I wasn't involved with those sacrifices," she said, shaking her head slightly. "When it came out on television I realized what had happened."

She explained that she had not been involved in the kind of Santeria that involved human sacrifices. She had been involved, she said, in "Santeria Christiana"—the religion Constanzo had introduced her to a year earlier.

"When all of those sacrifices were made, when all those things came out on television—all of those things weren't true," she said. She squinted, threw her head back and looked wide-eyed. "What was found in my house were not satanic objects. They were saints—Saint Francis of Assisi, Saint Barbara, Santo Nino de Atocha.

"I practiced Santeria—Christian Santeria—as of a year ago," she said again, slipping into the logic of the sliding scale. "El Padrino was involved in Palo Mayombe."

A reporter asked her who had killed Mark Kilroy.

"Adolfo."

A reporter asked her how she felt about the killing of Kilroy.

"I feel sorry, because, when he disappeared, I was trying to help the family."

She didn't explain what she meant by that, and, strangely enough, no one pressed her on it.

Speaking in some moments in a voice cracked with emotion, at other moments in what seemed like a sort of Mexican Valley talk, she said, "When I saw the things on the television, watching all the sacrifices and like that, I just . . . it was amazing."

Asked if she had been in love with Constanzo, she said, "I did not love him, but I followed him."

As a postscript before being led from the room, she said, "If I had known it was like this, I wouldn't have been in it."

The reactions of the Mexican and American reporters

were very different and very telling. The Americans were disturbed and, when pressed, admitted that they were frightened by her almost unearthly calm.

It was one of those moments at the frontiers of cultures when people can see into each other's eyes and speak the same words and still have little notion what is in each other's hearts. The Mexican reporters saw it very differently.

Yes, it was as if she were trying to dodge some charges for stealing tires, one of them said later. That's what she was trying to do. Dodge some charges.

They used Palo Mayombe, maybe Abakua, all that stuff, Aztec heart-eating, whatever. They used it to smuggle dope. They used it because it worked. They used it because it scared the shit out of the cops, and it kept the cops away from them.

They did everything else. They paid the cops. They flew at night. They went out with the paper plates on stakes and waved in the dope with flashlights.

The voodoo was just one more element. The sacrifices were just one more step toward making it perfect.

And they got caught. So what does one expect people to act like when they get caught?

At that moment, when she had been led from the room and the story already was singing out over the phone lines to the world, one would have been hard put to say with authority which culture had been affected more profoundly by Constanzo's power.

The Mexicans took it all in course, believed in most of it, saw it as a fairly predictable element in any serious criminal conspiracy. They believed in it, and so they were less shaken by it on that day.

The Americans, meanwhile, always seemed to have a great deal at stake in their ardent, cocky, self-assured assertions that voodoo was all a bunch of primitive mumbo jumbo, the empty even laughable belief system of simple peoples. And yet they were the ones, that day, who were so disconcerted that they couldn't even express their feelings.

How could she have had anything to do with those bodies and still speak of the cult and its beliefs in this voice of girlish innocence? Wouldn't the enormity of the crimes produce at least *some* visible aspect of depravity and horror in her bearing? Was she in fact innocent?

Was she some exotic form of psycho? Immediately, the press was full of crude speculation about "multiple personalities" and other pseudoscientific nonsense.

However cheap and nonsensical, the pseudopsychological explanations seemed to bring some balm to Western minds. Bad science, even ridiculously bad science, was easier to accept and handle than the other deeply disturbing specters that Sara seemed to raise for people.

Especially for those few who had seen Mark Kilroy's body in the earth, El Dubi and Sara both were profoundly discomfiting figures. El Dubi admitted freely he had been present for it. No one who saw the body believed it was mutilated after Mark was already dead. There was no rational explanation for their conviction that he had been tortured while alive. But something in the body seemed to scream it.

If Sara is dismissed, if Sara cannot be assimilated yet, then take El Dubi. He was there. He took part. It means almost nothing to him. It's yesterday's news. Old business. What happened to Mark Kilroy was an ordinary event in the lives of those who killed him.

In general, the people of Matamoros reacted to Sara's performance in the terms of their culture. They flooded into Our Lady of Refuge Roman Catholic Cathedral, which towers over the main plaza of Matamoros, lighting candles in record numbers and buzzing devoutly beneath the priest's sonorous incantations.

As for Aldrete, they had no confusion of feeling. She was a trickster and a witch. "The people here want her burned in the plaza," said a farmer, Jose Luis Martinez. "The people of Matamoros are afraid of her being alive in jail because she can still have contact with others and influence them."

Across the river, Jim Kilroy's plaintive query summed up the most profound and troubled kind of pondering that decent normal ordinary American middle-class culture could bring to bear on a life like hers:

"It's very sad," he told a final press conference. "She was going to a good college, and she was a good student. But she fell off into the deep end because of drugs. I would like to ask her, 'Why?' How did we let that happen?"

The prognosis for the legal cases of the people who were arrested was cloudy. By now they had all been charged with homicide—Mexico's most serious crime. It carries a maximum sentence of forty years in jail.

The cult's religious practices were not likely to figure importantly in their legal fate. As Mexican human rights advocate Teresa Jardi pointed out, "These Satanic practices do not interest the law here, they make no difference. If there was homicide and illegal burial, and if they confess, they are responsible."

But even a confession can mean little in Mexico. The problem is that there is no public trial in Mexico, and the pervasiveness of corruption makes it almost impossible to predict outcomes. In early 1988, the nation of Mexico was outraged when Alejandro Braun, son of a wealthy Acapulco family, confessed to the brutal drugging, raping and strangulation murder of an eight-year-old girl.

Braun was convicted of the crime at midyear. By the end of the year, however, two appeals court judges had granted a transparent appeal. The judges were convicted of bribery soon after, but Braun was safe and sound, outside Mexico. When the outcry dies down, and when he returns, he will be just as safe, since Mexican law will not allow him to be retried.

A week after the last press conference, when the story already was dying out of the media, Cameron County Sheriff Alex Perez's assistant told him he had a call waiting from a woman claiming to be Constanzo's mother. Perez took the call. He asked a few quick questions. It was Delia calling from Miami. She wanted the body. Perez was confused at first. Your son's body. Yes, of course. Your son was not killed here. He was killed in Mexico City. Yes, of course, I know that, I read the newspapers. I watch TV, the world knows how my Adolfo died. Then you must call Mexico City. But I am an American citizen. You should help me get the body back. No, call there. Don't call here. We don't have anything to do with your son anymore. Call Mexico. I must have the body. Can you help me get it?

In mid-May, the Texas Rangers apparently tried to salve their wounded honor, still smarting from their rejection by authorities in the Rio Grande Valley. The rangers had suffered a crushing humiliation three years earlier in the matter of one Henry Lee Lucas, a mentally deficient wall-eyed drifter whom they had presented as the confessed culprit in hundreds of murders all over the United States and Mexico. Other law enforcement authorities, notably Jim Mattox, had exposed Lucas as a fraud and, although it had not been Mattox's aim to do so, the exposure had made a laughingstock of the rangers.

In mid-May after Mark's body had been found, the rangers leaked a map that had been drawn two years earlier by Lucas. Lucas had penciled in areas of a map of the Southwest to show where he supposedly knew child sacrifices were being carried out. One circle was just outside Matamoros, in the area of Rancho Santa Elena.

Of all the objects that were smashed and burned and exorcised at Rancho Santa Elena, only one was removed by the men of Benitez Ayala. The nganga. A few days later, reporters visiting the ranch to check on the exorcism story noticed that the heavy iron cauldron was missing and asked where it was. They were told it had been "destroyed at another location."

On a later occasion, another reporter asked where and how the nganga had been destroyed. He was told no one knew. That it had been lost. That it was gone.